Praise for *Where Earth Meets Water*

"Padukone has created a rich cast of unforgettable characters.... Her debut novel demonstrates an understanding and appreciation of the cultures of both America and India, a sense of the world as a powerful place, and the redeeming values of adoration and belief in the person you love. A powerful read for those who enjoy beautifully written multicultural fiction."

—*Library Journal*

"[*Where Earth Meets Water*] is compelling as [Padukone] writes with grace and wit about grief, moving on, and accepting love."

—*Booklist*

"[*Where Earth Meets Water*] has an elegance that defies the bread-crumb trail Padukone leaves for readers...this story of learning to love what you have should not be missed."

—*RT Book Reviews*

"Smart and insightful. A worthy addition to the burgeoning field of new Indian literature."
—Gary Shteyngart, *New York Times* bestselling author of *Absurdistan* and *Little Failure: A Memoir*

"Padukone offers a gripping tale of one man's haunting sorrows, the wounds that bind a people, and the redemptive power of love. An unforgettable debut by a very promising young writer."

—Patricia Engel, author of *It's Not Love, It's Just Paris* and *Vida*

"Pia Padukone adeptly captures the aspirations and heartbreak of her engaging characters."
—Manil Suri, author of *The City of Devi*

Also by Pia Padukone:

Where Earth Meets Water

THE FACES OF
STRANGERS

PIA PADUKONE

MIRA

Recycling programs
for this product may
not exist in your area.

ISBN-13: 978-0-7783-1805-7

The Faces of Strangers

Copyright © 2016 by Pia Padukone

For questions and comments about the quality of this book, please contact us at
CustomerService@Harlequin.com.

www.MIRABooks.com

Printed in U.S.A.

First printing: April 2016
10 9 8 7 6 5 4 3 2 1

For my mother, Nina, who started my story.
For my daughter, Salma, who continues it.

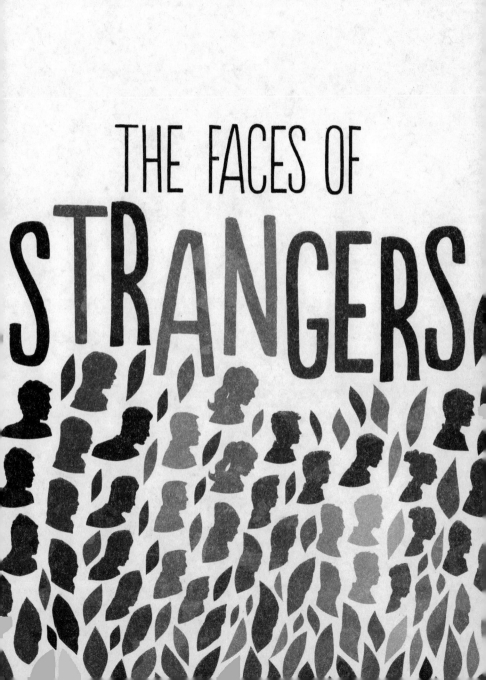

NICO

New York City
November 2013

The day begins wrong. Instead of the bright sunlight that usually breaks through the slats in the blinds and filters playfully across the bed, ominous shadows stand sentry in the corners of the room. Instead of the sharp fragrance of coffee, the earthiness of sweat fills the air. Nico won't notice the difference until later, when he sits alone in his living room staring at a paper cup of coffee long gone cold. Normally, he will reach for his BlackBerry before he reaches for anything—or anyone—else. He will have been alone in the bed for at least an hour anyway, as Ivy will certainly have left early to get in a run or a sunrise Pilates class. Normally, he will brush his teeth with one hand while scrolling through emails with the other. But this morning, he allows himself to lie back against the pillows as he smiles up at the ceiling.

This is where it all begins, he thinks to himself. *I wonder if presidents ever just take a moment to reflect.* It's a few minutes before he notices the silence. Usually at this time, the students entering the school directly across the street will reach a deaf-ening crescendo. This morning, there is only the constant ping-buzz melody from the BlackBerry on the bedside table.

But today, the messages can wait. Nico wants to luxuriate in the day, in the anticipation of what is sure to be a land-slide mayoral election. This morning—the morning that will change his entire life—Nico wants to take his time. He stretches his limbs carefully, one by one, listening for the tell-tale crack in his lower back that has lingered since his very last wrestling match in college. He showers, taking care to wash between each toe, over the points of his pelvic bones, massaging the tender dip at his temples. He flosses—a rare occurrence, but he wants to feel clean right down to his gum line. He shaves carefully in front of the foggy mirror, marvel-ing that he has managed to make it this far without check-ing his email, voicemail, the news. He concentrates instead on his sideburns, recalling Ivy's insistence that he edge the razor at an angle, shaving half an inch shorter than normal so as to give his youthful face a sense of gravitas.

Never underestimate the importance of appearance, Ivy has stressed. *People need to trust you. They need a strong, secure man to lead them. Physical appearance is half the battle. Don't forget that infamous Nixon-Kennedy debate.* Nico has drunk the Kool-Aid. How you look matters almost as much as what you stand for. He has allowed Ivy to tote him around town, spending thousands of dollars on bespoke suits and fitted shirts. He is, frankly, embarrassed at the amount of money he has spent to clothe himself, wondering each time he handed over his credit card for a new suit for a photo op or a speech, whether he should have gone into high-end fashion instead. He has allowed Ivy free rein to ensure that he presents himself with his best polished Italian handmade shoe forward. He has allowed for haircuts at abhorrently inappropriate prices, a straightedge razor shave by a hip Hasidic Jew on the Lower East Side, once even a manicure in a cheap Korean salon with bright fluorescent lights in Queens. He has allowed these changes for the betterment of his public image. But he has his boundaries.

One afternoon, Nico had been standing statue-still as a tailor measured his inseam.

"I was thinking," Ivy had said, holding a teal-and-brown-striped tie against Nico's jaw. "Maybe you should think about reverting to Nicholas. Nico is who you were as a little boy. Nicholas is stronger, more masculine. It stands for something. I looked it up. It means people's victory. How perfect is that?"

At this, Nico had shaken his head adamantly until the tailor had asked him to hold still. For the past eleven years, he has been Nico Grand. The name is a vestige from the semester he spent in Estonia as an exchange student. He was dubbed from the moment he'd set foot in the Sokolov household.

"No," he'd told her, surprising himself. "I've always been Nico. People trust Nico. He's down-to-earth. He's a people person. I'm not Nicholas anymore. I'm running as Nico Grand."

Ivy had shrugged. "Suit yourself. No pun intended," she'd said, turning back and busying herself with the carousel of ties. Nico knows he is lucky to have Ivy, but if he's honest with himself, he feels stifled by her intense motivation for him to succeed. He has wondered whether she would have given him a chance if he hadn't been in the limelight from the start of their relationship; whether or not he would have been interested in her in the first place. Sometimes he thinks of Ivy as an accessory: a beautiful, sparkly thing to wear on his wrist like a charm bracelet or good luck amulet.

When they'd first met, at that very first press conference,

Ivy had shown genuine interest in his politics. As a representative from the comptroller's office, she'd asked several follow-up questions about the Navy Yards, the project Nico had invested in on behalf of the Housing and Parks Protocol. When would the project be completed? How could they ensure that the neediest causes would receive priority access? Had they done their due diligence to determine the lowest income threshold? She'd been engaged and ardent, and Nico had been drawn to Ivy like a magnetic pole.

He can't pinpoint for sure when the change happened exactly, but at some point, the impetus to represent the people began to dissipate into Ivy's desire for status and power. Nico didn't originally enter politics for the fancy clothes, the beautiful girl or even the prestige. No, in fact, it was the other way around. Once he realized he had the charm and the charisma he needed to lead, he made the decision then and there to use it for good. Upon his return from his high school semester abroad in Estonia, the confidence he'd gained gave him the strength and conviction to run for student body government and truly make a difference. Even at age seventeen, he had set up an anti-bullying initiative, lobbied to introduce school-issued ID cards that could be scanned upon entry in order to monitor and incentivize attendance, and had even set motions in action to challenge the caliber of standardized testing in public schools across the city. At that age, he wanted to be the voice of the people—high school people—and he had worked tirelessly throughout the remainder of his time at the Manhattan High School of Science, into college and his first job on a real city campaign that would set the stage and prepare him for his future. Now the city knows Nico Grand, mayoral candidate, tireless crusader for the underdogs and hopeless, who won't sell out the middle class or anger the one percent in order to make a dime or prove a point.

Nico hears the front door open and Ivy's heels click against the floor until they reach the bathroom door and her keen gray eyes meet his in the mirror. "Here," she says, holding out a paper cup of coffee. "Your machine broke this morning."

"Thanks. Can you put it on the sink?"

"My hair's going to get all frizzy in the steam," she says. Nico puts down his razor to take the cup from her. "Are you almost ready? There's already a line of photographers waiting outside for you to cross the street and cast your vote."

Of course: on Election Day there is no school. There are no clusters of schoolchildren across the street, no *thunk* of a handball as it ricochets off the narrow alleyway, no squeals of children as they're tagged by *It*.

"The obligatory photo op." Nico sighs. "What do they think—that I'm not going to do my civic duty by voting for myself?" He rubs some pomade from an oversize tub he has purchased from the Hasidic Jew into the roots of his hair.

"Just play the game," Ivy says. "It's your day, baby. You're here."

Nico sips at his cup. "Thanks for the coffee," he says. "Come here." He reaches for her but she arches backward as though about to dip under a limbo stick.

"Your hands are all tacky from the gunk," she says, grimacing.

Nico returns to the mirror, raking the razor across his face to make tracks in his stubble.

"You're ringing," Ivy calls from the bedroom.

"It's probably Mason," Nico says. "I'll call him back." But Ivy has already pressed the answer button and hands the phone to Nico. She lingers nearby, leaning in the doorway of the bedroom, taking diminutive but deliberate sips from a bottle of water. Nico bristles each time she raises the bottle to her lips. He has extolled New York City's tap water as some of the best tasting in the world, yet Ivy always insists on drinking bottled water. It's irresponsible and wasteful, he argues, and he makes a mental note that he has to change her ways once and for all now that as a public figure, his—and his girlfriend's—every move will be scrutinized, dissected and judged.

"Mason, can I call you after my vote?" Nico tucks the device under his ear and hops into a pair of boxers. Somehow, through the crispness of fall, a large black horsefly has found its way into the apartment and is buzzing lazily through the tepid air that hangs like a cobweb as steam drifts out of the bathroom. Nico waves the fly away, irritated at this potential blemish on this otherwise felicitous morning.

"Dude, where have you been? I've been trying for an hour."

"I'm just trying to get a little Zen over here before what is sure to be a big day. What's up?" Nico tugs at the dry cleaning plastic that sheathes his victory suit, as Ivy calls it. He can feel his impatience mounting. He yearns to be calm and controlled today.

"There's an issue." Nico's press secretary, melodramatic on the best of days, speaks in a tone that can only be described as shrill.

"Unless you're calling to tell me that your numbers were all wrong, let it go, Mase. We're golden. Five-point spread, remember? It's the magic number." Nico counts to ten before releasing his breath. Perhaps coffee isn't necessary today, he thinks to himself. Adrenaline is enough. He is a shoo-in. Polls taken days before elections are rarely wrong.

"Well, we're going to need more than magic today. When

were you going to tell me that you have a kid? With some European supermodel?"

"This isn't the time for jokes, Mase. I'm tightly enough wound as it is." Nico dodges the fly that swings toward him in the mirror. He adjusts his tie and smiles at himself. Appearances.

"Tell me you didn't know about this. You didn't know, right?" Mason's breath catches between his words.

"What the hell are you talking about?" Nico pushes air out of his nostrils and swats at the fly as it veers toward him once again.

"It's not a joke, Nico." The words hang in the air; Nico feels like swatting them, too. "Some bored paparazzo decided to do some sleuthing on you. And he had absolutely impeccable timing."

"Paparazzo? Sounds like a dirty Guzman ploy to me. I can't believe they're playing at this on election morning. Give that asinine campaign advisor of his a call and tell him that a supermodel is just cliché. And remind him—ideas, not incumbency. Just to drive it home."

"Cliché or not, it's all Channel 1 is talking about. Turn it on."

"I don't have time, Mason." But Nico can feel something turning in the air. There shouldn't be a horsefly in November. His coffee machine should be working. He should be able to breathe.

"Well, you have to find the time, Nico. As soon as you step outside your apartment, the cameras are going to be on you like stink on shit."

Nico can barely squeak the words out. "What—what supermodel are they saying?" He finds his legs and sinks his tailbone onto the bed.

"Some Russian lingerie model—Maria? Marie?"

He can feel the blood drain from his face. He feels as though he hasn't used his voice in days. "M-M-Mari. Sokolov. She's Estonian," he croaks.

"Potayto, po-fucking-tahto, Nico. Jesus Christ, it's true? You're her baby daddy?"

"No! For God's sake, stop being so vulgar. I haven't seen or even talked to her in something like ten years. She was my Estonian exchange partner's sister. We barely even talked when I lived there. We just…" And then it hits him. Actions have reactions; isn't that one of the basic laws of physics? Snippets of Mari's body flash against the backs of his closed eyelids like a strobe light: curved ribs, pursed lips, steely gaze. When he opens his eyes, Ivy has moved toward him, but he holds his hand up to ward her away under the pretense of swatting away the fly that has become more brazen with its advances. Ivy's eyes narrow in deep concentration as she attempts to read Nico's face.

"It couldn't be. There's no way." Nico hears himself say the words out loud, but the words that rush through his head are, *Of course there is a way.* Tucking the BlackBerry under his ear, he opens his laptop, angles it away from Ivy and types *Mari Sokolov* into the search engine.

The last time he'd Googled Mari, he'd been a junior intern on a tense campaign trail for a congressman who had no chance of getting reelected. Surrounded by take-out cartons in a nameless motel chain with the ghostly glow of the television flickering in the background, Nico had jerked off to her image on top of a morose bedspread. Back then he had needed to take the edge off a particularly grueling day of press dockets, speeches and a neck cramp from sleeping on the campaign bus. He'd found Mari parading around the internet wearing ethereal, lacy undergarments that left little to the imagination, but helped him perform—though rather perfunctorily—that night. He woke up the next morning feeling rejuvenated, but that had been the last of it. Now, the hits reveal that her promotion to a Victoria's Secret Angel means that she will wear more clothes rather than simply lingerie.

Nico clicks rabidly as Ivy shifts and sighs loudly on the other side of the laptop lid. He alights on the celebrity gossip website DishIt.com.

Dark Angel Mari Sokolov's ten-year-old daughter, Claudia, accompanied her mother to the Haute Couture Awards last Friday. Until recently, when Sokolov has been seen dining and yachting with Spanish media mogul Javier Pizarro, Sokolov has been notoriously single for the past decade, and has kept the identity of her child's father confidential. Rumors of the father's identity have included British multimillionaire Eric Rausch and Persian model Feni Rahman, though Sokolov has denied both counts. Both the Sokolov women wore Dior.

"Nico, man, we'll figure it out," Mason says softly, breaking into Nico's thoughts. "But I can't cover your ass properly unless I know the truth."

"But this is insane. There's no proof of anything. I knew her when I was sixteen. It was a lifetime ago. I didn't even start it. *She...she used me.*" There are a thousand things to say, and Nico is saying them all at once. When he closes his eyes again, Mari has disappeared, but the infamous Latin term flashes in his vision like an LED sign: *ignorantia juris non excusat.* Ignorance of the law does not excuse.

"So you *did* have relations with her."

"Stop talking to me like some Clintonian. It's not like that. It's not like anything!"

Ivy is searching Nico with her eyes and she sits on the armchair facing him on the bed just as he slams the laptop shut.

"Look, I think it's best if you forget about the photo op

for now. Lay low for a few hours until I figure some things out. Promise me you'll stay put."

Nico promises. Mason hangs up, but Nico keeps the phone to his ear. He wants to keep this to himself for as long as he can. The moment he puts the phone down, Ivy will rush in and insert herself into the situation, demanding to know every last iota. But there is nothing Nico can do now to stave her off. She will find out eventually. She'll try to make sense of it all calmly and rationally at first, like the lawyer she's been trained as, but eventually her anger will mount and she will erupt like a steam kettle. And just as Ivy will find out, so will everyone else: the whole city and constituency, his family, Paavo.

He thinks back—it's been what? Over eleven years since he was in Estonia for the Hallström program, a third of his life ago. He has memories of Estonia, the long bovine vowels that make up the language, the burn of Viru Valge as it traveled down his throat, and of course, Paavo, his exchange partner. He hasn't spoken to Paavo in a few years. There'd been a rift, and while Nico had tried to understand and repair it, things just got so busy. He was writing speeches, and then he was making speeches, and before he knew it, he met Ivy and she was encouraging him to run for city office. Which he's doing now. Or at least he's trying to.

He feels a cold chill run through his entire body, as though he's sitting on a roller coaster and it has just peaked at the top of its parabolic climb and is about to tip over. Is this what his sister Nora wanted to talk to him about a few months ago? That must have been it. Unlike him, Nora has stayed close to Paavo. Their bond—once created when Paavo had first come to New York those eleven years ago—has strengthened over the years, and Nico is ashamed to admit that she now knows more about Paavo's life than Nico does of his own exchange partner. Nora knew, and despite the code of therapist-patient ethics to which she usually steadfastly adheres, she had suggested rather intently that Nico reach out to Paavo and Mari. Until now, Nico had no idea as to why.

But he'd tried, hadn't he? He'd emailed and called. He'd even gone to Estonia to meet with Paavo face-to-face and when Paavo hadn't been there, Nico had returned to New York City and thrown himself headfirst into schmoozing with politicos and potential donors. He got too busy mobilizing field organizers and wooing supporters to follow up. He's been too busy cozying up with Ivy in trendy restaurants with overpriced cocktails. He's been too busy choosing his bespoke suits and neckties.

He stares at his suit where it hangs on the rack, looking shameful and despondent. It, along with the other beautiful garments in various shades of gray that he'd had to learn upon their purchase—charcoal, ash, smoke, birch—has cost hundreds of dollars. It feels like such a waste, like everything else he has worked toward: the campaigning, the speeches, the countless hours he has spent on his public image. It is all about to come crashing down. He clutches the phone to his ear and nods, concentrating on a spot on the floor. If he can carry the farce on a little longer on the phone, he can buy some time before he's forced to face Ivy. If he continues pretending that nothing is wrong, maybe he can start believing his own lie.

But he can't deny what happened in Estonia all those years ago. He can't help but catapult his mind back to his junior year of high school when he stepped off a plane onto a sliver of land half the size of the state of Maine. It had been an experience, as he told his mother it would be when he had signed up for the exchange program. But apparently this experience has stretched far beyond the year that the program was supposed to take place. Nothing could have prepared him for how the Hallström student exchange program would change his life.

August 2002

HEADLOCK12 would like to chat. Accept?

HEADLOCK12: Hi…is this Paavo?

EESTIRIDDLER723: Yes. Is this Nico?

HEADLOCK12: It's actually Nicholas.

EESTIRIDDLER723: In Estonia, the name is Nico.

HEADLOCK12: I kind of prefer Nicholas. Anyway, Ms. Rothenberg sent me your screen name, so I thought I'd say hi. How's it going?

EESTIRIDDLER723: Hi, it is nice to talk to you. I look forward to coming to New York.

HEADLOCK12: Same. And I'm excited about Tallinn.

EESTIRIDDLER723: So you are a wrestler?

HEADLOCK12: Yep, I'm on the team at school. I've won my division a few times. But mostly it's just nice to be a part of a team.

HEADLOCK12: What about you? Do you play any sports?

EESTIRIDDLER723: No. I am more intellectual.

HEADLOCK12: Ouch.

EESTIRIDDLER723: Oh, I did not mean to offend you. Perhaps I should say that I am not much of an athlete.

HEADLOCK12: Gotcha.

EESTIRIDDLER723: I'm actually quite poor at sports. My father was always trying to get me to play football—what you call soccer. And I was always trying to be the goalie so that I didn't have to run. I'm more into riddles.

HEADLOCK12: What, like, why did the chicken cross the road?

EESTIRIDDLER723: That's a joke. I mean brainteasers. Like, when you see me, you don't see anybody. When you see everybody, you can't see me. What am I?

HEADLOCK12: I give up. What?

EESTIRIDDLER723: Fog.

HEADLOCK12: Ah, I get it.

EESTIRIDDLER723: I'm as big as a house, as light as a feather. What am I?

HEADLOCK12: I'm not very good at these. What?

EESTIRIDDLER723: Smoke.

EESTIRIDDLER723: So is New York like it is in the movies?

HEADLOCK12: I guess that depends on the movie. But it is the best city in the world. No offense.

EESTIRIDDLER723: None taken. I can hardly compare the likes of Tallinn to a bustling metropolis like New York.

HEADLOCK12: Your English is very good.

EESTIRIDDLER723: Thank you. In Estonia, we take lessons since the first standard. It's compulsory in all schools here. I have been reading English books all summer.

HEADLOCK12: You really are a bookworm. :) It's cool that you read in English too.

EESTIRIDDLER723: I am fluent in Russian as well. It was compulsory until 1991 but I speak it because my father's parents are originally from Russia. They don't speak Estonian.

HEADLOCK12: This might be a stupid question, but is Estonian hard to learn?

EESTIRIDDLER723: I don't really know. I grew up speaking it. But I will help you. You will take a class while you're here.

HEADLOCK12: Cool. Hey I gotta run, but I guess I'll see you at orientation?

EESTIRIDDLER723: A free trip to Berlin. No complaints from me.

HEADLOCK12: Yeah, totally. See you then.

HEADLOCK12 signed off.

EESTIRIDDLER723 signed off.

NICHOLAS

New York City
September 2002

The morning that Nicholas Grand set off for a semester in Estonia was like every other. At the table, his father, Arthur, chugged coffee in an effort to use the bathroom as the first step in his morning ablutions. His mother bounced around the kitchen like a pinball, pocketing a ring of keys, absently fingering the same gold-starred studs in her ears that she wore every day as she sorted through a stack of bills. His sister, Nora, pulled at a stray thread in the tablecloth, mussed and unsettled by the anticipation of the first meeting of a support group for other people just like her.

Although it was only eight o'clock, the air was already hazy and hot—an unseasonable September morning. Nicholas could feel perspiration collecting in his armpits as he sat slumped in a chair like the melted butter that was pooling in the dish on the table. Stella swooped in and collected the butter crock, depositing it in the fridge.

"Mo-om," Nora bleated, her tone echoing a pair of bellows

fanning a fire. "I kept that out on purpose. I hate hard butter. My toast always tears."

"That butter was Dali-esque—practically drinkable," Stella admonished. "Nicholas, did you eat? It's a long flight."

"There'll be food on the plane, Mom." It took effort just to speak. Nicholas felt as if he was talking through a bowl of tepid soup; the humidity had already risen to unspeakable levels. One of the few comforts of going to a place as random and as far north as Estonia was that the country scarcely appeared to even have a summer at all.

Stella paused in her undulations to place a maternal hand on Nicholas's shoulder. Her hand hung like a wet mop against his damp T-shirt. "Are you sure you don't want me to go to the airport with you?"

"The program is sending a car. Don't worry. I'll be fine."

Stella pinged over to her daughter. "Nora, don't be late for your first day of group," she said. "First impressions are lasting."

"It's not like they're going to remember who I am," Nora said. She collected her wet hair into a tight, tidy cocoon against the nape of her neck with one hand and stroked the little black notebook by her side with the other. "It's downright cruel, making us sit around learning new faces when we can't remember the ones we are supposed to know."

"Remember what Dr. Li said about seeking support from others who understand," Stella said, putting her other hand on her daughter's shoulder. "It'll be good to have some cohesion and routine to your week. I'm sure it'll get easier."

Nora rolled her eyes. "I better go get ready," she said. "Have fun in Commieville, Nicky."

"STD!" Nicholas shouted gleefully.

"Seriously? You're actually going to call that out every time?" Nora asked.

"Ste-re-o-typed. STD. Every time you make a generalization about Paavo, yes, I will. In fact, anytime anyone makes
a generalization about him. It's not fair. We don't know anything about him. So be nice."

"What kind of a name is Paavo?"

"STD!"

"That's not a stereotype," Nora pointed out. "It was a
question of clarification. If you're going to shout out that of-
fensive acronym every time, at least let it mean something."

"Whatever," Nicholas said. "I better head down, too." The
family clustered around him, administering kisses and hugs.

"Try everything once, Nicholas," Arthur advised. "This
is the opportunity of a lifetime. I wish I'd had the chance to
do this at your age."

"Call us when you get there," Stella said. "Maybe we
should have gotten you a cell phone."

"Mom, I'll keep in touch. I'm sure the Sokolovs have a
telephone. It's not like I'm going to the Amazon or something." Nicholas crawled his way out of the huddle. "I'll see
you guys in December."

Nicholas had been hoping to catch his breath on the drive
to the airport. His mother had insisted on coming down to
the street to see him off, and he'd been embarrassed when she
pulled back from the hug that had lasted a few beats too long
to see tears shimmering in her eyes. He reminded Stella—
again—that he would only be gone for four months. But once
the driver of the shiny black Town Car deposited his suitcase
in the trunk, he was surprised to feel the tiniest lump in his
own throat. He'd even gotten a little emotional the night
before, hanging out with Toby and his wrestling buddies.
In the den, Carmine's eyes were already glazing over from
the pot he had smoked before arriving at Nicholas's house.

He was a large, lunkheaded boy with an exceedingly good nature. From the moment Nicholas had met him, he'd reminded him of Lennie from *Of Mice and Men.*

"Hey, Lefty, you gonna wrestle over there?" he asked Nicholas, prodding him in the side with his elbow.

"I don't know," Nicholas said. "Paavo said his school doesn't have a team, but that he thinks there are club teams around the city I could join. Though I gotta say it doesn't seem worth it."

"I bet your coach would be happy if you kept it up," Toby pointed out. He grabbed a handful of potato chips and fed them to himself one at a time somewhat daintily, rubbing his hands together to shed the excess grease. "Though in a country of a million and a half people, the odds of finding another left-handed wrestler in your weight class are pretty slim."

"Forget wrestling; I bet the girls are smoking," Chen said.

"What about the sister?" Carmine asked. "Didn't you say she's a model or something?" He tried to sit up slightly but his heavy shoulders pulled him back into the sofa.

"That's what Paavo said. But that doesn't mean she's hot," Nicholas pointed out.

"Lefty, please," Toby said, grabbing another handful of chips. "Of course she's hot. Estonia has more models per capita than any other country."

"Why and how do you know that?" Nicholas asked.

"Common knowledge," Toby shrugged. "And *Maxim.*"

"Yeah, but Estonia has like, a million people," Nicholas said.

"Exactly. And with that statistic, it means that a higher percentage of them are hot. The odds are in your favor."

"Yeah, go give up your V card, tiger." Carmine growled, and the boys joined in, ribbing and poking him.

"How do you know I still have it, jackass?" Nicholas shot

back. He still did, of course. Though he'd dated a modest number of girls, he hadn't gotten anywhere near losing his virginity. He had to admit, the prospect of starting new in a place without a shared history was exciting. He'd be the new kid, an exotic American. He could use that to his advantage.

Nicholas looked around at his friends and felt a pang of sympathy that they would be left behind in the drudgery of the eleventh grade at the Manhattan School of Science while he went forth into the world to learn new things and gain invaluable experiences. Who knew if they would ever be the same together again—shrewd, calculating Chen; sharp but lazy Carmine; and affable, overachieving, ever-loyal Toby. Even saying goodbye to them had been a strange departure from their straight-faced, unemotional relationships. Nicholas felt tears pricking at the corners of his eyes and turned his head away to take a long swig of soda, but the bubbles released up his nose and pressed upon his tear ducts even harder. Chen had even hugged him properly instead of issuing the closed-fist punch trademarked by adolescent boys who refused to show any form of emotion.

But Nicholas had to be strong. He couldn't walk into this new experience weak-kneed and watery-eyed. He stepped into the car, welcoming the time and the space during the ten-hour flight to Tallinn to gather his thoughts and expectations, but he realized he wasn't alone.

Barbara Rothenberg was pressed compactly behind the driver's seat, her stilt-like legs crossed at the knee. Her perfectly coiffed static helmet of silver hair curled just beneath her chin and neckline, defining her as one of those women people called "handsome," especially with her judicious use of pantsuits. She reached over to Nicholas and pressed his biceps with her hand, as if assessing him for a fight. It was a strange greeting: a cross between a hug and a handshake. Despite having met her a few times, the director of the Hallström program remained a complete mystery to Nicholas.

"Aren't you excited?" Barbara asked, her keen gray eyes glistening. "Aren't you positively bubbling over? How are you? How are you feeling?"

After that setup, Nicholas thought, you weren't really allowed to feel anything else. "I'm good," he said. "I think it's going to be great. I'm really stoked for the experience. But I didn't realize you were taking me to the airport."

"I escort all students on the first day of the semester," she said, using her index finger to scrub at some lipstick that had strayed onto her incisors.

The last time Nicholas had seen Barbara had been at the home visit this past June. He had skipped wrestling practice and headed home to find Stella frantically tossing throw pillows into what she hoped would appear to be an intentionally haphazard pile, collecting magazines into two teetering but thoughtful towers flanking the coffee table and slicing lemons into circles before the doorbell rang. Barbara not-so-surreptitiously gave Stella a startlingly disparaging once-over from head to toe before she stepped inside. The home visit, she had told Nicholas, would be a mere formality since his grades had already been vetted, he'd passed all three of his one-on-one interviews, and now they just had to meet the members of the family who would host one very lucky boy from either Estonia, Poland, Hungary, the Czech Republic or Russia. Nicholas would go to his home for four months, and then he would come to stay with the Grands for the remainder of the school year.

It had been clear that Barbara was trying to remain solemn, but the pretense fell immediately after she walked through the entryway that led from the elevator into the apartment.

Nicholas always steeled himself when friends visited his home for the first time. He knew that the apartment that his parents had purchased many years ago, when New York City was considered a den of iniquity, had been a wise decision. The soaring ceilings took breaths away, the cavernous foyer was the size of most people's entire apartments, and the fact that his home had three living rooms awed most visitors to the Grand home into silence. When the elevator door opened to deliverymen, Nicholas watched them peer past him into the living room as though they were taking in a Victorian room replication in a museum. Nicholas watched Barbara's eyes travel the length of the molding along the edges of the ceiling and into the center, where they stood.

"This is lovely," Barbara said. "I've never seen anything like it."

"Thank you," Stella said. Nicholas could anticipate exactly what his mother would say next and nearly mouthed the words along with her. "We bought it a long time ago and we got lucky. Who knew Flatiron would blow up like it did? You should have seen this neighborhood when we first moved in. We were scared to walk down the street."

"Indeed. Our fair city has come a long way." Barbara stared, quite unselfconsciously, even though this was against one of the tenets of the program. *We're all different,* Nicholas had heard Barbara chant on more than one occasion, *and there's no reason to stare or to wonder. So ask the question rather than keeping it in. It's why we're all here—to learn about one another, about the differences in our cultures, and why we eat and wear what we do and why we prefer and believe in certain things.*

"Please, come in. I'm Stella. And of course, you know Nicholas." The three settled on the pair of couches in the formal living room, a plate of water crackers, a crumbling

wedge of Parmesan and a perspiring pitcher of iced tea between them.

"I have to tell you, Stella. We love Nicholas at Hallström.
He's the perfect candidate. He has an impeccable school record, and he's a varsity athlete, well-spoken, conscientious.
I've conducted countless interviews for these coveted spots,
and there aren't many youngsters that tick off so many of the
traits we like to see in our exchange students. You've got a
bright one on your hands." Barbara pressed her hands into
her lap and forged onward before Stella had a chance to ac-
knowledge the compliment. "We make these home visits to
ensure that your family has the capacity, ability and desire
to host a student from another country. Other than the permission slip, we have no idea whether candidates' families
even *want* to be a part of this program. Why—" and here she
tittered "—a few years ago, before we implemented home
visits as protocol, a young woman arrived from Warsaw without anyone to pick her up. When I drove her back to the
program's office—poor dear felt so abandoned—to call her
host family, the candidate's mother hadn't even known her
daughter had applied and gotten into the program. What a
mess that was."

"Can I choose where I get to go?" Nicholas asked.

"Unfortunately not," Barbara said. "We match candidates
up with who we think they are best suited, personality-wise.
It's not really a question of where you're going, because you'll
have a chance to travel in Europe on sponsored trips to visit
Prague, Budapest, St. Petersburg, Tallinn or Warsaw. The
focus is on getting to know people from another culture. It's
about letting someone in. These are things that you can't pick
up in books or movies. They are life experiences, nothing
you can study or learn. Regardless of where you go, Nicholas, you will learn invaluable lessons about your exchange

partner, his culture and about yourself during your time in the program. Herman Hallström, our founder and benefactor began the program in the post–Cold War era, to attempt to create an understanding between the United States and the countries of the Soviet regime, forging connections and creating ties between countries that had previously been enemies. Mr. Hallström wants to recognize the students, the children of the next generation who will become the politicians, the teachers, the lawyers and the champions of the future to take charge of this change. It's no longer the Cold War era, thank goodness, but it is about making the world smaller. It's about bridging the gaps between us in this great wide world in which we live." Everything Barbara said sounded like a rehearsed speech or as though it was being dictated from the FAQ section of a brochure for the program.

"Well, we're delighted to host a student, wherever he's from," Stella said. "Let us show you the rest of the house." They took Barbara through the other two living rooms that extended from the first: a casual television den and then an office/library, with a computer and shelves of tightly packed books. In this room, Barbara stared extra hard at the framed Saul Steinberg *New Yorker* poster with its view from Manhattan as the center of the world.

"You might consider taking that down," she said, strolling past Stella. Sometime during the tour, Barbara had begun leading the way, and Nicholas and Stella had been relegated to following meekly behind her, feeling guests in their own home. She stopped in front of the foyer and thanked them each formally before pressing the button for the elevator.

A few weeks later, she'd called the house and Nicholas picked up the phone. Barbara had been simultaneously bubbly and composed on the other end, a cheerleader on Park Avenue. "I have some exciting news for you, Nicholas," she'd said. He could hear the clacks from her strings of pearls as she fussed with them against her neck. "First of all, you're in. We have officially accepted you to the program. And second, I have your assignment for next year. You're going to Tallinn!" All he could think about was the fact that he didn't want to be kicked out of the program for his ignorance; where the heck was Tallinn?

"Oh," he'd responded. "That's cool. Tallinn..."

"Estonia," she finished for him. "Can you imagine?" Nicholas had already started imagining the whimsical steeples of Prague or the onion domes of St. Petersburg. Tallinn had been the furthest option from his mind.

"Why, uh, why Estonia?"

"Remember, I make my matches based on people, not on places. This partnership is one of my favorites. You're going to love him."

"What's his name? The guy, my partner?"

"Paavo. Paavo Sokolov, and I think you're going to get along really well. You remind me a lot of one another. I think there's going to be some common ground. I can't wait for you two to meet."

Nicholas pictured the Estonian as the Beast from the Disney movie, hulking and wrapped in furs, brooding in a corner. *STD*, Nicholas thought, mentally rapping himself on the knuckles.

"Same," he responded. "I've never been to Estonia. It should be a good experience." That was the key to handling Barbara; approaching everything as an experience and welcoming everything that life handed to you, including hours of studying, constipation, a strange assignation in an exchange program. As soon as he'd hung up, he'd dashed off for the World Atlas and located Estonia, a tiny nostril of a country overlooking the Baltic Sea. It felt as remote and punitive as if he were being sent to Siberia, another fictional-sounding place that Nicholas couldn't locate easily on a map. But backing out at that point would have appeared shortsighted, against everything the program stood for. The explicit agreement Nicholas had made when he handed in his application to Hallström had included accepting any assignment he would be granted.

So he was stuck with Estonia and he was stuck with Barbara spouting her enthusiastic rhetoric on the ride to the airport. It felt as if this trip was already off to a bad start.

PAAVO

Tallinn
September 2002

As far as Paavo was concerned, the Hallström program was off to a terrible start. He'd been paired with a wrestler, someone with whom he couldn't imagine having the slightest bit in common. His parents—particularly his father—didn't seem to have any interest in hosting a boy from New York in the least. All Leo seemed interested in lately was spouting anger toward the Estonian immigration authorities. He seemed to be getting sourer by the day. And it seemed as if he was drinking more, too. Most importantly, Paavo was disgusted with himself. He'd applied for the program thinking it would help—anything had to help. Paavo was growing more skittish and cowardly by the day. If he continued like this, there was no way he was going to survive the program to the very end. Paavo opened the sofa bed in the den and pulled a fresh pair of sheets over the creaky mattress, taking care to tuck each corner in tightly. Nico's flight was scheduled for on-time arrival, and Paavo wanted everything to be perfect. He wanted to erase the first impression of the program from Nico's mind. He wanted everyone to forget what had happened at orientation. Not that Paavo could forget it himself. It kept repeating itself over and over in his head like a broken record.

In the last week of August, Paavo had flown into Berlin along with the rest of the students participating in the Hallström program. Rolf, a diminutive Hallström employee, met Paavo at the gate, looking almost as blasé as a teenager himself. Rolf herded Paavo through Brandenburg Airport, landing him in front of a dormant baggage carousel and telling him he'd have to wait there while Rolf collected the other European students from their flights. After speakers had gurgled something about a flight arriving from New York City, the gaping mouth of a conveyor belt began spitting out bags and Rolf herded the rest of the European students toward them. Barbara Rothenberg, the program director, who had interviewed Paavo for the program the previous semester, was leading the New York students. The Americans were moving in slow motion, having arrived in Germany that morning, red-eyed and jet-lagged.

"Come, come," Barbara said, gathering them all together in the wingspan of her arms. Paavo could barely tell the difference between the Europeans and the Americans. He knew there were two girls and two boys from each continent. There was one boy wearing a bandanna around his neck— Paavo thought he might be Russian—who caught his eye. The boy's nostrils flared before he looked back down at the floor and then at Barbara, who was starting what appeared to be another rehearsed speech. Paavo felt a shiver down his spine, an all-too-familiar feeling. He had a flashback of fleeing down Toompuiestee, his knapsack banging against his back in the hopes of losing the gang.

"Students, welcome to the Hallström program. As you know, you have been selected carefully by a group that judged your academic record, your character and your moral persona to be of great value to the future of relations between America and each of your respective home countries. This is the first day of what should be a very exciting year ahead of you all. Today you meet your counterparts, those young men and women who will become your brothers and sisters for the next nine months. You will go to classes together and learn together, join activities together. You'll make friends with one another and introduce each other to new and unique experiences. You'll learn about one another's cultures and have an insatiable desire to teach your friends back home what you learn. It's just the beginning. Let's do introductions."

Paavo knew it was irrational but he hoped the boy with the flaring nostrils wouldn't be Nico. He fixed his stare on another boy. This boy was all lean muscle, which he wore well. He was strong without appearing formidable. He seemed confident in his stance, though he rubbed the sleep out of his eyes. When he looked up and saw Paavo looking at him, he smiled, and Paavo looked away quickly, embarrassed to be caught staring.

Barbara extended her right hand toward the bandanna boy, who turned his head away although it appeared that she was going to start with him. Paavo could see a crisscross of holes in the boy's left ear, leàding up to the helix of his earflap, as if something very tiny had been digging for treasure and hadn't quite hit the spot. A trace of a tattoo caressed the nape of his neck like an extra piece of cloth or a thatch of hair that hadn't been brushed away after a haircut. Paavo bit his lip and steeled himself for the introduction.

"Everyone, this is Peter," Barbara announced, as though

he was her own son. "He's from St. Petersburg." Paavo realized he'd been holding his breath; he released it slowly and
took in cool sips of air. This boy would not spend the next
four months in his home with his family. Paavo would not
be sent across the ocean to be raised by this boy's mother,
who, it seemed, didn't appear to be doing much mothering
at all. Paavo cupped his elbow with his palm, congratulat-
ing himself with this victory.

"And," Barbara continued, "this is Evan, who will be your
program partner." Evan stepped forward in unsure, jerky
movements as though he'd just learned to walk.

"Hi, Peter. It's nice to meet you." Evan said, holding his
hand out. Peter scowled while shaking his hand.

"It's Pyotr," he said in heavily accented English. "Peter
is so common."

"Pe-eter." Evan smiled, pleased with himself.

"Pee-ott-urr," the boy said, shaking his head and knot-
ting his eyebrows. "Roll the *r*."

"You'll work on it," Barbara said, ushering them to the side
together. The girls and the other boy were appropriated—
Sabine to Jess and Anika to Malaysia. Barbara guided the boy
who had smiled at Paavo toward him as her finale.

"Nicholas, everyone," she said. "You're paired with Paavo
from Tallinn." Nicholas smiled broadly at Paavo, who remained tight-lipped and nodded his greeting toward his host
brother.

"Once everyone has located their luggage, it's time to head
straight to orientation. We have a busy few days ahead of
us before the semester starts." Barbara herded the combined
group out, with Rolf bringing up the rear.

"How was the flight?" Nicholas asked. It looked as though
his face would cleave into two parts from the breadth and
strength of his smile.

Paavo's face remained stoic and unchanged. "Unfortunately, quite bumpy the whole way. These Polish pilots don't know what they are doing half the time."

Nicholas raised his eyebrows and licked his lips. Apparently Estonians had STDs of their own. "You ready for orientation?"

"I suppose so. What are they going to tell us that we don't already know?"

The Hallström program orientation was scheduled over two days, with a few hours scattered here and there for sightseeing and getting to know one another. The Berlin Hallström corporate office was an imposing metallic building that glinted so brightly in the sun's rays that it was impossible to look straight at it with the naked eye. Rumor had it that when the architect was drawing the plans, Hallström himself had insisted on using the most reflective steel in order to create an edifice that dominated the skyline in more ways than one. However, the building was so lustrous that it had succeeded in causing arson; on more than one occasion it had set fires in a few surrounding buildings, melting plastic chairs and beach umbrellas that had been placed on nearby rooftops. Hallström resolutely refused the fire department's suggestion to sandblast the facade, digging in his heels when the matter was taken to the city council.

The conference room reserved for the orientation was located on the corner of the forty-ninth floor of the building, with light striking against the sharp angles of the balconets so that Paavo had to squint upon entering the room. A long slab of wood constituted the table, the knots still visible but the grain polished and buffed. Around the table sat the Czechs, the Poles and the Russians in that order, geographically from West to East, congregating like a tiny Eastern European Bloc. The American counterparts bookended the Bloc in designer swivel chairs, each of them guarded and their spines straight as they waited for orientation to begin. Barbara had disappeared once they'd arrived, but Paavo could hear her in the hallway, delegating the staff and ordering more ice and soft drinks.

In her seventeen years working as the coordinator of the Hallström program, Barbara had ushered in all types of students. With her keen sieve-like manner, she had succeeded in plucking the right type of student for the program, though their shared characteristics were invisible to the untrained eye. They were all model students, their grade point averages vetted and culled from a stack of applications by a team hired expressly for this mundane responsibility. The students have arrived in packs, or alone, with overstuffed suitcases as though they had been summoned to an expedition down the river on the Amazon instead of into the conveniences of cosmopolitan cities. They have arrived wielding only a simple backpack, causing host parents to worry about hygiene or whether they might have to coax their exchange student to change their undergarments. They have been sent home early for misconduct, which mostly consists of smoking pot or excessive drinking. They have received commendations, accolades, and have been recommended for honors programs at universities. They have been preppy, athletic, rebellious, lazy, overweight. They have come with eating disorders and autoimmune diseases. They have come with clean bills of health. They have come resplendent in designer clothing, exuding riches from every pore and orifice. They have come needy, some almost destitute, but no matter, because entering the hallowed fold of Hallström levels the playing field. They have all come with open minds, with open hearts, of that Barbara is sure. They have come with good intentions, the desire to lead, to fulfill the common Hallström goal.

As he stood upon the threshold of the room, Paavo couldn't imagine these ten people having anything less in common, not to mention how uniquely disparate he felt amongst them, like a lamb amongst wolves. Paavo glanced at each of the students already seated; the Polish and Russian girls flanked the Czech boy on either side. Pyotr's face appeared sour, as if he were constantly being forced to chew on lemons. Paavo made his choice to settle directly across from the Russian girl, a decision he immediately regretted because of her hair. It was so long and ratty that he almost wished he'd sat next to her so he could pick apart the tangles with his fingers. Nicholas settled in next to him and reached over immediately to the small bowls of snacks placed in a straight line like a dividing border between themselves and the rest of the group. The room was eerily silent, waiting with anticipation for their leader to enter the room. Barbara entered the room squinting, and held her hand up to her forehead like a visor.

"Looks like we're all here." Though she smiled, there was something chilling in her look, as if even though everyone had made it into the Hallström program, she was still constantly assessing and appraising every one of her recruits, to ensure that she had made the right decision.

"Now," Barbara said, standing in the front of the room and gripping the chair back in front of her, "let's reintroduce ourselves to one another, just in case we have forgotten names or faces." Paavo was secretly glad for this, as he had forgotten everyone's name except for mawkish Pyotr, who sat sullenly between the girl with the unkempt hair and Nicholas.

One by one they were reintroduced as partners: Pyotr-Evan, Sabine-Jess, Tomas-Justin, Anika (Unkempt Hair)-

Malaysia, Paavo-Nicholas. Each time Malaysia's name was mentioned, whether it was during a roll call or introductions, Paavo found himself stumbling over the concept of her. Malaysia was a slender black girl, with hair that puffed out around her head like a cloud of spun sugar. Her skin was darker than any Paavo had seen before. He hadn't encountered anyone quite like her, and not just because black people were few and far between in Estonia. What kind of a name was Malaysia, he wondered. She was clearly not from the country; their people were tawny-skinned with eyes that seemed to screw together at the corners. He had to force himself to stop looking at her; as if she could sense his gaze, Malaysia lifted her head and shifted her body to face the opposite direction.

Paavo stifled a yawn behind his hand and sat up so that his spine pressed against the back of the seat. It was the only way that he was going to get through this session. He could feel the creep of sleep start behind his eyelids and he twitched his mouth and licked his lips, willing himself to wake up.

Barbara was warming up. She looked out over her audience as though surveying her kingdom. It appeared that there was something there that just wasn't right. She honed in on something—someone—seated in the center of the table, and before Paavo knew what was going on, she was walking toward Evan. She held her hand out expectantly and Evan looked up.

"Give that to me *now*, Evan," she said, her voice like stone. Paavo leaned forward. What did the boy have in his possession? A cell phone? Cigarettes? Drugs? How had she even seen what he'd held in his lap? All the students leaned forward and craned their necks to see the contraband in Evan's hands. He handed over a small book and looked up at Barbara, his eyebrows knitted with confusion. Barbara held it up in front of her chest. It looked like a guidebook. The words *Understanding Russian Culture* were typed across the front in a firm, Communist font. "*This*, ladies and gentlemen, will *not* be tolerated. Do you understand?" Some of the students nodded, though Paavo didn't understand; perhaps it had a false cover and was hiding something else. But Barbara held the book over her head and marched to the front of the room, shaking it so that the pages flopped from side to side.

"This is poison," she said, her voice rising an octave above its normal pitch. "This type of book is what CliffsNotes is to literature. It's demeaning, it's degrading and it's uncalled-for. Hallström is about understanding. It's about bridging the gap between cultures that have for the past few decades been estranged, unfriendly and misunderstood. It's about breaking down all the stereotypes that books have printed or movies have compounded. If I see anything like this again, we're going to have serious words about your future here. Is that understood?"

There were soft murmurings throughout the classroom. Evan looked down at the ground, as though he were about to crumble into tiny pieces. Even Pyotr looked as though he had softened during Barbara's speech. Barbara lifted the book into the air again with both her hands, and with one swift motion, the book was torn right down its spine into two halves. She tore the pages from the binding in pieces and chapters and tossed them into the trash bin at the front of the room.

"I apologize for destroying your property, Evan," she said. "But that trash doesn't exist within the Hallström walls. This should mean more than a bolster on your college applications or simply for just a *cool* experience." Paavo flinched at the older woman's use of the word. It seemed forced and neglectful, creating an even wider gap between her and the students.

With the room shocked into silence, Barbara segued into a long lecture about social and cultural anthropology, about the strength of unique comprehension across borders. She reviewed the scheduled outings, check-ins, protocol for what to do in certain situations, difficulty in school, financial issues. Although each of the students had read all this in their course packets, she rehashed etiquette from both host and guest point of view, and though she stressed constantly that neither of them were to think of themselves as hosts and guests, she didn't change her choice of verbiage, either. What to do in a cultural conflict, what to do when someone wasn't understanding you, what to do when you had a problem only your parents could solve but they weren't there, what to do if you needed something your host brother or sister couldn't help you with. Barbara drawled on and on, her shiny hair reflecting the fluorescent lights over their heads.

It was when Barbara addressed bullying that Paavo felt all the air rush out of him. Pyotr had been sneering all morning; whether it was at Paavo or whether that was just the general look on his face, Paavo couldn't tell. But it reminded him of the gang at home. It made him remember things like the raised scab on his right knee. Things like the memory of the trash cans behind the Kadriorg market, and how the boys had threatened to stuff him into one of them and seal the lid shut. They'd seemed friendly enough at first, surrounding him on his walk home from the bus stop on the last day of school, bumping into his sides good-naturedly so that passersby didn't suspect that he was being walked against his will. In fact, it looked as if the pack of them were all walking together, toward a unified destination and that Paavo was happy to be right in the middle, the most popular boy of all. The gang was thickly cut, each of them like great slabs of black rye bread, and their identical brush cuts made them indistinguishable from one another. They were cartoons of themselves with their soldier-like severity and their fierce blue eyes stabbing into him with each glance.

But as soon as they cleared the busy stretch of Narva maantee, the boys flanked him on all sides in a most unfriendly manner, pulling at his knapsack, tugging at his collar. *Russian Rabbit,* one of them hissed in his ear. *Half-breed.* He flinched as a stubby finger traced figures into the back of his skull. *Know what that says?* another asked. Paavo shook his head. *Eighty-eight. A lucky number,* the boy said. *Next time, I'll ask you why.* As they reached Toompuiestee, the pack of boys shrugged him off like a scratchy sweater. Paavo had kept his head down to the ground the entire time, looking where his feet were stepping rather than the direction he was going. When he lifted his eyes once all the boys were gone, he realized that he was going the right way. They had steered him to the start of his street, which was a blessing and curse. They knew where he lived.

Once, just after he had returned home from school without incident, he'd happened to glance out the window to see one of the boys across the street. The boy looked harmless as he leaned against the gate of a garage, smoking a cigarette nonchalantly. He didn't tap the end of his cigarette for a long time, waiting for the ash to collect and when he did release it, he caught it in his cupped palm and turned toward the garage gate, his back to the street. Paavo couldn't make out what he was doing and he waited hours until the boy had left to make sure that he was truly gone before opening his door and approaching the gate. The number fourteen had been written in cigarette ash. Another number. Paavo felt as though he were being numbered, like a cow in anticipation for slaughter. A chill ran down the back of his neck as though someone were watching him. He didn't know what the number meant, but he ran back into the house and cried in the kitchen, not because he was scared, but because he was a coward.

The next morning, on the first day of summer vacation before his Hallström year, Paavo found that he couldn't leave the house. He loitered around the living room, toeing the carpet in his football cleats until his mother asked him to remove them lest he tear up the floor or go down to the pitch once and for all and stop floating around like a specter. He went into the den, the room that would become the exchange student's in a few months, and dragged his fingers across the books lined up like soldiers on the shelf. Leo's deep obsession with rummage sales and secondhand shops had resulted in an overflow of cheap, dog-eared books that no one would ever read. Perhaps this was the summer to change that. Paavo selected the first three from the top shelf and sat down at the bottom of the case. *How to Code, Computer Programming Made Easy, The Software Inside Hardware.*

He spent the summer inside or on the back porch as snowy feathers floated through the air from the neighbor's chicken coop next door, his face buried in a book. His naturally pale skin grew even more luminescent. The house had been his; Mari had spent most of her time in studios, returning home late at night from photography shoots, her face caked with makeup and her toes throbbing from being jammed into sky-high stilettos. Reading was the guise; he knew his parents wouldn't challenge him to go outside or find a summer job, and even Leo stopped his refrain of telling him to go down to the football pitch and play a game or two when he recognized that his son was studying without being told to do so. It wasn't that Paavo was a particularly keen student in general, and certainly hadn't professed any passions about anything much.

But the computer books had whetted Paavo's interest. At breakfast a few weeks before, Leo had been complaining about the government-funded computer initiatives that were being put in place in order to compensate for a lack of physical infrastructure and a workforce with limited education.

"They're giving our jobs to machines," Leo thundered, pounding at the newspaper on the table so that his teacup jumped. "They're making a mockery out of hard work." But Paavo had always believed in knowing your enemy. So he read everything he could about computers, including the endowments that had been granted at the Tallinn Institute of Technology.

After he'd exhausted reading the computer books at home, he ventured out to the Tallinn Central Library on a few furtive and brazen occasions to learn more about the information age. He collected a stack of books on programming, wiring and hacking, stowed them in his bag and headed toward the World War II section of the library. He had some research to do, namely on numbers. Eighty-eight was comprised of the eighth letter of the alphabet, *H*, which when doubled, stands for *Heil Hitler.* Fourteen: the number of words that create the doctrine established by David Lane, a white supremacist who had become one of the voices of the contemporary Nazi party.

"We must secure the existence of our people and a future for white children." Paavo whispered the words out loud to himself in the cool stacks of the library over and over before shaking his head as if to release them from his entire being, replacing the slim volume in its place on the shelf and slipping onto a bus back home to Kadriorg.

Across the conference table in the orientation, Pyotr blew air out of his mouth, which was still curled in its perpetual sneer. Pyotr's hulking frame, his hunched shoulders, his Cro-Magnon brow—they were all too reminiscent of the gang back home. How had Pyotr made it into this program with his belligerent face and his uninterested countenance? Paavo lowered his head down between his knees and took deep breaths.

"Are you okay?" Nicholas whispered.

"Fine," Paavo said, without looking up.

"Do you need some air? We should probably ask for a break." Nicholas glanced up toward Barbara, who had just dimmed the lights and was pulling up a PowerPoint presentation on the screen.

"Just taking everything in. Probably should have had some more breakfast." Paavo raised his head and grabbed a handful of pretzels from a nearby bowl. The saltiness seemed to calm something in him as he crunched and tried his best to concentrate.

At the afternoon's first set of icebreakers, the students had to share something about themselves that no one else knew. He watched the intensity in Sabine's eyes as she searched for something interesting to share with the group, how Pyotr chewed on his bottom lip and scowled in thought. Paavo wondered what might happen if he divulged the truth: "I'm Paavo from Tallinn. I am happy to get some distance from home because I am being harassed and bullied by a group of neo-Nazis who want me to join their gang."

He could only imagine the drama that would ensue after that admission. His parents would be called; they might force him into that all-American practice of going to therapy, lying vulnerably prone while a man or woman analyzed every word out of his mouth. He would be monitored carefully for the rest of the program in case there were signs of weakness or breakdown. That was the last thing he wanted, so he kept his mouth shut and said the following: "I'm Paavo. I'm from Tallinn and I really like riddles."

Halfway through the session, Paavo had to use the bathroom. He slipped out of his chair and found the men's room down the hall at the curve of a corridor. He stared at himself in the mirror. His face appeared wan and washed-out, as though he hadn't slept in days. He rubbed his eyes, and pinched his cheeks, coaxing the blood to flow through his veins. The toilet flushed, and Paavo flinched. He hadn't realized someone else was in the bathroom with him. Pyotr opened the door to a stall, zipping his fly and grinning—or was it sneering—at Paavo.

"Pathetic," Pyotr said, as he stood in front of the sink alongside him, wiping something off his face. His eyes met Paavo's in the mirror.

"Excuse me?" Paavo felt his voice squeak, and Pyotr turned to face him.

"I said, 'pathetic,'" Pyotr said again, wiping his hands against his thick trunk-like thighs. "This whole thing is just pathetic. As if we don't know how to behave. Adults never give us enough credit."

Paavo watched him as he smoothed down his sweater, and rubbed at the tattoo on the back of his neck. Those certainly seemed like numbers printed at the base of his skull.

"Did you hear me? I'm talking to you," Pyotr said. "Hello?" The set of Pyotr's jaw was all too familiar. He even had a crooked smile like the gang leader. Paavo could feel his stomach start to fall. He put his hands up in front of him for mercy, and began backing away, his desire to use the bathroom long forgotten.

"Yes, yes," Paavo said. "I'm just... I'll see you back in

there." But Paavo's foot caught on a cleaning mop that leaned against the wall, and he fell backward. The last thing he saw before his head hit a stall door was Pyotr's face. Then everything had gone dark.

NORA

New York City
September 2002

This was what life after the accident felt like to Nora, as though a switch had been flipped and the spotlight on her life had been turned off. She constantly felt as though she were wandering around in the dark, groping for answers, reading faces, trying to make sense of what had happened in her brain. She'd certainly made sense of her feelings in the year since the accident, and she could communicate how frustrated and helpless she felt. Perhaps she would do well in the support group after all; these things always tried to get you to connect with your feelings. But would acknowledging the feelings help them go away?

After her brother left for the airport, Nora spent a long time lying on her back in her bedroom, clutching her black notebook and staring at her wall of quotes. It had been about a month after the accident that she had first starting writing directly on the wall in permanent marker. She'd done it out of pure rage at first, scribbling angsty snippets from whiny bands that all her friends listened to, and then graduating to more philosophical lines. Words of wisdom from Shakespeare and Sonic Youth each bore equal presence on the wall. It would be another six months before she would abandon the wall altogether and whitewash over it in another fit of frustration, but for now the wall was her own personal therapy.

Her mother had told her not to be late for the group, but she dawdled, opening her notebook and flipping through the pages. She hated overhearing her parents talk about her as though she wasn't *right there*. They discussed her at length— out of concern, she had to admit—but it was still humiliating. She had already started living away from them in college. She'd already staked her independence. But after the diagnosis, she found she couldn't return. She'd been intimidated by the prospects of all those faces: her suitemates, her professors, her thesis advisor. At the end of the summer, once her arm had fully healed and her skin had grafted itself back into her own cells, she called the registrar and told them she was taking the year off. It would be a setback, and it would certainly be embarrassing, Nora knew, but it wouldn't be as tragic as returning to a campus filled with people who called out to her but whom she couldn't greet back.

Her stay in the hospital had been over a year ago, but it still felt as if she had just returned. From time to time, her leg pulsed as a cruel reminder of the accident. As if she could forget. In the first few days of her stay at St. Paul's General, doctors had all tried their luck at diagnosis. They asked her to recall the specifics of the accident.

"I was crossing the street at Fifth Avenue and Twenty-Fourth Street and a car barreled into me. I remember flipping over onto the hood but not much else after that."

They asked her to recall what she had been doing, where she had been going.

"I'm home from college on spring break. I have to go to Myrtle Beach with my friends. We're leaving. They're going to leave without me." She had attempted to rise out of the bed, but her wrists and ankles had been tethered there beneath the blankets. They asked her to recall her name— "Nora," she'd scoffed. They asked her to recall the names of the people standing in front of her. "Dr. Li, Dr. Charles, Dr. Kelly." They asked her to name the couple sitting on either side of her bed, each holding one of her hands. She rolled her eyes. But when the request was repeated, she stared into each face with determination and focus for what felt like hours before she turned her head, slumped back into the pillows and said that the exercise was stupid. The woman had broken down then, biting her hand so as to contain her tears, and the man had come over from his side of the bed to comfort her. Nora had watched all this, as she had watched Doctors Li, Charles and Kelly exchange glances and purse their lips before they scribbled copious notes into their individual ledgers. One of them picked up the phone in her room to make a page, and in moments, a flurry of men and women in white coats descended upon the room.

After a number of days, questions and tests, the team of neurologists and orthopedists gathered the man, her father Arthur, and the woman, her mother Stella, into the hallway to deliver their diagnosis in hushed, hurried tones. Arthur had erupted in the hallway at the mention of the words. "That's ridiculous. Nora knows why she's here. She knows her name. She can remember what color her sheets are, what kind of cake she had on her fifteenth birthday. She knows who she is." This time, it was Stella who calmed him, walking him into the stairwell, where his angry shouts echoed and bounced off the landings and banisters.

In the end they told Nora everything, from her broken

femur to the damaged sliver of fusiform gyrus in her brain. How could such a tiny piece of spongelike matter make such a difference? The doctors had tried to soften the diagnosis by reinforcing the fact that Nora could still function regularly on a daily basis. She could eat, study, get a job, find a husband.

"Not really sure how that one is relevant," Arthur had smirked in the hospital room while Stella held her daughter's hand. "Everyone knows you would have no trouble in that field even with a bag over your head." The neurologists weren't entirely certain of the long-term effect this might have, but the terminology was enough to scare the Grands: brain damage. Nora had forced herself to smile at her father's attempt at levity, but brain damage was brain damage. Whenever people mentioned it, there were always a few shocked moments thereafter, with audibly sharp intakes of breath and sympathetic sighs exhaling them.

By the time Nora was released into the care of her parents and a borrowed wheelchair, she had lost all track of time. Her father wheeled her from the elevator and into the foyer, where her eyes lit on familiar things. She took in the pile of colorful throw pillows in the corner, the twin towers of stacked magazines on either end of the coffee table, the plush couch that had long since broken its spine but was so comfortable that the Grands couldn't bring themselves to part with it. Even the word *familiar* had become familiar to her. She cherished the word now, because when the doctors used it, it meant that she was doing well, that she could identify things. *Familiar* was always one step closer to being normal. From the threshold of the dark dining room, she could hear whispered rustlings and excited murmurs.

"She's here," a voice whispered. She turned to look back at her father, that not-quite-yet-familiar face, but one she was retraining herself to know in the antiseptic starkness of the hospital room. He smiled down at her and pushed her farther into the room, where a flashbulb went off, illuminating a few bobbing balloons and a group of people gathered around a large cake.

"Welcome home!" they chorused together, and broke into embarrassed giggles at their seemingly rehearsed symphony. Nora knew she should smile so she did, but there was a halting in the way her cranial muscles worked, taut and obdurate, as though coming out of hibernation. She engaged her brain, forcing her lips to purse together and show her teeth, but she didn't mean it. She didn't even feel it. Seven strangers smiled back at her. She turned back to look at her father. He licked his lips and smiled even harder, glancing at the woman who stood just off to the side, methodically massaging each digit of her fingers as though she were taking a tally. Nora could see the gold stars twinkling in the woman's ears. She smiled harder at their presence, at their continuity. She was forever grateful for those gold stars that helped her identify her own mother.

A boy approached her, holding out his hands. "Welcome home, Nor," he said. "I really missed you." He bent over to hug her and the floral smell of Pert Plus mixed with the metallic scent of the oil he used to clean his flute wafted off him. Her brother, Nicholas. She remembered the scent in the hospital room as he had sat by her side, watching her concernedly and narrating the play-by-play of his recent wrestling matches. Her own brother had been distilled to a smell. She found herself hoping that he kept up with flute practice and being that hygienic boy whose sweaty wrestling practices encouraged him to wash his hair every single day. As he leaned in to her she put her arms around him and breathed him in. She wanted to pack this smell, to put it in a little atomizer and spritz it every so often so that everything around her smelled just like him. But that left six others. Behind Nicholas came a tall girl with a cleft chin. She had sandy hair and wore a retainer across her top teeth. When the girl bent down, she whispered, "Claire" in Nora's ear, like a blessing. Nora looked up at her best friend, grateful for the answer to an unasked question. Claire tightened her grip on Nora then, and Arthur had to put his hand on Claire to remind her that Nora was still very weak.

"Sorry," Claire whispered, backing away, her eyes glittering with tears, the ridge of that perfect cleft chin quivering with sadness. One by one the others came forward—her friends and classmates from high school, from her childhood, from the building. They each whispered their names in her ear like an invocation, and Nora felt glad that she'd had each of their names on the tip of her tongue as they leaned down. All except one; when the last boy approached her, she flinched and turned her head down. She hadn't meant to be rude, but she couldn't place anything about this boy, from his polo shirt to his porcupine hair. His arms were reaching out to embrace her, but this boy couldn't look more like a stranger to her. He looked up at Arthur before he came any closer to Nora, his eyes beseeching him. Nora couldn't see behind her, but Arthur had shrugged his shoulders sadly and shaken his head. Stella had whispered, "Maybe later, Jason. She's probably exhausted."

Jason backed away, nodding, and joined the group of girls and Nicholas, who were still using the dining table as a sort of barricade between them and her wheelchair. Nora turned her head slightly and whispered toward her parents. Whispering was all she seemed to be capable of right now. It seemed to be the only tone appropriate for the situation. Anything more and everything would appear normal. "I need a minute, Dad."

Arthur patted Nora on the shoulder and swung her chair toward the hallway. As she passed the group of people, they were all nearly indistinguishable in a huddle. There was only enough time to recognize that her brother was wearing a maroon hoodie with Harvard emblazoned across the chest before she was wheeled down the hall to her room. The late-afternoon light softened the walls, glancing off a window outside to illuminate all the framed photos on the walls and on her shelves.

"Just wheel me to the vanity. I can take it from there. My hands are fine, you know." She shook them jazzily.

"I know you can do it, honey. I just don't want you to tire yourself out."

"I have to get used to it." He parked her where she had requested and kissed her softly on the cheek. "We'll be in the dining room. Just call if you need anything."

Nora nodded and waited until the door had clicked shut. Once she was alone, she looked up. Purple bruises blossomed under her eyes and her lips were red and chapped. Her cheekbones looked all wrong to her, as did even the color of her eyes. They had been brown, she'd thought. But now they looked gray. She was looking at a stranger. This face was unknown to her. This face, this entire temperament was like an arranged marriage to a person she would have to spend the rest of her life with, sight unseen. She shut her eyes, turned her wheelchair away from the mirror and buried her face in her hands. She didn't want to look at herself anymore. She didn't want to look at anyone.

Everything felt drained—her brain, her heart, her tear ducts. There was a tentative knock at the door, and when it was pushed gently open, Harvard walked in, wafting that burnished flowery aroma.

Nora looked up. "Nicky...?" she asked.

He nodded. "Here's how I see it, Nor. I figure that now we're even. You're face blind. I'm left-handed. The playing field has finally been leveled."

"How is that leveled?" Nora said. "Being left-handed is not an affliction."

"I can't tell you how many wrestling matches I've lost because of it," Nicholas said.

"Last I checked, being left-handed wasn't classified under brain damage. And when's the last time being left-handed ever caused social suicide? 'Cause that's what this is, you know. I'm fucked."

"It's not that bad. It'll get easier. It's just hard now 'cause it's new. Look, I got you this," Nicholas held out a small black notebook toward her. "I thought it might help."

"What is it?" Nora took it from him. The pages inside were blank except for the first one, which had Nicholas's name on top.

Nicholas Grand
5'10"
Hazel eyes
Broad shoulders
Handsome
Stunning smile

"You're too young to be resorting to the Personals section. What is this?"

Nicholas grinned. "It's a face book. You make notes on people. That way, you can put the descriptions to the faces." Years later, when that ubiquitous social media site would seemingly take over the world, Nora would remark that if only her brother had taken his idea to the internet, *he* might have been the millionaire by his thirtieth birthday.

"And I see this one has been written extremely objectively," Nora said, arching an eyebrow.

"Well, you can amend those based on whatever helps you remember." Nicholas grinned.

"Thanks, Nicky."

"We can go back out and start working on it together," Nicholas said, nodding toward the door. "Starting with Jason. How about ape-like?"

"I know Mom and Dad did it to help, but I didn't ask for all that." Nora sighed, waving her hands in the direction of the dining room. "I didn't even ask to come home from the hospital. I would have been fine sitting propped up in that bed for the rest of my life, with the doctors shining their little penlights in my face, whispering all around me like I had lost my hearing. Gesturing toward me as though I had gone blind. No, asshole, I can hear and see just fine. The problem is that I can't remember your face."

"The mind is funny," Nicholas said. "Your brain is probably exhausted from everything that's happened. You'll be okay, Nor. We'll all help you."

She looked at his sweatshirt. "What happened, did you get into Harvard while I was in the hospital, boy genius?" Nicholas looked sheepish.

"No, this is the one Claire gave you. I stole it while you were in there, 'cause it smelled like you." He raised his arms above his head and peeled it off, offering it to her. She accepted it and buried her nose in it.

"Now it smells like you."

"Really? What do I smell like?"

"Pert Plus and flute oil."

He sniffed under his arms. "Add it," he said, nodding toward the notebook. Nora scribbled down the observation onto Nicholas's page. "What about me? What do I smell like?"

Nicholas leaned toward her and breathed in. "Raisins."

"I don't even like raisins."

"I know. That's what's ironic."

"I can't believe I didn't recognize Jason. That was some mind fuck."

"It's okay. It'll take time. Though if you ask me, Jason is definitely worth forgetting."

"I guess that's one way of relegating an ex-boyfriend to the recesses of your mind. Or literally forgetting about him altogether." Nora smiled at her brother, but she could feel tears building in the back of her eyelids, threatening to weaken her resolve, forcing her to screw her eyes shut and bury her face in her hands. Nicholas held her tight, and while she tried to hold her tears in, they burned her eyes as they trickled out from behind her fingers.

The ironic thing was that when Nora was in high school, she'd known every single person in her graduating class of five hundred. She'd started introducing herself to everyone and, by the middle of her freshman year, waved to everyone in the hallways. That overfriendliness had begun as a defense mechanism at first. Saying hi to everyone seemed less obnoxious than saying hi to no one, so she began associating herself with them all—the cheerleaders, the football players, though she'd never been to a school game. She waved to the kids who dressed in black trench coats and who played that fantasy card game Magic on the sixth floor outside the English department. She waved to the theater kids, and the preppies, and even the teachers—the ones she'd had the years before. The ones she'd inherit the following one. She'd felt strange doing it at first, waving and acknowledging everyone. But that had been in high school. That had been before the accident.

Shortly after she'd been brought home from the hospital, her parents had given her space, encouraging her to take all the time she needed to heal. They let her postpone her return to college until she felt ready. But at the end of what would have been the second semester of her junior year, on a dark overcast Saturday afternoon, Stella had silently placed a few books on Nora's bed and walked out of the room. Nora had waited until her mother's footsteps had faded away down the hall before she vaulted herself out of her desk chair and limped over to read the titles. *Facing Your Fears, Understanding Facial Recognition, Face Prosopagnosia Down.* Nora had seen it as a personal affront. *This is what you have,* the books were calling. *This is your new label and you can't shed it until you recognize who you have become.* She needed some kind of protection from the elements, from herself, even, so she'd cracked open the covers and learned how to combat this feeling—this feeling of helplessness, of unfamiliarity. There were tricks and tools you could use. But a lot of it relied upon good friends and people that you could trust inherently. And at the time, she wasn't sure she could get that. She didn't know how to talk about her situation. She couldn't very well introduce herself to some stranger that didn't have any specific identifying demarcations and expect them to become friends with her.

She rolled over now and hugged her knees to her chest. *I can't do this.* She swallowed hard, pushing back tears that were poised to spill. *It's too difficult. I want mandatory name tags. My brain hurts.* It was exhausting, having to focus even harder on everything all the time, to have to imprint someone's face onto your brain. It wasn't the way it used to be, where you made casual eye contact upon meeting someone. Now she was forced to devour faces with her eyes.

After a few silent moments of crying, she sat herself up and went into the adjoining bathroom. Her face was tan from the summer, but crying had whitewashed it so it appeared pale and gaunt. She squeezed her eyes shut and examined herself in the mirror. Thank goodness for that beauty spot right on the crown of her cheekbone. But she would never forget her own self, would she? She gripped the edges of the ceramic basin with both hands, feeling as though she herself might sink through the tiles. Her mascara was bleeding down her face; she looked like a sad clown in a Marcel Marceau sketch. A limp washcloth hung from the edge of the sink where she'd left it this morning, and she polished her face with it. A new person appeared, clean of the mask of makeup. It was so surprising to her how different she looked without it, completely new, washed out, as if she'd just been born. But that thought made her start crying all over again. *How can I not even recognize myself,* she asked through blurry vision as she stared menacingly at the mirror, engaging with it, pushing herself to recollect some aspect of who she was, what she looked like. She used to think her features were so striking, but clearly they weren't. Clearly her features looked to her naked eye like anyone's features, because she didn't even look like herself. Not to her, anyway. When was this going to stop? Would this eventually turn into a dull headache that might only pierce the edges of her memory? Her memory was the one thing she had. Other than faces, she remembered everything. Vacations, graduations, those mundane family moments that suddenly seemed so precious. It was faces that escaped her entirely.

She felt daunted by the day's task of attending this group, already drained by the prospect of conjuring features, memorizing jaw formation and the way dimples poked like divots into faces. She would have to concentrate extra hard when someone addressed her, her eyes keen for signs of nail biting or cuticle peeling that might tip her off on his or her identity. She had promised her mom and Dr. Li that she would attend the group and see what it was all about. She hadn't promised to commit to it, but if Dr. Li thought it would help, she would go. Maybe she'd start to feel a little like herself again. Maybe that light would finally start to turn back on in her life.

NICHOLAS

Tallinn
September 2002

When Nicholas's plane departed after the hour-long stopover in Stockholm, the light had already been waning, highlighting islands floating like clusters of paint chips. Tiny crystals of ice spider-webbed across the glass window, splintering the dark outside into tiled mosaics of uncertainty. With the plane starting its descent over Tallinn, the sun was completely gone, and Nicholas felt the darkness seeping into his chest and sticking to his insides, eclipsing light and hope. He had considered that he might be homesick, but he was more fearful of the unknown, of the foreign, of the discomfort that might await him. He stretched his arms overhead, his fingers striking against the light and air panel. As the plane circled over a postage-stamp-sized tarmac, the fear saturated him completely like a sponge. He focused on shaking it off with the same concentration he used to approach a wrestling match: fiercely and with conviction. But fear clung to him like a straitjacket, pinning his arms to his sides and rendering him helpless.

As he stepped through the doors of the plane, warm air whipped through the slats of the air bridge, attacking him like another fold of ammunition. Even the immigration hall with its warm halogen lights didn't soften the pall that seemed to have settled over him. He handed over his passport with his Estonian visa plastered inside. The control guard scarcely glanced at him or the pages inside before stamping it heavily and passing it back across the divider. Nicholas felt warm and turgid from the compression of the plane as he made his way down a long ramp that led to Arrivals. The hall was practically empty; just a few limp businessmen holding laptop bags and searching for their drivers; flight attendants walking briskly past him, their heels clicking against the floor as they wheeled their bags away from the airport as fast as they could.

Either the passengers on his plane had been incredibly fast to collect their belongings, or no one had checked in any bags. Nicholas's suitcase was the only one making a plaintive, circuitous path, and as he pulled it off, he noticed Paavo walking toward him. Paavo was even wirier than Nicholas had remembered, as though the slightest flick of a finger might upset him. His fine, blond hair was so light that he appeared bald. He remembered how Barbara had mentioned her pleasure with this partner match, how much she had thought Paavo and Nicholas would have in common. Nicholas could hardly believe that he would share any common ground with this boy. He remembered how skittish Paavo had been at orientation, how pale and wan he'd looked, and how that hulking Russian student had come bursting into the conference room to announce that the Estonian boy had passed out in the bathroom. Paavo had been all right—mostly dazed and extremely embarrassed. But Nicholas couldn't help but think that he'd gotten the short end of the exchange student stick.

"Nico," Paavo said. "Welcome."

"Nicholas." He gripped the handle of his suitcase and put his hand out. "Paavo. Good to see you. You feeling better?"

The boy nodded and looked away. "It was nothing that day. I hadn't eaten." He took Nicholas's hand and reached for the suitcase handle with his left. "Was the flight all right?"

"It was long," Nicholas said, stifling a yawn.

"I hope you are hungry. Mama has been cooking all day for your arrival."

"I'm starving. I slept through the meals."

"Come," Paavo said, turning toward the door. "Papa is in the car outside."

"I forgot how good your English is."

"I told you—mostly everyone in Estonia speaks English. After all—" Paavo turned around to face Nicholas, who stopped short behind him "—it is easy when there are only three words in the English language. What are they?"

"Huh?"

"It's a riddle."

"Oh. I give up."

"The English language," Paavo exclaimed triumphantly. "Get it? One—The. Two—English. Three—Language?"

"Right," Nicholas said, forcing a smile.

"Anyway, you'll pick up some Estonian while you're here. I think you're taking a class at school. But I can teach you some things, as well."

"I'd love that." Secretly, Nicholas wanted the information, vocabulary and pronunciations to travel by osmosis from Paavo's brain to his own so they could skip all the embarrassing times when Nicholas would feel inferior to Paavo, when he would feel beholden. Nicholas had a good ear—that's what Senora Hall told him in Spanish II—but he wasn't sure where his talents lay in a language that sounded as though it had more vowels than consonants.

Nicholas followed Paavo meekly toward the door, feeling as though he were being brought to the gallows. In the small embankment outside baggage claim, the brisk air sent a shiver down his spine. Was it still September in Estonia? It felt so much colder. He zipped his jacket up to his nose, breathing in the salty, damp flavor of his unwashed self. He squinted at the streetlights; their contrast against the inky sky was blinding. A small brown Lada chugged at the curb, streaked with gray stripes of dirt as though it were aging. Paavo swung his suitcase into the trunk and nodded toward the passenger seat.

"Please sit in the front."

Nicholas opened the door and ducked his head, folding his legs in front of him. The car was warm and smelled like petrol and peppermint. "Papa, Nico. Nico, this is my father, Leo." The man in the driver's seat looked nothing like Paavo. He was broad and brown and hairy, reminding Nicholas of a big Russian bear. Leo grunted and grimaced, which Nicholas translated into a greeting and a smile. The evasive Estonian smile would emerge eventually. Coaxing it out of Leo would be one of Nicholas's first challenges in the Sokolov household. Paavo's father pulled at the gears, squeaking the car out of the airport road and onto a slip of a highway.

"Don't mind the car," Paavo said. "Papa refuses to trade in his trusty Russian beast for something a bit more modern." Leo threw off a few long sentences into the air. Nicholas tensed at the sound. Was that English? He couldn't be sure. Paavo sighed from the backseat and spun off a few of his own, ending with, "Papa, English please. For Nico."

"Nico, I am saying," Leo said, shifting the car into the

next gear, "that this car has been with us for the past fifteen years. There is no problem with it."

"It's actually Nicholas," he said. "And hey, I'm with you. If the car gets you from point A to point B…" he said.

Leo glanced at him. "How was the travel? Are you wanting tired? Wanting sleep?"

"I'll be okay," Nicholas said, though the moment he uttered the words, he found himself stifling a yawn. "What time is it anyway?"

"Eighteen thirty. We'll take it easy tonight. Mama's made dinner and you can go to bed early. There is a mall where we shop." Paavo pointed. "And they are building a market there. And another mall there." Shadowy, mountainous structures sulked in the recesses of deep parking lots. Silhouettes of cranes stood out against the harsh blaze of floodlights. Nicholas could see large pits below them, which would eventually be filled in with cement and the foundations of more shopping centers.

"You've come at an interesting time," Paavo said. "The city has finally begun to fix some of the damage done by the Soviets, so there's a lot of building and renovating going on." The land was otherwise flat, but punctuated every so often with a slightly taller structure in the process of being overhauled. There were cranes and heaps of construction material all along the side of the road. The entire city was in a state of flux.

"They have made the old salt-storage building into a museum of architecture, and we have a new multiplex in the city with eleven screens," Paavo said. "I'll have to take you there." Nicholas nodded, deciding not to share the fact that there were numerous movie theaters in New York City that boasted multiple screens. Old brick buildings that had been factories, storage space, silos, were being converted into retail space, lofts and offices. In ten years, when independent businesses would start to do the same to factories and large building spaces in the outer boroughs of New York City, it would be considered "hipster" and all associated retail and services would be priced at triple their actual value.

Tallinn didn't look very different than Queens, especially near the airport. The existing buildings—from what he could tell in the darkness with intermittent streetlamps shining through—were monstrous industrial edifices, looming in the background as the trusty little Lada zoomed down the road. There was a cloak of darkness settled over everything, as though in September, the country had already settled into hibernation.

Nicholas had been anticipating a long drive, like the one from JFK to Manhattan that could take more than an hour. But the industrial-sized buildings began to shrink in stature, the road narrowed, and soon they were driving over cobblestones.

"We live in Kadriorg," Paavo said. "One of the nicest neighborhoods in all of Tallinn. We are very near the park, where there is a castle and a pond and most importantly to most Europeans, a football pitch." Modest wooden houses began to flank them on either side of the road, making Nicholas feel as though he was entering a fairy-tale village. The houses differed in color, size and design; they'd just passed a moss-green cedar-planked one across from a humble mauve ranch-style. Nicholas found himself disappointed when Leo parked the Lada in front of a plain brown wooden cottage, turned the engine off, and the three sat in the silence as the muffler slowly ticked to a halt. Nicholas dreaded going back into the darkness, but Paavo and Leo had unloaded his suitcase and were waiting for him on the driveway.

"Come, come," Leo said. "We will be late for dinner." He

held his arm out toward the front door, where a tall woman stood. Her hair was either so blond it looked silvery or so silvery it looked blond. Her rosy cheeks were the only color she wore. Her lips held the trace of a smile, but her head was erect and alert as though she had been trained not to slacken her facial muscles. Nicholas had studied the Dust Bowl in United States History the year before; that famous photo of the woman staring into the distance with children clutching at her shoulders reminded him of the woman's hardened face.

"Tere," the woman called to him. "You are welcome." She nodded, as if she were calling a puppy home from its romp outside rather than her new adopted son for the next four months. Nicholas approached her, and at the threshold, wafts of cooked meat mixed with the stark coolness of outside air. "I am Vera, Paavo's mother. Welcome to Tallinn." She held out a small posy of orange marigolds. "This is the traditional welcome here in Estonia. You are very welcome to Tallinn and to our home."

"Thank you. It's good to be here." He accepted the flowers, clutching them in his fist and expecting to be enveloped into her chest. Instead, she stepped aside so he could enter the house.

He had imagined a warm, cozy gingerbread-like house with antiques on the walls and framed black-and-white photos yellowed with light. But the decor was minimalistic; the white walls provided little dimension to the room, the dining table took up as much room as it needed and while there were casserole dishes and pots on the table, everything else was concealed behind cabinets and drawers. He had only been in Estonia for an hour, but Nicholas furiously missed the chaos of his home.

The same lump that had arisen in his throat when Stella had hugged him goodbye appeared in his throat again, but he swallowed it back. There was no way he was going to cry now. But his body was bucking being here. The tears he blinked back had sent some kind of signal to his stomach and it rumbled like an approaching storm. He had slept through the meal services on the plane, and he was ravenous. He swallowed the saliva that had been collecting in his mouth. He felt light-headed, as though he might faint right there on top of the table.

"Would you like to eat first, or sauna?"

"Sauna?" Nicholas looked around, bewildered.

Vera swiped an errant piece of hair away from her forehead and placed her hands on either side of Nicholas's shoulders. "And will you have coffee or *kvass*?" Nicholas spun around to Paavo, who was stepping through the door, lugging his suitcase with him.

"I… I don't know. What's *kvass*?"

"We have a sauna out back," Paavo said, breathing heavily from the weight of Nicholas's suitcase. "It was actually the first on our street, but since then, the neighbors have been building their own. It's sort of like our religion. In Estonia, we believe any bad day can be made right with a sauna. It's absolutely best after a long flight. Unless you'd like dinner first?"

"I am pretty hungry."

"And *kvass*, is like nonalcoholic beer. Papa makes his own. It's delicious. You should try it." Leo had already poured a stein, which he held out to Nicholas.

"And Nico," Vera said. "What would you like to—"

Paavo interrupted. Nicholas was able to decipher the difference between the Russian he had spoken in the car to his father and the Estonian he spouted out now. Both had been delivered rapidly, and both had left Nicholas wondering how in the world he was going to catch on in four months' time. Vera pursed her lips and spouted something back. Paavo shook his head. *"Lõõgastuda,* Mama," he said, pressing his hands in downward motions like undulating waves. *"Lõõgastuda."*

"My son is telling me to relax," Vera said. "You, too, Nico. You relax. Okay?"

"Sure," Nicholas said, though the instruction made him tense a bit more, his back going rigid against the chair.

Vera began carting dishes to the stove, ticking the burners on one at a time. Nicholas sat at the round table in the middle of the kitchen, gripping the mug of *kvass* with both hands. The ale had a pale yellow tint with tiny effervescent bubbles escaping to the top of the glass every so often. He lowered his mouth to the lip of the mug and took a sip as Leo and Paavo watched. Caraway seeds and yeast filled his mouth, as though he were drinking a loaf of rye bread.

"What do you think, Nico?" Paavo asked.

"Nicholas," he said under his breath. Nicholas wasn't sure at what point it would become awkward to correct everyone about his name, though he felt as if he'd passed that point already. It was too early to concede, though in a few days, it would get too frustrating to correct everyone at school, and he would only be referred to as Nico from that point forward.

"It's refreshing." The room deflated, as though it had been holding its breath. Even Leo, who had gripped the steering wheel tensely and barely glanced at Nicholas during the drive, seemed to have engineered himself a new, scowl-free face. The table was silent as Vera reheated the pots on the stove one by one, lids rattling as steam pressure built up beneath them.

"Where's, um, Marie?" Nicholas took another sip of *kvass.*

"Mari," Leo corrected. "She is model."

"She has been in St. Petersburg for the past few days for some new fashion magazine. She'll be back tomorrow," Paavo said.

If Nora felt like the spotlight on her life had gone out, Nicholas felt as though there were three trained on him. He had fumbled Mari's name, been unable to correct the Sokolovs about his own and could feel the drilling intensity of three pairs of eyes since he'd set foot into the kitchen. He felt exposed and naked, as if he was wandering the streets in a dream. As he looked around him, he realized that the contours of this room were all he knew in this country. He didn't know his way around this town, or even around this house. Nicholas felt as though he had been set loose in a place that could consume him unless he was very careful. Leo pulled him out of his thoughts by plunking a clear bottle down on the table.

"Here is good stuff," he proclaimed. "Now we make you good Estonian man with hairy chest."

"Viru Valge," Nicholas read aloud. "Vodka?"

"Your initiation into Estonia," Paavo said, grinning at his father.

Standing at the sink with her back to the table, Vera raised her voice like a dagger in the air, stabbing with its elongated vowels. Paavo responded in English.

"No, of course, Mama. He doesn't have to if he doesn't want to." Paavo looked at Nicholas. "You don't have to if you don't want to." Nicholas shrugged; while the vodka might rankle Vera, this appeared to be the way to Papa Leo's softer side.

"I'll try it," he said. Leo grinned, revealing stained teeth as though they had been steeped in tea, frozen in sepia for posterity. He lined four tumblers along the edge of the table.

Vera shook her head. *"Mitte minu jaoks."*

"Oh, come on, Mama. Just one to welcome Nico."

She sighed and turned to face them, closing her eyes as she held her hand out for the glass, as though she were receiving a rap on the knuckles in penance. Nicholas looked around at the faces, Vera's resigned and tired, Paavo's shining and expectant, and Leo's suspicious and taut.

"*Terviseks,*" Leo said, raising his glass and looking Nicholas squarely in the eye.

"*Terviseks,*" they echoed obediently. Nicholas let the liquid slide down his throat like a luge. The burn in his throat wasn't new; he had done shots at parties before, but never with adults as chaperones, as instigators.

"More?" Leo asked, lifting the bottle.

"It's very good," Nicholas said, holding his glass out.

"No," Leo said as he tilted the bottle into Nicholas's tumbler. "The best."

Vera placed the dishes in the center of the round table. "Okay, enough drink. Now we eat. As we say, *head isu.* Eat well."

Paavo reached for a plate of dark sliced bread. "Have some homemade *rukkileib.* And there's pork and potatoes in that dish over there. And you must try the *sult.* It's very Estonian." Nicholas was passed a clear, jelly-like substance wrapped around chunks of white, fleshy meat. The dish quivered as though it were terrified to be consumed.

"This all looks wonderful. I'll start with the pork, I think," Nicholas said. "I need something hearty to stick to my bones." Vera gave him a tight smile as she passed him the platter of pink meat with a hard shell.

"The skin's the best part," Paavo said, tapping his knife against it. "It's Mama's specialty. No one can get it like her."

"Nico, tomorrow after school, Paavo and I take you for ID pickup from city office," Leo said. He hadn't touched his plate, but had refilled his vodka tumbler three times since they had sat down at the table.

"I believe Hallström has already applied for one on your behalf," Paavo said. "So we just have to pick it up."

"What do I need the ID card for?" Nicholas asked.

"Every Estonian has one, including visitors who will be here for a long time. You need it for everything—voting, parking, transportation," Vera said.

Paavo shoveled *sult* into his mouth. Nicholas could barely stand to watch him. He reminded him of Figaro, Toby's cat, lowering his lynx-like head to lap up food from a bowl on the floor. He turned his head to watch Vera and Leo, who took large forkfuls in silence, the clicking of their jaws and soft clash of teeth the only sound in the room. From somewhere in the hallway, or the living room, Nicholas presumed, there was the gentle ticking of a clock. The warm meat and the doughy potatoes stabilized his stomach but weighed down his head. His eyelids felt as though they were dripping vodka. He shouldn't have had that third glass.

"I'm so sorry to be rude," he said, breaking the silence. "But I just can't keep my eyes open anymore. Could I—"

"Sauna!" Paavo cried. "It's going to help you sleep through the night. It helps with jet lag."

"Not tonight, man," Nicholas said. "I want to try it, but I'm so tired."

"Don't bully him, Paavo. Let the boy sleep if he wants to sleep," Vera said.

"I will turn steam off," Leo said. He got up from the table and disappeared into the backyard, letting the door slam behind him.

"Come on." Nicholas followed Paavo down a long hallway. The streetlamp outside cast long amber strands of light into the darkened room, so that Nicholas could see an armchair, a bookshelf and a computer table without a computer tucked into the corner. A sofa bed was opened out already and sheets were tucked into the mattress with tight, crisp corners.

"Don't even bother turning on the light," he said to Paavo. "I just want to sleep."

"Don't you want to brush your teeth or change your clothes? I can loan you some pajamas if you don't feel like unpacking."

This was not the time to let Paavo know that Nicholas slept in the nude. "Sleep," Nicholas said.

"Unfortunately, this room doesn't have a door. It is our family room, but we put this curtain up for you," Paavo said, pulling a dark piece of what looked like blackout curtain from where it had been tucked behind a rod. "Whenever it's closed, no one will come in or disturb you."

"Thanks, man." Nicholas sat on the edge of the bed and felt the ropes of sleep tugging at him to lie back. "I'll see you in the morning."

"Sleep well, my friend," Paavo said. "I will be right upstairs, the first door on the left. Knock if you need anything." In his dreamlike state, Nicholas understood a whole new meaning to the term nodding off.

In the middle of the night, Nicholas awoke, regretting his refusal to sauna before bed. He lay awake in the dim darkness, the hazy gleam of the streetlights filtering through the gauzy curtains. The ceiling was pockmarked, and Nicholas stared at the constellations of stains above his head. The bed had been comfortable for the first few hours of sleep, but once the jet lag had begun steaming off his warm body, he'd wrestled against the lumpy mattress. Poking a tentative foot outside his blanket, he pulled it back in. The air was frigid outside the little cocoon he'd spun in the sheets from tossing all night. He peered at the electronic clock in the corner of

the room, its glaring red numbers mocking him. He threw
the covers off and began searching for the light. Ten minutes passed before Nicholas realized that there was no light
switch in sight, not behind the curtain rod, not anywhere
a light switch should be found. The streetlight would have
to suffice. He located his suitcase where Paavo had placed it
under the window and pulled out a fleece and a pair of track-
suit bottoms. His room didn't appear to have drawers or even
a closet, so Nicholas began stacking his clothes beneath the
window in short towers of T-shirts, sweaters and jeans. He
left his boxer shorts in the bag; he wasn't sure how private
this den without a door really was. As he moved to build his
fourth pillar of clothes, he sensed something. He peered out
into the street, but all that was there were the dust-smeared
Lada and other quiet houses with formidably shaded windows. He cocked his head and listened hard. There was something on the other side of the blackout curtain.

"Hello?" He wasn't sure how far his voice would travel
in this house, so he spoke barely above a whisper. He felt
silly being afraid, but he also felt silly being here in the first
place. He should have stayed in bed, in the warmth, in his
unconscious. He should have stayed in New York.

"*Tere?*" a voice called back, filling in the darkness. The
curtain was swept aside, and all Nicholas could see were a
pair of milky-white legs shining in the light. He felt momentarily blinded before he could follow the slim line of a
body up to a face.

There were dashes of color. The girl's lips were too pink
to be naturally colored—her lipstick appeared to have faded
over time. But her blue eyes were bright and glistened like
jewels, accentuated by striking teal eye shadow in the deep
crevices of her eyelids. Her hair was just as light as Paavo's,
though it had been bronzed with golden streaks. It was pinned

in fat whorls which had probably at one point been strategic, but now pieces of it were falling down and onto her shoulders, giving her a shipwrecked look. She wasn't as pale as Paavo; her complexion was more olive, similar to Leo's tinted skin. The rest of her was clad in a skintight black skirt and top. Other than her pale legs and face, Nicholas couldn't tell where the black curtain ended and she began. In the dim streetlight, the girl stepped down into the den, coming into full view. "You are Nico," she said. "Welcome to Estonia. Sorry to frighten you."

"Mari?" he asked, forgetting to correct her on the pronunciation of his name. "It's nice to meet you."

"And you." She was like a cat stalking its prey, surrounding him on all sides with her bright, azure eyes even though she hadn't moved. "Did you have a nice flight?"

"Can't complain," he said. "I fell asleep pretty early. But it seems like jet lag is getting the better of me."

"It always does." She smiled. She reached her long fingers behind the bookshelf and flicked a switch, flooding the room with light. Nicholas flinched and closed his eyes. When he opened them, Mari was perched on the corner of his bed. "Don't let me interrupt." She gestured toward his open suitcase. But she was a tigress, and Nicholas knew better than to turn his back on a tigress unless you wanted to be hunted. He felt vulnerable as he stooped into the case, feeling the broad stretch of his tense shoulders and back and how his fleece tugged at his waist.

Mari rubbed at her eyes, as if trying to rid them of their color. She yawned widely and unselfconsciously. "I took an earlier train back," she said. "The session was brutal. I just wanted to sleep in my own bed."

"I know the feeling," Nicholas said.

"Day one, and Yankee Doodle is homesick already?"

"I'm just tired." Nicholas furrowed his brow. He began folding his T-shirts with more care than he would without an audience. "So you're a model. What's that like?"

"Exhausting. Demoralizing. Disgusting." Mari looked as though she should be holding a cigarette between her slim fingers as she spat the words.

"So why do you do it?"

"Because it's so fucking glamorous," she said, turning to smile at him. "Since you're up, you'll be the first to find out. I'm going to Moscow in the spring."

"Cool. Have you been there before?"

"Of course." Mari rolled her eyes and sucked in her breath. "But this isn't a vacation. It's work. I've been chosen to move there, to model full-time. Moscow is a stepping-stone to Paris. And Paris...well, you know Paris."

"I know Paris," Nicholas said. He spoke slowly and clearly, so as not to stumble and say something else that might make him sound ignorant. "But I'm guessing Paris means something more than just the Eiffel Tower in this case?"

"The Eiffel Tower is so gauche," Mari said. She pulled at a loose thread from the sheet on the bed and it came loose in her hand. She offered it to Nicholas, and he accepted it in a cupped hand. "Paris is the start of everyone's career. If you're sent there, you're practically made already."

"Made. Like, into a model?"

"Yes." Mari sighed. This wasn't going well. Mari already seemed exasperated with him, and she had only been home for fifteen minutes. Time passed between them. It was quieter in Tallinn than it was back home. Nicholas yearned for a siren or a car alarm, some semblance of life outside these four walls.

"What do you think of our fair city so far?"

"I haven't really seen any of it," Nicholas said. "We just

came straight from the airport and had dinner. Your mother is a great cook, but that vodka really packs a punch. I could barely keep my eyes open."

"Well done. You probably passed Papa's test by having a drink with him. I have to say that you're more of a sport than I had you figured for."

"What do you mean?" Nicholas stopped folding and sank down on the bed, facing her.

"I'm impressed that you are here in the first place. That you're trying something out of your comfort zone." Mari inspected the underside of one of her manicured nails.

"Isn't that the whole point of Hallström?" Nicholas asked.

"Well, sure. I just think it's laughable that it's an exchange with Americans. You probably already think you're hot shit."

"I... I don't," Nicholas said. Although he'd never considered himself particularly patriotic, he could feel the pride—or was it anger?—bubbling inside him and threatening to rise to the top. "I don't think I'm anything."

"Please. I've been on countless shoots with models from the US. They stand separately from everyone, constantly looking in the mirror, appraising and judging everyone with their eyes." Mari was standing on the other side of him now, her legs as slim as stalks of sugarcane.

"Are you sure that's not just a model thing?"

"Maybe," she said, a curl swinging in front of her face. She made no effort to swipe it away. "Maybe not." She moved toward the curtain where she turned and smiled sweetly. "I can warm you some *piim* to help you sleep."

"Piim?"

"Milk."

"No thanks. There's no need to babysit me," Nicholas said, turning to face her fully for the first time.

"I just want to make sure you have everything you need.

I'm your host sister, after all," Mari said. In the austere glare of the overhead light fixture, her makeup looked clownish. *"Maga hästi.* That's 'sleep well.' Hope you're taking notes. There'll be a test, Nico." She winked and stepped outside the room, pulling the curtain closed behind her. Nicholas blinked in the light. He could hear the tip-taps of her heels ascending the stairs and the door closing gently overhead.

Then it was silent again. It was as though she'd never been there in the first place. Nicholas felt for the light switch behind the bookcase and snapped the light off. He lay back in the bed. The entire encounter had felt like a scene out of a movie, where a siren appears to completely distract the hero from the task at hand. He leaned his head back, feeling the pillow accept his weight, as he considered what in the world he'd gotten himself into.

LEO

Tallinn
September 2002

Leo had gotten himself into a holy mess by marrying an Estonian citizen and staying in the country after independence. He'd committed himself to a life in a country that didn't even recognize him. He looked around, shaking his head. All around the yard small pieces of white fluff floated in the air, as if dozens of dandelions had been blown and the seeds danced about the grass. The sun was barely up; his family was still asleep upstairs as he assumed the American boy was in the den. He yawned and stepped into the yard, gripping his cup of tea as though it were a lodestone. A syrup-like layer of dew coated the grass. He pushed his feet into the lawn, his feet dampening with the moisture as he approached a clump of the fluff.

"Damn it," he growled under his breath in Russian. "Damn those damned birds." He stalked to the fence and peered over the boards, some moldy and chewed away by termites in places. He made a mental note to speak to Kunnar about the fence, but he weighed the other topic in his head, as well. What was more important—the fence or the chickens? One had to choose their arguments; ensure the priority. Perhaps it was the fence, so essential to demarcating his property. But those chickens made such a ruckus as well as a stink. They had to go.

Leo had become quite proficient in choosing his arguments. Each day's Russian-language newspaper reported a new slew of insults toward his people. In his heart, he felt Estonian, but when policies were created stating otherwise, separating the Estonian wheat from the Russian chaff, he couldn't help but feel rebuffed by the country in which he'd spent most of his life. The small gray passport that lay side by side with the three other red passports in the vault in the master bedroom was like a spit in the face. When the family had traveled to Riga for the children's school holidays last summer, and previously across the sea to Finland for a long weekend, the border guards flipped through its pages searching for visas while impatiently waving the rest of the family through. It appeared that the country—his country—was doing more and more to make him feel insufficient, unnecessary. He felt like the outsider in the family. There was a game he used to play when Mari and Paavo were small—which one of these objects doesn't belong with the others? It was always him, glaringly. He could barely stand to look at the newspaper anymore. It was ripe with arguments waiting to explode over the breakfast table that continually minimized his presence in Eesti, if he was even allowed to call it that anymore. The night before Nico arrived had been the penultimate clue that he was wearing his family's patience thin. He had sat down in his chair at the dining table, glowering over the layered tower of *kasukas* salad of smoked salmon that Vera had prepared especially for him, and grabbed at the sliced *rukkileib* she'd placed beside it. With his other hand, he tossed the newspaper onto the table. He'd folded the pages to frame an article that proclaimed that six thousand Estonian-born Russians had failed the citizenship test to date.

"There," he'd sneered in Russian. "And I'm supposed to compete with those numbers?"

Vera served herself and passed the platter to Mari, who took a modest dollop of *kasukas* on her plate. Vera settled back, chewing her food meticulously while Mari picked at her already-meager portion. Lately, his daughter seemed to want nothing to do with them. Leo was disappointed that his eldest had grown into a full beauty. She had piercing blue eyes and a dainty mouth and a figure that he ensured was well attired when she left the house. Leo had not wanted a beautiful daughter. Nor did he want a homely one, but there had to be something in between. Beautiful daughters were nothing but trouble, and this one was poised for it. At least she had funneled her beauty into something concrete; Mari's modeling career was beginning to take flight and her ads had appeared in *Anne & Stiil* and *Naisteleht* and her face had taken up prominent real estate on the side of bus shelters. Leo had swallowed the silence that followed his indignant proclamation and thrown the paper under his feet in disgust.

Leo watched the chickens now, clucking and pecking. A few of them bobbed toward him, cocking their heads hopefully. Leo stalked the length of the gate, noting where the paint had scratched away or where the wood needed to be replaced, never once taking his eye off the chickens, which also followed him as he moved. He bent down where the fence led toward the back of the long yard, where the wood had truly corroded, and ran his hands over the decaying boards. Behind him, the walls of the sauna he had built by hand when they had first moved into the house were still solid; a gentle breath of eucalyptus and birch bark puffed through the slats of the wood, aerating the insides of the sauna and perfuming the air. Leo crouched and shook his head at the base of the fence, where a hole as big as two fists allowed him to see the birds in Kunnar's yard, bobbing and searching in vain for any scraps that might have lingered in the dull grass. That's when he saw it: a single egg, nestled amongst the crocus bulbs on his side of the yard. He startled at first, as though a tiny little bird beak might begin to press through its porcelain shell. But then he knelt down, set his teacup down in the grass and scooped the egg up in his palm. It was still warm, as though the hen had just lifted her bottom from it moments before. He cupped it within his fingers, imagining it as a butterfly or something that might take flight.

His family would have been shocked to see him hold something so delicate. Leo made quick, definitive movements, rarely lingering, barely faltering. He declared decisions before he'd necessarily even made his mind up. To have been caught cradling an egg as though it was an infant might have lost him years of curmudgeonly credibility.

Inside the house, he held the egg up to the sun that was just beginning to stream in through the kitchen window. The egg was dark in this light, impenetrable to his naked eyes. He rifled through the kitchen drawer and found the stovetop lighter that Vera used to relight the pilot light when it went out and held it up behind the egg. Immediately, it lit up like a bulb. Leo could see the dark yolk within, strands of tissue that held the yolk and its gelatinous membrane together. He peered at it as though through a microscope, taking in the contours of the goop inside, how it formed itself around the yolk and floated there formlessly. It was safe.

Leo listened for signs from upstairs but there was complete silence. He took a bowl out from the cabinet over the sink and looked at the egg in his cupped palm. He moved his wrist up and down, flexing and stretching. Leo had one chance at this. His wrist felt ready, so he held it poised over the bowl.

The egg white dripped down the side of the bowl, but the yolk had found its way into the bottom of it. Leo smiled, pleased with his technique but twisted his lips at the mangled carcass of shell in his hands, which he slipped into the wastepaper bin. He fished out a shard of eggshell from the bowl and turned on a small skillet. A pat of butter melted effortlessly; the fat sizzled as it spread out across the pan. A purist, he slid the egg into the pan and let it cook on its own, the butter bubbling around the sides as the yolk took shape and form.

He had never tasted anything like this before. He understood the allure of fresh eggs now. It tasted like morning had burst open in his mouth; the woodsy, farm-like flavor couldn't be bought in the cardboard egg cartons Vera brought home from the store. This was natural and real. This was how eggs should be eaten. He savored every single bite until it was gone. It wasn't until after he had finished that he realized he hadn't even used any salt or pepper for flavoring. He could hear footsteps from overhead now, so he rinsed the bowl in the sink and set more water on the stove for a second cup of tea.

Vera creaked down the stairs, her steps heavy with sleep. She appeared in the kitchen, her hair mussed, her robe pulled loosely over her shoulders. She smiled at him. She had once again forgotten to take her makeup off the night before, and there were shadows of the black kohl she used to edge her eyelids smudged in the hollows beneath her pupils.

"Have you made yourself breakfast?" she asked in Russian. "What a surprise."

"I didn't know when you'd be up, so I made myself an egg," Leo answered.

She opened the fridge and stared into it, as if an answer would form before her eyes. "We were out of eggs."

"Oh." Leo couldn't bring himself to tell her the truth, not after he had lambasted the chickens in the yard for weeks. "There was one...in the very back...in a bowl." With her makeup smudged like this, Vera resembled an angry raccoon. Her lips were so tight they appeared sewn together.

"Levya..." she trailed off, watching Leo's face carefully.

Leo's face paused over his teacup, the darks of his pupils watching her like an animal. "Yes?"

"Don't be upset."

"At what? What did you do?" Leo lowered the teacup to the table and placed it a few inches away from him. He planted his feet firmly into the wooden floor, bracing himself for her to speak.

"I didn't want to say anything last night in front of Nico, but I got you another test date. For citizenship."

Leo felt his head expanding. He pursed his lips and was grateful that the porcelain cup wasn't between his fingers. He was sure his grip would have otherwise shattered it. "Why— Vera, why would you do that?"

"It's time, Levya. It's been a few years since you took it last. You can't avoid it forever. You and I both know that you're as much of a citizen of this country as any of us. You've lived here for forty years. This is home. Just because our asinine government decides to make a stupid law shouldn't make you a pariah."

"Pray tell, my Estonian goddess," Leo sneered, leaning back against the stove. "When am I scheduled to participate in this little charade?"

"You have time," Vera said, approaching him. She patted his arm as though she were about to administer an injection. "It's not until November."

"November?" Leo snorted and turned away from her, pouring more tea and spooning a glob of blackberry jam into the cup. He stirred it vigorously, sugary liquid slopping around the outside of the rim. "I'm supposed to learn this godforsaken language in three months?"

"Oh, don't be like that. You already know a great deal," Vera said. "We just have to soften your pronunciation, polish the edges. I'll help you."

Leo shook his head, hunching his shoulders up around his ears. Vera stepped behind him, letting her arms envelop his stocky figure, allowing her hands to trace the elastic waistband of his pants, dipping a finger beneath the drawstring. Leo tensed against her touch.

"Remember when we used to play Defector?" she murmured into his broad back. "Remember how innocent we were? How we had no idea what it meant?" During the Soviet tightening of the borders, a handful of rebels slipped through the cracks. Ballerinas, chess players, fighter pilots—they all sought lives outside the Iron Curtain. While the Soviets tried to keep the news of defections under wraps lest others get ideas, the news inevitably traveled fast, inspiring excitement, support and very often jealousy amongst those who remained in Soviet-run countries. Defection was easily translatable into a children's game. All you needed was someone to flee, someone to assist and someone to pursue and ultimately banish them to Siberia, a chalk-drawn square demarcation in which miscreants had to sit for the rest of the game if they were caught.

Vera had been a petite child, and therefore an obvious choice to play the Defector attempting to flee the oppressive Soviet regime. She was nimble and could fit into suitcases, squeeze into bicycle baskets and wooden boxes, contort her limbs to accommodate any mode of transport. It was mostly other girls who were forced into Aider/Abettor roles, pushing the wheelbarrow, riding the bicycle or "driving" the getaway car. When boys played the role, they impatiently hoisted Vera onto their shoulders or cradled her in their arms, clutching her desperately as they weaved and dodged their pursuers. Burly Leo was always cast as a KGB Minder, keeping a lookout for those on the lam. It was in the small courtyard behind the imposing block of gray concrete apartments where both Vera's and Leo's families lived that Leo literally first began to chase his future wife. Paavo and Mari cherished their parents' love story—their romance that began as a game and blossomed into reality.

"So?" Leo asked, his voice gruff with annoyance. He was well versed with Vera's tactic of tapping into his soft side, which she managed to locate from time to time underneath the hard armor that appeared to have toughened over the past decade.

"Remember how you used to chase me? I miss that," Vera said, letting her voice drop into its husky timbre, a pitch that usually brought Leo to his knees.

"That was a long time ago. When we were young and stupid," Leo said. "When the KGB called the shots and we stood to attention. When I was a citizen. When I had rights." Leo tensed his body against hers.

"That's not quite how I recall those years before Independence," she said, releasing her hands completely from around him. He turned to face her. "In fact, I remember some pretty miserable times. Or have you conveniently forgotten them?" Leo looked down at his hands and shook his head.

"I don't have time for this right now. I have to go to work. That is, if they haven't found a red-blooded Estonian to configure bus schedules in my absence," Leo said, clearing his throat. "Did your daughter come home?"

"She's my daughter now? What did she do?" Vera smiled, attempting to break the tension as she dabbed at the spilled tea with a dishcloth.

"As long as she's that pretty, she's your daughter. I will reclaim her when her looks go."

"Levya! That's terrible!"

"It may be, but I can't deal with a pretty daughter gallivanting around town. It's dangerous. Beautiful things don't ask for attention. You damn well know what I mean. You need to have those talks with her. You know, the ones about the fine balance between flaunting her body and not letting men have what they want."

"Wow," Vera said, leaning back against the sink with her mug and surveying Leo. "You have managed to be incredibly insulting in the past fifteen seconds. That's a record, even for you."

Leo frowned. "I am just trying to keep her safe. It worries me, Vera. This situation, it's not easy for me. The fact that she's beautiful is a gift, and it's a blessing that she's able to make some money from it. But that doesn't make it any easier to digest the fact that she may be traipsing about town with God knows who doing God knows what. Not to mention what people might be saying about her."

"So what do you suggest—that we stop her from modeling? She's making good money from it, you know. At least it keeps her out of trouble and away from loitering with her useless friends in Freedom Square."

"Fine. Fine. Let her make money. If she's talented, she's talented."

"I have a great solution," Vera said. Leo leaned in toward her. "Trust her. How about that?"

"'Trust' is an interesting request from someone who just made me an appointment behind my back," Leo retorted, his nose in the air. "I just don't have time to worry about this, Vera. I have enough to worry about with Mari. And then there's Paavo. The boy spent the whole summer reading books. I don't think he went down to the football pitch once. I don't think he ever met friends. He needs to leave the comfort of his own backyard." At this, he looked back through the screened-in porch. The fluff was still floating about, as though a chicken were plucking itself on his roof and sending the feathers cascading down below them, an early snow day in September.

Vera shrugged. "It's a phase, Leyva. He will spread his wings. New York may be very good for him. Go and take a shower before the boys wake up. And Levya, please don't stress about the test. I'll help you. We all will. Besides, I think you know more than you realize."

Leo took in a deep breath. He hesitated before leaning over and kissing his wife gently on the lips. "Have a good day, *armastatu*." Vera smiled at his use of the Estonian word. She tried to pepper their Russian conversations with as many Estonian words as she could, but it was especially poignant when he made the effort on his own. At least he was trying.

PAAVO

Tallinn
September 2002

There is no try. At some point in his life, Paavo had lived by
the *Star Wars* credo. He'd once been capable of everything,
or at least he'd possessed the self-confidence to think he was.
He'd approached each experience and opportunity fearlessly
and was prepared to fight whatever he thought might come
in the way. But since the gang had started its advances toward him, his confidence had run for the hills of Narva, its
tail between its legs. At first, Paavo figured he would just
avoid the boys, make sure that he stayed out of their way.
But it appeared that it wouldn't be that easy.

Now it was the first day of school, and Paavo had to ven-
ture back out there once again. The best part of participating in the Hallström program was that Nico was here. Well,
Nico and really, that Sabine girl from Prague. When he'd
passed out in the bathroom and Pyotr had run back to the
conference room and announced that the Estonian boy had
passed out, Sabine had been the first one on the premises.

Paavo was just opening his eyes when he heard her enter the bathroom, taking tentative steps toward him, and then kneeling down on the cold tile floor next to his head. She'd made a pillow from her cardigan and placed it gently under his head. She put her hand over his mouth, testing for the warm puffs of air that emanated from his lips. She put her own fingers over her lips, guiding him not to move, even though his hands instinctively moved toward his waist as she tugged his belt off, whispering, "Relax. I'm just easing any restriction." Then she reached down and lifted his legs a few inches off the ground. Paavo had been awed by Sabine, how she'd taken charge without waiting for an adult or further instructions and by her serene, methodical manner. How had she known that the fear of walking back into the conference room pained him more than his ankle where he'd turned it on the bathroom doorjamb? "Don't worry, your pride can be healed," she'd whispered. Paavo would repeat the mantra to himself over and over in the years to come. Barbara and the EMT had found them there—Paavo lying back and Sabine elevating his legs as she encouraged him to take deep lungfuls of air. The EMT had commended Sabine in a thick German accent—raising Paavo's legs above his heart had been exactly the right thing to do. "From verr did you learn zis? Das ist perfekt tek-neek." By that time, of course, the blood had rushed back into Paavo's system, and he sat up and promised a very stricken Barbara that he was fine—he just had low blood sugar and needed to eat something, that he would be able to continue on with orientation. It was just too bad that Sabine lived four whole countries away. It felt good to have an ally for once.

But Nico could be an ally, too. Paavo's heart leaped a little, thinking of his presence here. He wasn't sure whether or not they might get along, but at least he had a travel companion to get to and from school. He didn't have to be alone any-more; there was strength in numbers. And Nico was a wres-tler. It was as though the Hallström program had provided him with his very own bodyguard.

Paavo sat straight up in bed, gripping the edge of his blan-ket with his stubby fingers, the nails bitten down past their keratinous whites. The bluish haze of night was still settled over the world outside the window, blurring the outlines of the houses and cars across the road. He could hear motion from the kitchen just below his room. Leo and Vera were up, communing, combining, collaborating. Paavo could hear the grinder's powerful blade come to a shuddering halt and Vera's breathless curses. It was *kasha* for breakfast today; the fatty fragrance of melted butter and hot rough-cut buck-wheat seeped into his room. He should rouse Nico in case he wasn't already awake. After all, they couldn't be late on their first day.

Not that Paavo was particularly looking forward to it. He washed his face in the hall bathroom. His face looked wan and pulled. He had no idea whether the gang would be waiting for him with the start of the school year; he'd hardly given them a chance to bully him over the summer. He pulled on a pair of jeans and a jumper and headed downstairs.

Nico was already sitting alone at the table, mixing a bowl of groats rather aggressively with a spoon, as if it would some-how magically transform into ice cream or chicken noodle soup like that fable that Babu used to tell Paavo as a child. Paavo watched from the doorway as Nico sliced off three more pats of butter and dissolved them over the steaming buckwheat.

"Unfortunately, that's not going to help," Paavo said, smil-ing. "Butter just makes them soggier. They take some get-

ting used to." Nico turned toward him, his eyes still droopy
with sleep.

"They're not so bad," Nico said. "It's kind of like oat-
meal." He spooned some into his mouth, swished it around
with his tongue and took a long chug of coffee before swal-
lowing the whole thing down.

"Try this," Paavo said, opening a shelf over the sink. He
handed Nico a bar wrapped in red-and-orange plastic.

"Kamatahvel," Nico read. "Chocolate?"

"Kind of," Paavo said. "It's a candy bar. Mama and Papa
ate it when the Soviets were in power and chocolate wasn't
easily available. Break some off and let it melt over the *kasha*.
How did you sleep?"

"Okay," Nico said, looking sheepish again. "Though, you
were right. I woke up in the middle of the night and had
trouble falling asleep again. I guess I'll try the sauna tonight
after school."

"As I said, it's a religion here," Paavo said. "I'm sure you
will be a convert."

"I got to meet Mari, though," Nico said.

"So I did hear her come in last night. I thought I was
dreaming."

"You and me both," Nico muttered.

Paavo sat down at the table and broke a few splinters
of Kama bar into his bowl. He looked up at Nico, who
was looking back at him. It felt so awkward, having this
stranger in his home. Barbara had told Paavo how perfect
she thought the partnership was between these two boys,
but so far, Paavo wasn't sure where their common ground
might lie. Of course, appearances could be deceiving. On the
second day of orientation, Paavo had blanched when Pyotr
met him near the coffee urns at the back of the conference

room. But Pyotr's face had softened as he put his arm on Paavo's shoulder.

"Are you okay?" he asked. "I'm sorry I ran out of the bathroom like that. I was worried about you. I wanted to get help. I didn't mean to embarrass you in front of everyone." Paavo shook his head, concentrating hard on the piercings in Pyotr's ear and said it was nothing—that he was glad that Pyotr had gone for help, what if he'd hit his head or worse, that Pyotr had done the right thing. Pyotr wasn't such a bad guy after all.

"We should leave as soon as we finish. Are you ready to go?" Paavo said.

"I thought my Estonian class starts earlier than the rest of school. Your dad said he'd drop me on his way to work."

"I don't mind going early," Paavo said, shoveling *kasha* into his mouth. "I will help you find your way."

MARI

Mari had definitely found her way. At least, that's what her booker Eva told her each time she called to tell her that she had scheduled a go-see.

"This is your calling, pussycat," Eva said on the phone, her voice raspy from cigarettes. "You were born for this work. That face and that body... I'm just sad we missed out on the few years we had with you before Viktor found you."

But even though she was a verified, certified model, Mari had never considered herself beautiful. She knew she had a "look," which was what Viktor had told her the first time he'd seen her in Freedom Square. She knew she had a set of killer cheekbones, because her friends commented on them often and with great reverence. She knew she had height, because she towered over most of the boys in her twelfth grade class. And once she'd completed puberty, her lithe body had settled itself into a very comfortable size thirty-four, an enviable figure for anyone at the age of seventeen. But it still surprised her, the way that casting agents looked at her when she walked into a room, as though golden beams radiated from her body. It surprised her that people wanted her to wear clothes in an effort to get others to want to wear them, that people wanted to watch her walk down a long, narrow strip only to turn at the end and go back. It astounded her that she got paid for such simple tasks.

A few hours after she returned from St. Petersburg and met Nico, Mari lay in bed staring at the ceiling, unable to sleep. She could hear her father approaching on the stairs, his heavy footsteps nearing her door, and then pausing just outside. She tensed as the floorboards creaked. He continued down the hall toward the good bathroom. She glanced over to her desk, where the framed certificate leaned against a stack of books. "Highest Honors for Eleventh Year of Studies," it read. "Mari Sokolov." Not that it mattered.

The fact was that Tallinn was over. Estonia was over. Every year, the situation got bleaker and more desperate. There were barely any jobs available, unless you wanted to work in mining or the information technology sector, and Mari didn't want to do either. Instead of discussing makeup and clothes and boys, Mari and her friends discussed exit strategies. What could they do to get them out of Estonia? What path would they take that might lead them to the opportunity that would escort them out of the country? They spoke of politics, of studying abroad, dreaming up grandiose inventions that might bring them glory and fame outside these borders. A few students from the class above hers had succeeded. Laine Laanemaa's grandfather had left an inheritance so he could attend university in the United States, and Terje Raud's family had a printing factory in Riga, so she'd left to work there shortly after graduation. Everyone else had stagnated around the city, applying and reapplying for the same handful of jobs. And the gender gap was widening. Mari had read that Estonia had the highest gender pay gap in Europe; men made twice what women did for the same jobs. With the combination of lack of opportunities and only a fraction of the pay, what was the point in even staying here?

But Mari would soon join the ranks of Laine and Terje. Last October, she and her friends had been hanging out in Freedom Square when a man had approached them. He had been watching them—her, mostly—and she had a raw feeling in the pit of her stomach as he neared. *It's happening*, she thought to herself. *All those kidnapping drills and no talking to strangers when I was little and it's finally happening now that I'm seventeen.* The man was immaculately dressed, in a blazer that stretched cleanly across his shoulders and lambskin gloves that looked soft as butter as he peeled them off and reached into an inner pocket to retrieve a card. He extended it to her as he stood there amongst her friends and they giggled and whispered around him.

"I am Viktor. I own a modeling agency in Moscow. Will you come see me for a test?"

"What kind of a test?"

"A screen test," he said, gingerly putting his gloves back on as though he couldn't stand to touch any surface with his bare hands. "I want to see how you walk."

"Why do I need a test for that? I can walk right here. Watch." She stood up and grabbed a book from a friend's lap and balanced it on her head. She took a few unsure steps, but willed herself forward, walking almost the whole way to St. John's Church, where she regained her confidence, sashaying her hips back and forth and waggling her pert bottom to the hoots and whistles of her friends.

"It's a bit ungainly. And you are slightly pigeon-toed," Viktor said. "But I can train you to fix that." Mari felt a flush spread across her face, and she looked down at her feet, straightening them like alpine skis.

"Listen, only call me if you're serious," Viktor said. "I don't have time to play games. I need the next Carmen Kass." That caught her attention. Mari revered Carmen Kass. She was a Järva girl and had been the face of Dior for years. Mari loved the way Carmen floated upon a golden pond in the ads, her face, hair and skin aglow as though she were made of gold herself. Now that was a girl who had figured things out.

He left then, and Mari shoved the card into the pocket of her jeans, deflecting the attention away from her by joking around with her friends, mimicking Viktor's pristine gloves and dainty hands. She'd forgotten about the card for the evening, and it made a trip through the washing machine, emerging wrinkled and worn like an artifact, but the numbers were still legible. That business card was Mari's ticket out.

One afternoon, she decided to make history. That was how she thought of the call years later—just as Gavrilo Princip had decided to load his Belgian-made semiautomatic on the morning that he fatally shot the Archduke and set the first great world war spiraling into action. Only this time, there was no motorcade preceding her decision, no pomp and circumstance. The only sound was from the drone of the Cyprus-France football game projecting up the stairs from the den below. She could hear Paavo's quiet but insistent protests against a poor pass muffled beneath Leo's more aggressive jeers. She smoothed the card under her palm and dialed the number before she could change her mind. That call spurred the trip to the Mustamäe office, which was nothing more than a few square white rooms with a desk, a video camera and a still one perched on a tripod. This was his makeshift office, Viktor told her. He wasn't hoping to have to spend much time in Tallinn. It was a tertiary market.

Milan, London, Paris and New York were where all the action was. Even Moscow trailed behind. He hoped to find the next Carmen Kass, he reminded her. He hoped it might be her.

In his temporary office, Mari did in fact perform a series of walks in front of Viktor and his discerning assistant, Eva. "Be nice to Eva," Viktor warned Mari from the beginning. "She's rough around the edges, but she's my booker. You'll have to bend over backward to make her happy so that she sends you to the right places to make *you* happy." Mari was filmed walking in a straight line with a book on her head, holding stacks of them in her arms and again while wearing high heels. She was measured: height, waist, bust.

"Very good," Eva said without a trace of satisfaction, scribbling the numbers onto an index card. "A ten-inch difference between waist and hips. Maintain that, and you're golden in this business." Eva positioned Mari in front of the open window so that Viktor could scrutinize her face from every angle. He stood so close to her that Mari could smell his tangy breath. It felt as if he'd been staring at her for hours. Was he counting her pores? This is the best light, he told her. Natural light. No lighting designer can replicate it.

She hadn't told her parents anything about any of it. Not the fact that she'd been approached or that she'd followed up. She returned from the office triumphant and glowing, wielding a thin stack of stapled papers in her hands. Once she signed on with Viktor and his team, they would coach, shape and polish her facets so that she sparkled like the diamond he knew she could be instead of the one in the rough he had seen in Freedom Square. But since she was underage, the contract had to be cosigned by a parent. It had taken a few days to convince Leo to even look at it, but after some negotiations on Mari's part, he put on his reading glasses and studied the papers line by line.

"There's no way you're working your first assignment for free," he thundered. "You have to repay him after you've earned the overhead? What kind of business is that? So help me, Mari, if I ever even hear the word *nude*, I will pull the plug on this whole operation. Do you understand me?" Mari had nodded, but it wasn't enough. Leo had insisted on accompanying Mari to meet Viktor in Mustamäe so he could show off his breadth and the crushing grip of his handshake. Leo ensured the contract had been amended to his liking, and then Viktor, true to his word, had gotten to work, sending Mari out into the world.

NICO

Tallinn
September 2002

This wasn't technically Nico's first time in the world. He had traveled a fair amount with his parents. When the kids were younger, the Grands had visited all-inclusive resorts in Cancun, Nassau and Negril, with swim-up bars, eat-until-you-burst tropical fruit buffets and camp-like activities for the kids so that Stella and Arthur could snatch a few hours for themselves. Nico could conjure up the plastic scent of his water wings before he learned to swim. He could recall the time that Nora's nose had turned so bright red—it was the one spot on her entire body she'd forgotten to apply sunscreen—that Nico called her Rudolph for the rest of their time in Puerto Vallarta. As the kids grew older, the family ventured further, pushing themselves into activities rather than lolling on beaches. They camped in Yellowstone Park, hiked in the Atlas Mountains of Morocco and biked the lavender-scented hills of Provence. But as he'd always taken these adventures with his family, they remained a strong tether to his identity along the way. Whether he was sampling galettes stuffed with mushrooms that the Grands had harvested together from the woods outside their rented bungalow in Nevache Valley, or throwing tomatoes during the La Tomatina festival in Buñol, he was Nicholas Grand from the moment he buckled his seat belt on his way to the time he disembarked from the plane on the way home.

So it was strange to be remade in a mere few hours, to morph from one person to another. It was as though upon landing in Tallinn, Nicholas had been given an immediate makeover, a lobotomy, or even an entirely new brain in the cavity that had held his old one. The morning that he had left for the airport, he had been a wrestler in Div 1, played flute in Orchestral Band, taken a smattering of Advanced Placement classes and teetered on the precipice of popularity. He had been Nicholas. But now he was Nico, no matter how many times he tried to subtly correct Leo, Vera or Paavo. Even Mari had used the short form in the dead of night, when he had been too surprised by her arrival to correct her. While it was only his name that had changed, unlike Shakespeare, Nicholas felt that names did determine one's lot in life. There had to be a reason that the preppy kids back home at school had welcomed Charlotte James with open arms into their group as Charlie, while Charlotte Zinkoff had loitered on the periphery of a few social groups before redubbing herself Lottie, coloring her hair shades of pink and settling comfortably within the circle of skateboarders who spent most of their days performing ollies outside the doors to the auditorium.

Nicholas had to admit that while responding to Nico hadn't been instinctual, the name wasn't so bad. After telling the Sokolovs that he preferred Nicholas all morning, he decided to let it go. "Nico" was catchy, a new identity. It was one of those experiences that Barbara had said to wholeheartedly embrace. Nico could be a completely different person. It was pretty exciting to start fresh after sixteen years of living in the same identity. Did Nico make the same decisions as Nicholas? Would he assimilate faster into Estonian culture? Did Nico have a driver's license? A penchant for cigarettes? A girlfriend? What did Nico like? He asked himself as he brushed his teeth in the small half bath next to his den. Perhaps it might be easier to start with what we don't like, because pet peeves are harder to shake.

When it came down to it, there weren't many things that bothered Nico, or even Nicholas for that matter. One of his few pet peeves included Train Blocking, that most heinous of practices in which one stood directly in the center of the open subway doors that might only slide open for thirty seconds or so at each train station before sliding shut. Nicholas couldn't stand the selfishness of people who stood just inside the car, not moving to one side or another, not disembarking from the train, just standing there like guppies in a fish bowl, expecting passengers to move around them.

The other one was Slow Walking. Tourists were one thing—at least they had an excuse with their oversize cameras and their giveaway maps, taking everything in as they walked about the city dumbfounded. At least they were appreciating beauty, parts of the city that Nicholas knew intimately—the arches of the roofs of the buildings on Fifth Avenue, the simultaneous majesty and repugnancy of the gargoyles that perched quietly on promontories over their heads. It was the New Yorkers that he couldn't understand. Didn't people get tired walking that slowly? Didn't they have places to get to? Wasn't this the city that never slept? What *wasn't* the rush? Nicholas had learned how to skip-step around them, ducking quickly into the curb in order to overtake a lovey-dovey couple with entwined fingers, or worse, men in suits who looked too important to be ambling along, chatting brashly to one another in grating, raucous tones, relaying highlights from their weekends in the Hamptons.

As Nicholas and Paavo stepped out of the house on the first day of school, Nicholas braced himself to pace with his exchange partner. It would set the wrong tone to walk ahead of Paavo, as though he were trying to one-up him, when it was simply how fast he walked. Not to mention, Nicholas didn't know where he was going. But as they stepped onto the street together, Nicholas found himself smiling as he noted Paavo's long, loping strides.

"You walk fast," Nico said, in admiration.

"We must be on time," Paavo said, his eyes fixed and focused. "Especially on our first day. We must even be ahead of the clock if we can." Paavo led the way, but he appeared skittish, his eyes darting this way and that, searching the streets as if he'd dropped a penny, pointing his chin down alleyways and narrowing his eyes at shadows of trees.

At the crosswalk, as the light was blinking toward red, Paavo came to such a sudden halt that Nico bumped into him.

"What happened?" he asked. "I thought we couldn't be late."

"The light is red," he said.

Nico stared at him. "But there aren't any cars," he said, nodding toward the street. Nico had never met anyone so obsessed with punctuality yet so rigidly adamant about obeying the rules. He wondered if it was a remnant of Soviet times. He squeezed his eyes shut and mentally murmured STD to himself. Perhaps Paavo really just didn't like to be late. Perhaps there was a strict penalty for jaywalking in Estonia. But as soon as the light changed, Paavo picked the pace right off from where he'd dropped it, pulling Nico forward on an invisible chain just behind him. Nico was slightly short of breath as they neared a small bus shelter at the corner of a sleepy park where a few dog walkers herded their charges around on taut leashes.

Somehow, leaving the house had helped calm Nico's nerves. After he'd fallen asleep once Mari had gone upstairs, he had dreamed fitfully, waking every hour until the light began to glow from behind the curtains and the house had begun to awaken. He heard the slow, lumbering footfalls that had to be Leo, as he made his way to the kitchen in the morning. Half an hour later, Vera pattered past Nico's makeshift door. Their conversation traveled down the hallway, Leo's low ambling drawl paired with Vera's gentle supportive lilt. Toward the end of dinner the previous night, he thought he was just beginning to understand the difference between Leo's vehement Russian speech and the rest of the family's in Estonian. The Russian was hard with consonants, striking against the roof of Leo's mouth, while the lingering resonance of the doubled and tripled vowels in Estonian resounded like marbles to Nico's untrained ear.

Perhaps Nico felt on edge because he had to share a space with Mari, who had made him feel self-conscious and uncomfortable. Or perhaps it was that he really knew nothing in this city, in this country. He didn't even know how to get to school.

A bus turned the corner and the boys boarded it in the middle. Paavo handed Nico a ticket and showed him how to punch it in a machine mounted on a pole. Nico looked around at the rest of the riders. The bus wasn't crowded, but it was full of students and professionals who swayed as the bus made its way up a wide boulevard, flanked on either side by large buildings. Most of the riders were reading books or newspapers while a few others spoke softly to one another. The ride was short—too short for Nico to gather his thoughts and prepare for this first day. When Paavo nodded and moved toward the door, Nico was disappointed.

The bus left them at Freedom Square, a wide rectangular plaza with a rather hideous glass structure at its west end. Nico turned toward it, but Paavo tut-tutted.

"We can do the tour later. You have Estonian class."

Nico nodded. He arched his neck up to take in the bulb-like domes of the Aleksandr Nevsky Cathedral, an imposing white-and-black building that didn't appear to fit in with the rest of the decor in Old Town. Rust-colored steeples rose up as though planted centuries ago, beckoning visitors to walk the twisted streets dotted with cobblestones to discover the medieval treasures located within their clutches. Nico couldn't wait to explore, but he trotted obediently behind Paavo as he led the way into the labyrinthine streets. They made a number of turns and switchbacks, and just as Nico was about to say that he would have no idea how to return to the bus station without Paavo's guidance, they stopped in front of a small, nondescript building with a red door carved into it.

"Eesti High School," Paavo said, holding his arms out. The building took up only two stories; Nico marveled at how diminutive it was compared with the Manhattan School of Science and felt a bit saddened by Paavo's pride. "Come. We go in."

Nico always felt wrung out by the first day back to school; he'd felt that way since kindergarten. The summer made him anxious—so much could change in those two whole months. The early days of the school year were grace periods for new allegiances to be formed, old ones broken and truces forgotten. Last year, as a sophomore, he'd watched his best friend Toby get edged out from the group of kids he'd called friends since the first day of school. Nico didn't know what the big deal about those kids was anyway. They wore hiking backpacks ironically and they all had the same floppy dog haircut, even the girls. But over the summer, Nico had invited Toby to hang out with him and his wrestling teammates, who accepted him into their posse as seamlessly as he'd been let go from the first one.

Nico himself had a patchwork of friends—his wrestling pals, bandmates, arbitrary students in different classes. But he knew that in the early days, he could easily be traded in for a better model, that classmates easily crossed the great chasm from one clique to another. While Nico wasn't in the golden crew—so called not only because of their flaxen tresses, but also because of where they lived and their families' statures in society—he wasn't particularly unpopular, either. He'd had a few innocuous trysts with girls, mostly after downing a few tepid, watery beers at uninspired parties that a few acquaintances had felt they'd had to throw when parents went out of town. And while his virginity was still intact and he'd never really felt any peer pressure to lose it, he continued to feel a cool, somewhat reassuring trepidation when a girl flirted with him, something that seemed to be happening more and more often the longer he spent on the wrestling team.

The first day, for all intents and purposes, was a formality. It was filled with reunions, seating charts and book distribution, hardly any necessity to use your brain. It appeared to be the same way at Eesti High School. Normally, Nico would want to slump against a wall feeling everything sucked out of him, the way his tire deflated when he pushed the nozzle of his bike pump too hard instead of attaching it carefully. *Whoomp.* But at Eesti, things were different. From the moment Nicholas stepped across the threshold, it seemed that his reputation had preceded him. The students had known he was coming, and they had stormed him as an army would a fortress, stopping suddenly short before him. Even the teachers seemed impressed by his presence, asking him many questions about his life in New York City, his proximity to the buildings formerly known as the World Trade Center, if he'd ever met the president.

Despite the utter confusion and dull headache brought on by Estonian class, Nico had a rather triumphant first day. Estonian had too many cases for nouns, and it lacked harmony, unlike French or Spanish. Not to mention, it was a completely useless language; once Nico left Tallinn in a few months, he'd have no need for it ever again. But Nico had brought allure to the school. He was new and different. American. Students vied to sit near him in each of his classes; he'd held court before teachers walked in and asked everyone to settle. He was already more popular at Eesti High School than he had been at MSS. He'd walked from class to class feeling as though he were wearing an aura, haloed by all the attention. A boy named Heigi took a particular interest in Nico and insisted on escorting him around the school and helping him find his next class even though the school was so small that Nico had charted out each of its corners long before lunchtime. Heigi followed him around like a dog at his heels, peppering him with questions about the Empire State Building and the New York Yankees.

Over Heigi's incessant chatter, Nico was conducting his own observational study of the Estonians as he imagined Margaret Mead had done with the tribes of Papua New Guinea, scrutinizing their habits, food, customs, idiosyncrasies. Everything was blond: hair, skin, teeth. Nico felt as though everything and everyone in Estonia sparkled, that he needed sunglasses to look at anyone directly. And it wasn't just Paavo who was reticent and held a figurative cape across his chest as though he were about to reveal something dark and delicious about himself but never did. Nico was enamored by the way their stony faces filled with curiosity, hesitant to ask questions and then speaking in measured, even tones once they found the courage to do so. The silence that filled the air after he'd answered made him uncomfortable, as though they didn't think that his response had been sufficient. But eventually they nodded, weighing his words carefully in their minds. He finally understood how Nora felt, assessing people, making lists, keeping notes and observations, as he watched these young Estonians in their native habitats.

In the afternoon when the students were dismissed, Paavo found Nico in the darkening lane.

"Come," Paavo said. "We will go for a walk around Old Town before we go home. How was the day?"

"Good," Nico said. "But, dude, Estonian? Kicked my ass. I don't know if I'm going to make it through."

"I can help you," Paavo said, as he led the way up a long paved cobblestone alleyway. He waited for Nico to walk alongside him as they walked in tandem and approached a long, paved cobblestone street. "*Tere.* I'm sure you know that one by now."

"*Tere.* Hello," Nico answered.

"*Kuidas sul läheb?*"

"Yeah, you lost me," Nico said. They were walking up an incline and Nico could feel his breath quickening.

"It was 'how are you?'" Paavo said. He pointed out the black-domed church that appeared to stand sentry over the city. "There is the Aleksandr Nevsky Cathedral that we passed this morning. And here is the main square of the town, Raekoja plats." The only open space that Nico had seen since entering the narrow streets of Old Town loomed in front of him, holding a few lonely tables in front of some sleepy restaurants. "Stay with me. It is easy to get lost in these streets for your first time."

"I thought New Yorkers walked fast, but you are serious, man. You're on a mission," Nico said.

"There is a lot to see," Paavo said, glancing at his watch. "And we have homework." Paavo pointed toward a side street. "Let's go this way." Nico was walking so close to Paavo that he felt his body tense at the next turn. A group of boys stood at the corner, their backs turned toward Paavo and Nico. Paavo picked up his pace.

"Actually, this way. Quick, quick."

"What's going on, Paavo? Why are we running? We don't have that much homework."

"It's nothing," Paavo panted. "It's good to exercise, no?"

"Well, sure, but I thought I was getting a tour."

"Yes, sure. There is St. Olav's Church. The Russians used the tower to send messages during the Cold War." He pointed up at a tall metallic spire as he jogged quickly by.

"Hang on," Nico said, lagging back. "I want to look at it."

"There is time later. Or tomorrow. I want to show you this building." They approached a stained, gray building that took up the majority of the block, the windows on the street level boarded up. There were a few metal-framed terraces on the higher floors that looked as though they might come hurtling down at the slightest touch. "Around this way." Paavo led the way down a street and they found themselves in a back alleyway facing a set of stairs that spiraled down. Nico followed Paavo as they descended below street level into what appeared to be an abandoned cellar. Wooden boards blocked the rectangular windows and Nico was sure he heard rats squeaking in the corners. He wasn't skittish, but no one liked rats.

Paavo turned and smiled at Nico in the gloom. Why had Nico followed him down here unwittingly? What was about to happen? "This," Paavo said, smiling at Nico in the gloom, "is very special. Do you know where you are?"

"Not a clue. I need to catch my breath."

"This is the former headquarters of the KGB."

"No shit," Nico said, looking around. It was hard to see; the bulbs appeared to have been burned out, and the only light peeked from behind the boards in front of the windows. "It's just open like this?"

"Well, technically we're trespassing." Paavo smirked. "But I wanted to show you before the government makes it completely inaccessible."

Nico stepped forward and then immediately back as his foot hit something.

"I know there's not much to see," Paavo said.

"That's okay. It's still pretty cool." Nico walked around, kicking at the debris around him with his sneaker. "How long has it been abandoned like this?"

"At least ten years. There was a fight over who was going to own it after Estonia became independent. They're trying to make it a historic site. In a few years, I bet we'll have to pay tickets to get in here. That church I pointed out before? That was used by the KGB to send radio transmissions."

"Yeah, I barely saw it. You wanna tell me why we're running? Who were those guys?"

"I just saw some guys," Paavo said, running his fingers over dark spots on the wall. "Just some not-so-nice guys. It's not a big deal. It's just better to avoid them."

"Do they go to Eesti?"

"They dropped out."

"Are they bothering you?" Nico stepped closer so he could see Paavo's face.

"They're fine. They are just people I would rather avoid."

As the boys walked out of Old Town, Nico could feel the tug of winter once again. His skin prickled, craving the sun. It was a blot in the sky, huddled behind the clouds as though seeking its own warmth. The grayness of the day had been a precursor to the pitch that had now taken over the afternoon. Nico felt drawn and wan, his skin like paper in the drought of light. In the morning, the roofs in Old Town had been red brick, the sun pushing through to illuminate them, but now, everything was drab and colorless. The afternoon was like the opening credits of *The Wizard of Oz*, before Dorothy discovers the magical land of Technicolor. But he put his head down to fend off the breeze that had picked up and was snaking its way through the narrow streets of Old Town and followed closely at Paavo's heels out of the maze.

NORA

New York City
September 2002

Looking at a face felt to Nora like having to find your way out of a maze, the way a mouse in an experiment raced the clock in a lab. Nora had to add features, voice, stature and posture in adequate time before she passed that point of awkwardness where it became clear that she was scrutinizing someone a little too closely. Her brain felt scrambled; she couldn't think clearly, or keep up with what was being said to her before she could properly identify the appropriate person. But as difficult as it was to admit it to Stella, the few meetings she'd had with the group had been useful. For one, she hadn't felt quite as alone as she had before she'd walked into the meeting room at Mount Sinai. Even though the members of the group remained consistent, each meeting started the same way, with introductions. Nora didn't feel as helpless within the walls of that room as she did once she left the meetings. Nicknames were okay—there were no penalties for forgetting faces or names. And another thing, the girl

with the red hair had suggested using clues to identify people. Forget faces or body types, she'd said. Have your family wear jewelry, something that they always have on them
that can help you know who they are.

"Apparently," Nora said at the dinner table that evening, "I
need clues." Arthur stopped chewing and put his fork down.
It was the first time in a long time that Nora had shown any
sign of wanting to make progress. "Apparently, while I inherently know who you are, you can help me by being consistent and familiar so that I can recognize you. Ginger Spice
said that things like wearing glasses or having freckles are
markers that can help me identify you."

Arthur glanced down at his hands. "What about my wedding band?"

"Lots of men have wedding bands, Dad," Nora said.

"How about these?" Stella asked, pointing to the gold star
studs in her ears. "These pretty much go with everything
anyway. I won't take them off."

"I don't know, Mom. So you're never going to change
your earrings ever again? That's stupid. Maybe we should
just forget I said anything," Nora said. "I'm not a moron."

"Honey, of course not. But you know who we are within
the confines of this apartment. If we're outside, this exercise
can help. I think it's a great idea. And it can be our family secret. No one else has to know," Stella said, taking her hand.

"What if I don't shave my mustache?" Arthur offered.
"I've sort of been toying with keeping it around this time."

"What do you think, Nor?"

"That's fine," Nora said.

This evening, Nora lay in bed for a long time. Her parents
were due back from work in an hour or so, and the apartment was silent except for the clanging of some pipes in the
walls, which echoed through her bedroom. She thought she

should probably get started on dinner. While she only had group twice a week, she was satisfied to remain within the triangular path she'd forged between the library, the grocery store and the Grands' apartment. If she was going to stay home, she had promised her parents that she would read and keep up with her degree as much as she could on her own, and help with the shopping and make dinner each night. The library and the grocery store were relatively safe within the realm of her neighborhood. She didn't run the risk of bumping into many people she might know.

At least she didn't have to deal with the Estonian boy for another four months, when Nicholas returned with him in the new year. He would just be another face to remember. Rather, a new face to forget. She didn't have to worry about him until he was here in the flesh. But for now, there was something else to worry about. She reached under her pillow and pulled the corner of the envelope out between two fingers as through it were a piece of dirty laundry.

The envelope felt alive, as though it was throbbing from within. She knew its contents; she'd opened it the previous day when it had arrived in the afternoon post. She could feel the raised letters of the card under her fingertips.

Claire Evelyn French and Benjamin Jerome Reilly request the pleasure of your company at their upcoming nuptials.

The whole thing certainly wasn't news; Claire had gotten engaged the previous semester, though what the rush was to get engaged and then married while still in college, Nora couldn't quite understand. The fact that Claire and Ben wouldn't have children until at least a decade later was proof that they certainly didn't need to rush into anything.

But what was tacit in Nora's understanding was that she would be Claire's maid of honor. The two girls had imagined and envisioned this day for nearly as many years as they had been friends, and it certainly wasn't out of jealousy that she was having this reaction. It was out of fear. A wedding was a joyous occasion, but to Nora, it was almost worse than the prospect of returning to college. A wedding was a reunion. There would be hordes of their friends and classmates there. Familiar faces. That word had become anathema to Nora; *familiar* no longer existed.

After she opened the invitation, Nora grabbed her yearbook and began cataloging her friends in the face book that Nicky had given her. She started off furiously, with the zeal of a manic artist, copying names, analyzing hair color and eye position. She made a note to ask Claire for the guest list so she could include everyone from their high school in order to begin memorizing features as soon as possible.

Jason Levy (ex-boyfriend):
Porcelain skin
Underbite
Pear-shaped mole on side of neck

Jenna Raines:
Gap in top two front teeth
Cupid's-bow lips
Perpetually rosy cheeks

She had to be prepared; a maid of honor had to know faces and names, had to greet people. She would have to make a speech, referencing people in the room and hugging and kissing family and friends. But she wasn't sure she was capable of all that. And apparently, she wasn't the only one.

The buzzer to the apartment went off, startling her thoughts. "It's Claire," the tinny voice from the other end echoed through the speaker. Thank goodness for that announcement, Nora thought. It prepared her for who was about to step through the doors of the elevator. Her best friend stepped into the foyer, holding up a bag with the logo from the French bakery in Little Italy, an anomaly of a shop that had clung fiercely on amidst all the tourist-trap, Bolognese-bearing restaurants festooned with red, white and green flags ever since they had both attended preschool down the street.

"Surprise," Claire said. "I come bearing butter in pastry form." The two settled on opposite ends of the broken-in couch in the comfortable den, leaning against the arms with their legs entwined. Nora held her camera in her lap, feeding film into the spool.

"Ready for your close-up?" she asked. Claire brushed the crumbs off her lap and stood up. "Let's go near the window, where the lighting is best."

Photography was a relatively new endeavor that being a part of the group had introduced to Nora, though it was not for art's sake itself, but so she could literally put a face to a name. At the Chuck Close exhibit she'd attended with the group the month before, she'd learned that the artist suffered from the same disorder that they all did. It turned out that he was one of those annoying people who wouldn't allow a disability to just be. Close fought through it, forcing himself to paint faces so that he had to confront his demons head-on. *No pun intended,* Nora thought to herself. But the exhibit turned out to be helpful. Just like Chuck Close, Nora realized that a face wasn't so intimidating when it was two-dimensional, when it was capable of being flattened on a canvas or a photograph.

She took Arthur's old Pentax out of retirement from his office desk drawer and began cataloging her social and familial circle.

"Listen," Claire said, as Nora rewound the film before placing it in a canister to be developed. "This is by no means me retracting my invitation for you to be my maid of honor, okay? But I completely understand if it's too much right now. There's absolutely no pressure. I know you have a lot going on, and the last thing I want to do is to add to it."

"I'm fine," Nora said. "Or at least I hope to be by December 12."

"Really?" Claire cocked her head.

Nora pressed her thumb into the flakes left behind from a *pain au chocolat*. She poked her tongue around the corners of her mouth. She willed herself not to get upset. "Well, how the hell am I supposed to know? It's been over a year, Claire. Do you think I'm doing any better? Be honest."

"Well, that's why I don't want to add any more stress."

"I promise I won't embarrass you," Nora said, pulling her legs down to the floor and crumpling up the paper bag. Tiny pastry shavings scattered to the floor like snow. She looked at her friend, whose face was twisted in concern. Nora stared and stared at Claire's heart-shaped hairline, the tiny freckle on the end of her nose, the indent at the tip of her chin. Other than the fact that she knew that her best friend was sitting on this couch, she couldn't identify her at all.

"It's not that, Nor," Claire said.

"I said I'd be fine." One of the many awful aspects of prosopagnosia were that people treated her like a baby, as though it was more than just faces that she didn't know. They acted as though she'd forgotten how to live, how to behave around people anymore, that she couldn't remember how to hold a spoon or how to locate her nose.

The other end of the spectrum was that people thought

she was antisocial. They translated her avoidance of making eye contact as unfriendly and rude. No matter how many times she explained her condition she came away feeling as though it wasn't a disorder but just an invalid excuse.

Claire stood and hugged Nora and let herself out. The air was tense in the moments after she'd all but retracted her invitation to Nora to be her maid of honor, but Nora had to admit that she couldn't blame her. It was more than a title. She would be responsible for ushering in the bridesmaids, ensuring that they were dressed and ready. And she certainly couldn't do that if she wasn't able to identify any of them.

For now, she wasn't sure what she would do. Nora sat on the couch as the room darkened from the sun's descent behind the Hudson River. She held the invitation in one hand and her notebook in the other, as though her hands were a pair of scales.

NICO

Tallinn
October–November 2002

One of the best things about being in a country like Estonia was that one never had to choose between destinations outside Tallinn to visit on the weekends. The country was so small that it could be traversed from end to end in a matter of hours. There were three main highways that led out of Tallinn in a circle, and they met in the middle at the south end of the country. Turning west, east or south out of the city center would eventually result in meeting a road that led to Tartu. Nico was headed to the second-largest city in the country with the Sokolovs after Vera had suggested that he might like to see other parts of Estonia.

Leo, Vera, Paavo and Nico piled into the dusty brown Lada soon after breakfast as the sun peered over the edge of Kadriorg Park. Nico had eaten as much *kasha* as he could spoon into his mouth that morning, after crumbling an entire bar of the chalky Kamatahvel over the groats. He had a feeling that Leo wouldn't have much patience for pulling over for a snack stop along the way. Nico pulled the blanket over his knees that Leo had tossed behind him as he'd started the car. "Sorry—heat only in front." He was just getting comfortable behind Vera when the door opened next to him and Mari stuck her head in.

"Move over," she said. "You can't expect me to sit in the middle."

"I didn't even know you were coming," Nico said. "Don't you have a shoot?"

"Postponed," she said. "Come on, Nico, get a move on."

That Estonia was a small country was the only reason that Nico didn't complain about sitting in the cramped middle seat for the two-hour drive to Tartu. In an effort to give Mari space, he stayed as close to Paavo as possible, but the siblings fell asleep shortly after the car passed by the airport, both nodding against Nico's broad shoulders. Vera appeared to be asleep, too, small snorts emanating from the passenger seat from time to time. Nico tried to take in the scenery around him, as Leo and Nico's eyes met in the rearview mirror from time to time.

"Boring, no?" Leo said softly. Nico had actually been thinking that while the country was flat, it made the sky seem expansive and never ending. The clouds and the glow from the sun were ethereal. It felt as if they were driving on the edge of the world, making Nico perceive how large the universe was, and that there was so much more to life than he'd ever seen. Though they were on a two-lane highway, and the Lada didn't seem capable of going over fifty miles an hour, it seemed that Leo liked to speed, pushing down on the accelerator as hard he could. Other drivers moved out of the way, changing lanes and waving him on as he careened forward. As closed off as Estonians were, they were also incredibly polite.

"It's not so bad. It's a lot greener than I thought it would be."

"Most Estonia is trees. Untouched," Leo said. "Outside of Tallinn is quite beautiful. You will see. Vera has many plans for visitation. We will visit my parents in Narva."

"What about Vera's parents? Where do they live?"

Leo turned his head to honk three times as they jetted past a hitchhiker along the shoulder of the road. It was the fourth one they'd seen upon their exit from Tallinn.

"What's up with those guys?" Nico asked.

"What guys?" Leo asked.

"There are so many hitchhikers. Does no one have cars?"

"Not so many have. But it is easy to get a ride in Estonia. People are good and stop for them. If we had room, I would pick him up."

"Is that safe?" Nico asked. "Back home, picking up a hitchhiker is dangerous."

"Why?" Leo asked.

"I guess 'cause you don't know who they are, or where they're from, where they're going."

"Is the point," Leo said. "Otherwise, is no fun."

Just past Põltsamaa, Leo pulled the car over to the side of the road. There weren't many vehicles on the road, other than large trucks that appeared to be bringing goods to different parts of the country. Leo put his fingers to his lips and nodded to his sleeping family. "Come out," he whispered.

Nico eased Mari's head onto the back of the car seat and stepped gingerly over Paavo's legs out the door onto the road. "Are we here?" Nico asked. "I thought Tartu was a big town."

"Not Tartu. I will show you something special. Come." Leo walked toward a lush thicket of trees, which stood about a hundred feet from the edge of the road. Nico watched his shoulders retreat into the shadows before Leo turned back. "Come."

Just beyond the perimeter of the tall, slim trunks, the shrubbery created a canopy over their heads. Large boulders within the small, contained forest cast long shadows underneath logs, and sunlight filtered through the leaves above them. It was a few degrees cooler within the shelter of the copse than it was on the other side. Much like the streets of Tallinn, Nico felt as though he were entering a fairy-tale world, but this time instead of diminutive colorful houses, they were entering an enchanted meadow, where time seemed to stand still. The air in the woods was cleaner, brighter. Nico found himself taking great breaths of it as he walked, as though it would disappear unless he brought it all into his lungs. Leo continued farther into the woods, and Nico found himself having to jog over twisted roots and rocks to keep up with him. At a thicket of evergreens, Leo paused and waited for him.

"It's beautiful here," Nico said. "I would never have thought there'd be so much lushness to the country."

"The *most* beautiful country in the world," Leo said, smiling. In the few weeks he had been with the Sokolovs, Nico could count on one hand the number of times he'd seen Leo smile, and he felt pleased that he'd caught another sighting. The woods seemed to draw something else out of Leo; it was as though he'd morphed into a satyr, skipping about the woods without a care. The bottoms of Leo's pant legs darkened with dew as Nico followed at a polite distance behind. A few minutes into the walk, Leo stopped short and pointed.

"It is very Estonian," Leo said, removing a folded plastic bag from his pocket, "to collect mushrooms." He pointed out a layered mass of orange-colored foam. As Nico looked

around, there were clumps of them all over the mossy forest floor.

"Mushrooms?"

"To share your favorite mushroom spot, this is very special." He grinned at Nico and held the bag out toward him.
"We are like KGB when it comes to finding best mushrooms.
We never share this information with anyone. Now, Nico,
you are family."

"Wow. Thanks, Leo. Your secret is safe with me. I did
this with my family when we were in Provence," Nico said.
"In France they sauté them in butter and wrap them in a
dough, kind of like pizza."

"Is not same. Mushrooms are best in Estonia," Leo said,
digging a little into the dirt with two fingers. He unearthed
a long white root at the end of which was a tight little cap.
"It is religion here."

"That's what Paavo says about sauna."

"We have many religions in this country," Leo said, wink-
ing at him.

The two spent the next ten minutes gathering all the
mushrooms in the little clearing beneath the boulders. Nico
concentrated on collecting the orange ones as Leo foraged
in the clearing; digging beneath logs to find a variety of
mushrooms—oysters, morels, chanterelles—he showed each
type to Nico before depositing them in his sack.

"Thank you for showing that to me," Nico said, handing
his bag to Leo as they headed back. "It really meant a lot."

"How much?"

"Sorry?"

"I make small joke."

Nico grinned. "You really love it here, don't you?"

"Estonia is home. Best country in the world. Best beaches,

best forest, best islands, best culture, best vodka. But…weak history with bad rules."

"Right, citizenship. But you love your country. Can't citizenship be based on that? On like, knowing where the best mushroom spots are? And how to build a sauna? How important is language, really, when everyone speaks English anyway?"

Leo blushed. "Too bad you don't issue passports, Nico. Anyway, let us go back to the car. We will be late for lunch in Tartu."

As a family member, Mari was elusive. Sometimes she would join the rest of the family at the dinner table; other times she would be gone for great swaths of time at casting calls or studio shoots in a neighboring country. It was baffling to Nico that in Europe, it took the same amount of time to reach a whole other country as it did to drive across a single state in America, so it was often worth Mari's while to travel across neighboring borders.

But even though Nico had initially been intimidated by her cool, blasé aura and the vehemence with which she'd mocked him on his first night in her home, he was surprised that she always seemed to make herself available on weekends when the Sokolovs took their weekend jaunts. Whether she was warming to him, or whether she was truly not as busy as she claimed, Nico couldn't be sure.

What Nico didn't know was that even though Mari had intended to keep her distance from the young American, she began to find his presence comforting. When she came home late at night after a grueling day of travel, she slipped her shoes off just inside the door, paused at Nico's makeshift door and listened. There was something reassuring about hearing the rise and fall of Nico's breathing from the other side of the curtain, and she stopped there more often than not on her way upstairs. Nico had no inkling that his presence in the family comforted Mari, so he could support her meek brother, soften her bristly father and take some of the stress off her mother so that Mari could concentrate on her career.

Each Saturday morning, Nico found himself bookended by Paavo and Mari as Leo urged the little Lada down straight, cleanly paved roads that led as far as the eye could see. Vera was diligent in planning their jaunts, choosing a different destination, intending to show Nico every corner of the country. They strolled the cobblestone streets in Tartu, past students with their noses buried in textbooks in cafés and under trees. They walked barefoot in the cool white sands at Kabli Beach, their only company flocks of speckled grouse that congregated in the marsh grass below the dunes. They hung back on the rocks, watching the gray seals cavort at the edge of the ocean in Vilsandi National Park, as the wind whipped the sea into a frenzy, whitecaps and roiling waves churning toward the shore. They hiked the theater land around Rakvere, home to one of the earliest civilizations in the Baltic. They roamed the lush greenery of Saaremaa, the largest of the country's 1,500 surrounding islands, exploring the red bricks of Kuressaare Castle and poking their toes in the frigid, serene waters of the Baltic Sea. They visited Leo's parents, Paavo and Mari's Deda and Babu, in Narva, where they lived in an apartment amidst an immense block of communist-style housing, all gray concrete and right angles. They rode the ferry across the span of water to Helsinki—Leo sheepishly producing his gray passport at the ferry terminal—to spend a day traipsing the industrial neighborhoods that had sprung up near the docks.

Vera took her role as tour guide seriously, explaining the history of each place and why it was special. She explained how the tiny country had been overtaken and manipulated by hundreds of hands over the centuries: the Vikings at first, and then the Danes, the Swedes, the Germans, the Soviets. She spoke passionately about the resilience of the Estonian people over the years, despite the numerous changeovers that took place before their very eyes. Even though the family's weekend trips took them to every corner of the country, it was in their own neighborhood in Kadriorg that Nico got a sense of just what this little country had been through. As the family walked around the perimeter of the Tallinn Song Festival Grounds, Vera took him back to 1988 when hundreds of thousands of Estonians gathered to sing their hearts out in support of an independent Estonia.

"All those voices singing patriotic hymns together," Vera said, looking off into the distance. "It was the beginning of something very important. And then of course the following year, the Chain of Freedom."

"What's that?" Nico asked softly. He felt as though he were intruding on Vera's memory. Her eyes were misting, and she bit her lower lip in an effort to keep tears from spilling over.

"Citizens from Estonia, Latvia and Lithuania lined up to join the capital cities, holding hands in peaceful protest against the Soviet occupation," Vera said, sniffling. Leo put his arm around her, and bent his head so the others couldn't see his face. "Two million people holding on to one another, requesting for their countries to be free. It was beautiful to be part of this day. It led to independence. Do either of you remember it?"

Paavo shook his head and walked to the other side of Leo. Mari nodded slowly, concentrating hard on something on the ground. She grabbed her mother's hand, and the Soko- lovs walked together as a family, Nico following behind.

★ ★ ★

Right on time, the beginnings of winter arrived in Estonia in November. Nico was used to the wind tunnels of Manhattan that whipped through the canyons made by avenues, snaking from river to river, nullifying multiple layers of clothing to chill him to the bone. This cold was different than anything he had ever felt. It was as if he had let a flame lick the tips of his fingers and stuck his toes into the red embers of a fireplace.

It surprised Nico that it had taken him this long to get sick. The chill finally wound its way into him, permeating his bones, his body succumbing as it fell gratefully into the sofa bed with a croaking throat and a buzzing head. It felt as if Nico slept for a week, when it had only been three days. Vera attended to him, placing cold compresses on his sallow, drawn face and dosing him intermittently with marrow broth and a yellow fizzy drink that tasted too sweet to have any medicinal properties. Paavo brought him his homework, which piled up on the floor and was eventually kicked under the bed during one of his many trips to the bathroom. He slept in fits and bursts, plummeting into deep throes of delirious sleep, and fighting with his bedclothes, febrile and lathered in sweat when he was awake.

On the third day of his illness, Nico awoke to Mari peeking under his covers. He'd just been having a dream about her, in fact: he was crouching in his wrestling singlet on a runway, while on the other side of a wide chasm, Mari was walking sultrily on a wrestling mat, the points of her stilettos poking holes in the foam padding. In the dream, he had shouted at her to remove her shoes, as only rubber soles were allowed on the mat. It was always unsettling to see the person about whom you had just been dreaming in the flesh, as your mind attempted to unhinge itself from subconscious and reality, and doubly unsettling when the said person was reaching under the blankets for his feet. He startled, and curled his legs into a pretzel.

"That's completely unhelpful. Mama asked me to change you," Mari said, holding her hands out expectantly. She gestured for him to extend his legs and he did so cautiously, watching her every move. She grabbed hold of his socks with two disdainful fingers, stripping them off and tossing them to the floor.

Mari attended to Nico with a strange tenderness; in a moment she was a cat placing its jaws around the tender fur behind her kitten's neck to move it to a safer place, but the next, she could tear a mouse apart with the same razor-sharp canines.

"It was only a matter of time before the cold got to you. There's a pretty pathetic joke we have," Mari said. "Did you enjoy the summer in Estonia? No, I was working that day." She tugged another soggy pair of socks onto Nico's damp feet.

"What is that? Why are the socks so wet?" Nico rasped, speaking for the first time all day.

"Vodka socks," Mari said.

"Seriously?"

"Seriously. They help draw out the sickness."

"Does this really help?" Nico asked, pushing himself up on his elbows and trying to peer at his feet. "It sounds like an old wives' tale."

"Ask me that when you're feeling better." Mari cocked her right eyebrow at him and smiled her Cheshire cat grin.

"Isn't this kind of work beneath you? You're a big model now," Nico said, stretching his legs back out under him.

"Oh, is that what you think?" Mari asked. She pulled the blanket back over his legs.

"Aren't you? I've seen the billboards around the city."

"When my mother asks for my help, I give it. It's the Estonian way."

"So what's the point?" Nico asked. "Of all the glamour, all the pizzazz?"

"What's the point of my career?" Mari asked, disgustedly. "Thanks a lot."

"No, I mean, you have to get some perks out of it, right? Otherwise, you may as well rely on your high honors achievement." Nico bolstered himself with another pillow so that he could see her better.

"How do you know about that?"

"I have my ways," Nico said, arching his own eyebrow at her as though in reflection. "You're not just a dumb blonde after all."

Mari made a face at him.

"But seriously, what are you doing here anyway? I thought you had a big runway show in Riga."

"Canceled," she said.

"Again? Didn't that happen last month?"

"Mind your own affairs, Nico. And next time, change these yourself." Mari threw a pair of socks at him and stalked out of the room.

A few days later, Nico's head stopped throbbing long enough for him to close up the sofa bed and abandon the supine position he'd been in for days. He sat back into the couch, his bones slack as gelatin, and summoned all his remaining strength into his thumb to change the channel on the remote control. He settled on a football match where the ball was being passed and passed and passed.

Paavo sank down next to him. "Glad you're feeling better."

Nico nodded but didn't lift his eyes from the screen. "What'd I miss at school?"

"Not much. Heigi was asking after you. He practically followed me home to see you. I brought you some more assignments. They're in the car."

"Oh. Why?" Nico shifted on the sofa and placed the remote between them.

"Papa dropped me to school. And brought me home."

"Why?"

"What do you mean, why, Nico?"

"We usually take the bus. Why'd you take a ride with your dad?"

"It's just easier this way."

"It's not, Paavo. Tell me the truth. Why do you come with me to school an hour earlier than you have to be there?"

"I like having the company."

"Then why did we run from those boys on the first day after school?" Paavo remained silent. His pupils were the only things that moved as he watched the soccer ball being passed.

"P-Train. Level with me here. What's going on?" Nico searched Paavo's eyes. They weren't quite as volatile as Mari's but a steely blue that Nico still couldn't read after all these months.

Paavo sighed. "I just feel better with you there. In case."

"In case of what?" Nico sputtered.

Paavo pushed his hands between his legs and squeezed them together. "Just this group of guys that was hassling me last year. Bullies. They haven't bothered me since you came here, and I don't know whether it's because you're a wrestler, or because you're new or American, or what..."

"Who the fuck are these clowns? What the hell is their problem picking on you? Did you do something to piss them off?"

"You don't have to do anything specific to get on the bad side of neo-Nazis."

Nico's eyes widened. "You're being threatened by neo-Nazis? Like skinheads? That's serious, Paavo. You should report them."

"It's really not a big deal. They dropped out of school last year, and now they just hang out on the streets trying to get others to join their gang and causing trouble. What is the expression—their bark is worse than their bite? It will be fine. It's just easier when you're around. I know that's stupid."

"It's not stupid, Paavo. It's just not practical. I can't go with you everywhere you need to go, not to mention that I am not going to be here forever. And you can't hang out with your dad all the time. We have to figure this out."

"There's nothing to figure out. I'm a coward. Happy?"

"Not in the least. I'm fuming. We have to deal with this."

"I don't think you understand. These people, they don't fight fair. It's not that simple."

"You don't have to fight, Paavo."

"It's six guys. And me. What else am I supposed to do? I can't keep running away."

"Fighting would be stupid," Nico continued. "The first rule of wrestling is that you only begin fights you know you can win. You don't wrestle outside your weight class. You don't take on anyone who's not a fair match. You just need swagger. I can teach you swagger."

Paavo looked at the screen, where one of the players was being shown a yellow card. "I don't know, Nico."

"Look, when we get back to New York, you'll come with me to wrestling practice and Coach can teach you some things so you feel a little more confident. I can start showing you some holds now if you want. And you just need to know a few tricks. Like, if you have to get in a fight, always hit in the nose. That way you get enough time to get the hell out of there because the force creates tears to momentarily blind your opponent."

Paavo sighed. "Can't we just continue going to school together?"

"Sure. But at some point, I'm going to go home and you're going to come back here without me and you're going to have to go it alone."

LEO

Tallinn
December 2002

Leo had been going it alone for nearly twenty years. He had been singled out, his gray passport held out at border control like a penalty card at a football match. He had stumbled over Estonian conjugation at each and every grammar lesson Vera held in their kitchen as his children tried to quiet their snickers over his pronunciation. He could understand every iota of Estonian that was uttered on ETV, but he couldn't orchestrate the words to align in a cohesive sentence. It was as though he was living a life on one side of the country watching his family over a border partition on the other. And then this morning, he'd had to endure an additional insult for the fourth time.

Leo heard the door bang open in the kitchen. He replaced the hand that had been supporting his forehead with a tumbler of ice and vodka and let the cold crash against his skin. The house had been silent; the only sound he heard was Kunnar on his back porch as he tossed feed to his birds, the seeds chattering against the ground. There were footsteps in the kitchen, but Leo left the glass pressed against his forehead, letting the cold seep into his brain. He clearly had one. So why had he failed yet again? Why was he doing this to himself? The drudgery of shame was starting to feel old. What was the point of making him feel insignificant? Estonian was a useless language with extraneous vowels and redundant tenses. It didn't matter outside the boundaries of this insignificant slip of land, whereas Russian was spoken in a huge country, one that spanned millions of acres from ocean to ocean. He transferred the vodka to his other hand and stood up, the shame draining from his face. He walked down the hall to the kitchen, where Nico was sitting at the table, his own head in his hands.

"You're home early," Nico said, raising his head from his arms.

"I had to pick up my citizenship results from city hall this afternoon." Leo's voice was like gravel.

"Oh, right," Nico said. "How'd it go?"

"What you think?"

"Sorry, Leo. That sucks. Was this the third time?"

"Four." Leo swallowed what was left in his glass and poured another.

"Well, you can take it again, right?"

Leo snorted out his nose and took a large gulp.

Nico unzipped his bag and pulled out a roll of paper and tossed it on the table between them. Leo unfurled it and raised his eyebrows.

"You fail your Estonian exam, too, eh?" Leo tossed the paper back at Nico, the red number one glaring up at him. "Yes, but you are new. It's all right for you. It doesn't matter. Soon you will be rid of this language. This language is useless anyway."

"That's exactly how I feel," Nico said, turning to face Leo as he leaned against the sink. "Everyone here speaks English. Even the signs are in English. Estonian is completely ruining my grade point average."

"But for me," Leo continued as though Nico hadn't spoken, "I am worse. I'm old. It is too late. I've live here most my life, and still I am a second-class citizen. So what? I can't speak Estonian. Am I not a man?"

"I think you're just as much of an Estonian as everyone else here. You pay taxes, you work here and you've raised your kids here. I don't understand why they're making you jump through hoops to prove something to yourself."

Leo let out a large sigh and opened the liquor cabinet. He extended a bottle of Viru Valge toward Nico. "Drink?"

Nico glanced at the clock, in what he hoped was a furtive motion. It was just after four in the afternoon. "Maybe not," he said.

"Vera's not home," Leo said. "Don't worry."

"No, it's just that I have homework. Have to keep my wits about me." Nico smiled. "And isn't it bad luck to drink alone?"

"Not in Estonia." Leo poured himself a tumbler of vodka and leaned on the back spindles of his chair. He gulped down his vodka as though it were cold lemonade on a blistering day. "Tell me about Paavo."

"What about him?"

"He is so afraid these days."

"Yeah, he's a little tense. He needs to relax. I've told him that."

"But what is problem? He was not like this one year back. Once I had son who wanted to kick football, not speak riddles all day."

"He just needs to build up his self-esteem. He's going to

come to wrestling practice with me when we go home to New York." Nico saw Leo's gaze wander toward the vodka bottle. "Listen, I was thinking of hitting up Kadriorg Palace. Do you want to come?" The Baroque-style palace lay just a few blocks away from where the Sokolovs lived, a sprawling country home that Peter the Great had gifted his wife Catherine out of love. Only after it had been built did evidence that she'd had an affair with another man surface.

"No, you go on." Leo drained his glass.

"Come on. It might make you feel better. What puts things into perspective more than a cuckold?"

"A what?"

"You know—Czar Peter builds his wife a huge palace to prove his love, and then he finds out she cheated on him?"

Leo made a noise like a cat. Had that been a laugh? "Yes, it will remind me who was boss in Estonia for many years—Russia. I haven't been to Kadriorg in years. Come. I will get my coat." Once Nico heard the galumphing of Leo's footsteps overhead, he replaced the bottle of vodka in the cupboard and walked toward the front door. Two months ago, the prospect of spending time alone with Leo would have made Nico nervous. Perhaps he was finally making some progress.

MARI

Tallinn
December 2002

Mari's leg jittered against her desk. At an open call in Tartu a month before, she'd overheard a model say that fidgeting sped up the metabolism and helped her stay trim. But now Mari wasn't sure if she had always had this habit, or if she'd subconsciously picked it up upon learning of its effects. She picked at the edge of her desk. The laminate was peeling away from the wood. The curl of plastic seemed to mock her, as though it was corroding from disuse. When was the last time she'd sat here, other than to pore over proofs from a shoot? When had she last read a book, or anything of substance? During her first few calls she had brought along a battered paperback to pass the time, but after she realized that the models only toted glossies, she ditched the book and made it a point to pick up a few magazines before each call.

She silenced her leg by settling her free hand on top of it. Her skin was mottled and rough; there were stubbly patches she'd missed with the razor and her calves badly needed moisturizing. She shifted the phone to her other ear. She was still on hold—the third hold she'd been on since she'd called Viktor's office. She remembered a time—it felt like generations before—when her phone calls received precedence. Viktor would snap his fingers aggressively to silence his secretary when she entered the room during a coaching session. He turned his phone off when Mari was in the office, or ignored the other lines when she was on the phone. Mari had once captivated his complete attention. He had been laser-focused on making sure she wasn't heading to any call or shoot with the slightest hesitation or concern.

Everything seemed worn now, including herself; she felt as though her modeling career had been through the wringer, and was developing that gray pallor that was cast onto garments over time, tiny little threads pulling away from woven cloth. She sighed and stretched both legs out in front of her now, and something cracked in her pelvis, her lower back, she couldn't be sure. Her ligaments felt loose, as though a meat hammer had pounded and tenderized her joints like a slab of pork. It was true what was said about prodigies who skipped grades and were catapulted into classes ahead of their age; about army brats who traveled the world with their parents, clinging to the wisdom that the wide world had so much to teach them, but they didn't have a solid foundation on which to grasp ahold. It was true, too, of child models. While she'd only been modeling for the past year, Mari had missed out on her formal *saja päeva* ball, on being taken out by boys, on obsessing for hours over stupid details with her friends. Instead, her obsessions had been redirected toward booking shows, the arch of her foot, the circumference of her waist.

She sighed. *I'm hanging up by the count of ten.*

"Sorry, darling. Been utterly hectic." Viktor certainly didn't sound in the least bit harried or stressed; his voice dripped, as though he were midmassage. Maybe he was. "Where were we?"

"Next month's schedule." Mari began picking at the laminate again. She'd succeeded in lifting the entire upper right corner; she might as well finish the job now.

"Well, you've got Dove on the third, and then…then…" Mari could hear his fingers drumming against his own massive custom-made artisanal desk, which was most certainly not peeling. "I'm working on the rest."

"That's all? That Dove ad doesn't even call for models. It's an open call for real women. Dove doesn't discriminate." Mari pulled furiously at the laminate; a large strip of it ended up in her clenched fist. "What, am I not good-looking enough for the clients you're working with?"

"Oh, don't throw yourself a pity party, Mari. It's not becoming."

"Viktor, we're on the brink of a new season. I should have been cast in Spring Fashion by now. I should have had to turn down houses, because I couldn't handle the work."

Viktor chuckled. "Someone's been doing her homework."

"I'm not trying to be cute over here, Viktor. I'm trying to be indignant. I *am* indignant—you and Eva have to *book* me."

"I'm working on some really exciting things for you, Mari. You have to be patient. Let's talk at the end of next week. I think you're going to be pleased, and then you're going to be falling all over yourself in apology."

"I will come and polish your toilet in penance. But I'm getting bored and when I get bored, I eat."

"Don't you dare," Viktor said. It was the first time during the whole call that Mari had heard any emotion in his voice.

"Just do your job," Mari snarled, and hung up. She hadn't ever hung up on anyone before, but it was strangely satisfying. She stood up, stalking back and forth, kicking shoes out of her way, feeling steam mount in her nostrils. If she were a man, she would punch the wall. But she was a model.

Ha, she scoffed to herself. Some model. A failed model was more like it. She had promised her parents that she would try this for two years, and if her career hadn't taken flight by then, she'd have to return to school, return to life before the day in Freedom Square had changed everything. What's worse was that she would have to slink in sheepishly to a high school class two years below hers, leaving all that she'd learned about modeling behind by keeping her head down and her back hunched so as not to draw attention to herself. She needed to take control of her life, and if that was out of her hands, she needed the ability to control something else.

Was she not pretty enough? Could she not compete with the likes of Carmen Kass? If she wasn't as good-looking as her, Mari knew she worked at least as hard. She'd heard the story of when Carmen was just starting out in the industry at age fourteen and had her passport taken away from her in an effort to make her work cheaply. She'd threatened that agent with a knife until she'd gotten her way. That was a bit extreme, Mari admitted. But maybe she needed to up her game. Maybe she just needed more confidence to achieve what she wanted.

She heard a noise from downstairs. She'd thought she was the only one in the house, but she tiptoed down the back stairs and inched her way into the den. There, as though she were living a scene in backward time, Mari stood in the mouth of the den, watching Nico as he plucked his folded clothes off the ground in the same, meticulous way he had placed them there when he first arrived. This time the room was washed in the golden light of the late afternoon, and his hair was lit from behind, giving him a halo that followed him with each movement. Nico straightened up when he noticed her there. She liked the effect she had on him; his body had tensed in self-awareness from the moment she'd stood outside the den. He selected a pile of T-shirts from the floor and gingerly tucked them into his duffel bag.

"I feel like I've lived this scene before," she said. "Déjà vu."

"I was thinking the same."

"Shouldn't you be down at the football pitch?" Mari asked.

"I'm just finishing up here, and then I'm meeting Paavo and your dad in town for a beer. Paavo can't believe your dad allowed me to get away with not having had a Saku until now."

"I can't believe my brother had the balls to go to the football pitch by himself without his bodyguard by his side."

"Mari, you don't even know what you're talking about."

"I know that Paavo has been hiding in your shadow since you arrived. Come on, Nico, give me some credit. Not all models are airheads."

"I never said you were."

"So what, are you packing already?"

"Looks that way, doesn't it?"

"But you have a week here. You're not leaving for a week." Mari felt suddenly desperate. She'd known that Nico would eventually be going home, but like the end of her modeling career, or what felt like it, she hadn't realized it would come so soon. She watched him as he tossed in socks, and laid pants flat against the floor of the bag.

"Admit it. You're going to miss me." Nico raised his eyebrows and threw a sock at Mari. She grabbed it, giggling. What was she doing? She didn't giggle. She didn't flirt. She stayed on the periphery; at least, she used to. Now, of course, she was center stage, plastered across buses and billboards wielding a brown bottle of Vana Tallinn in front of her chest like an AK-47 and wearing a tiny little sarong as though

Estonia were a tropical island. She was making eye contact from behind last month's cover of *Kuula*, one of the very glossies she had purchased to bide her time in hundreds of waiting areas.

Standing there, watching Nico pack, all the thoughts in her head moved and shifted like puzzle pieces. Nico leaving marked the passage of time; a year and a half had passed since she had committed to modeling, to surrendering her childhood to Viktor and fasting and water and fidgeting. She had given her parents her word, but moreover, she had made a promise to herself. She could not go out of the modeling world being the face of a second-rate liqueur. She was bigger than that. She needed to leave a legacy. She would have to act fast. Mari broke her own reverie.

"When you're done, come upstairs," she said. "I have something for you."

Nico smiled. "I knew I'd wear you down. You're not the ice queen you try to be."

"Just remember which one of us freaked out when we first met," she said, turning on her heels.

"That's not fair," Nico sputtered. "You snuck up on me in the dark, in a place I didn't know." But Mari was already gone.

Fifteen minutes later, Nico stood outside her closed door. Soft music with vaguely French lyrics emanated from behind it. She opened it before he'd even finished knocking, smiled at him, hooked her two fingers into the collar of his crew neck T-shirt and pulled him inside. Mari hadn't turned on any lights in her room, allowing the floodlight that Kunnar had installed over the henhouse to cast long cants of broken light against the carpet, broken up into individual rectangles by the vertical Persian blinds. She shut the door softly behind him and leaned against it. Nico stood in the center of the carpet, bathed in the slatted light. He'd flinched at her touch; his face contorted as though he were awaiting torture. He looked stricken, but mostly he looked confused. Mari placed her finger in the hollow where his collarbone dipped. She continued the line down his chest, feeling the goose bumps that dappled upon his skin before her finger even reached there. She heard the breath catch in Nico's throat as her finger paused at the button of his jeans. He hadn't been undressed since he was a child, when Stella made all his decisions for him. The sensation was strange, as though he should have been taking over in order to voice his autonomy. But he stood mute, like the metal wand at the airport, watching as Mari's hands traveled all over him, unbuttoning and sliding cloth from his skin, waiting to see if she would set off an alarm. His entire body was tense and buzzing, as if she had released a hive of bees within it. As soon as she leaned forward and placed her mouth against his, his body went slack like that game of Trust that Coach had made the team play during practice, where you put your arms out, close your eyes and fall back into the arms of the person that you pray is there to catch you.

It felt like hours later that he emerged from a conscious slumber, but Nico knew it was only twenty-two minutes from the large red digital numbers blinking like a witness on Mari's desk. The clock was placed atop her towering stack of modeling papers, as though to remind them of the dwindling aspect of time, that she couldn't stay forever young with taut skin stretched over her cheekbones like a fresh canvas, that the sinews in her muscles would one day atrophy and her hips would one day lose their flexibility.

Nico would have been lying if he said he hadn't imagined

this before. In fact, he had imagined it many times over as he lay in the cold little pullout bed in what felt like the banished part of the house as the rest of the family slept upstairs. He straightened himself up from the bed, propping himself on one elbow. His chest was tacky with sweat, and his temples pulsed with adrenaline. Next to him, Mari was asleep, her body heaving up and down as though in distress. He poked her to make sure she was all right, and she turned away from him toward the wall, pulling the blanket over her shoulders. The house was still; their bodies hummed with the two lights that combined and settled over them: the blue haze from the floodlight and the orange glow of the setting sun. He felt caught within the sheet's clutches, everything all crunched together like a trap. Nico felt a conflicted tide rise in him, the ebb of wanting to stay by her side. Moving from the bed would be criminal. It wasn't like leaving her with a full sink of dishes. And yet he felt the flow of wanting to disappear, especially if she was faking it and giving him an out, allowing him to slink out of the room in order to minimize the drama that comes with the aftermath of such an act.

He edged his head toward her moist shoulder and brushed his lips against it. No response. He pulled himself out of bed in a single motion. She still hadn't moved. He wanted to tell her so many things, that she was so much better looking without all that makeup, that the whole thing was so much better than he could have ever imagined, that he wondered how long she'd been planning that... Instead, he closed the door with a gentle click. He stood outside her door, naked, pale and shivering.

The lower part of the house was unaware of what had transpired overhead. But as soon as Nico got to his room, waves of panic overwhelmed him. It was as though he had dreamed the whole thing, or had an out-of-body experience. A swarm of questions hung around his head like pesky gnats. Was that it? Sex? It was over, just like that? Why was there so much buildup? Had he been any good? Was Mari's response positive? Had they used a condom? Would it happen again? Was she his girlfriend? How should he behave when he saw her again?

With all the rush of emotions and hormones, he couldn't help but feel like a walking cliché. Of course the big American jock had traveled to a foreign country and slept with the gorgeous, foreign, exotic girl. Wasn't that practically written in the stars by some bad made-for-television movie? Perhaps, but at the end of the day, Nico was a cliché who had slept with a model. And as far as bragging rights went, they spoke the loudest.

His clothes were still in the six piles for each remaining day of the week he had left in Tallinn, but the ones he was wearing were still caught between the claws of the tangled sheets. He picked up the stack for the next day and somehow managed to fold his body into them. He passed his hands over the vodka for his father, the matryoshka dolls for Nora, the crocheted tablecloth for Stella and nestled them all carefully back within the folded clothes, padded by sweatshirts. He had to remember to return the down jacket he'd borrowed from Paavo before he left.

Paavo. Shit. But he didn't necessarily have to find out. Nico certainly wouldn't tell him, and he couldn't imagine Mari wanting to, either. Nico closed his eyes and breathed in and slowly out. He mumbled his wrestling incantation— Defend Until the End—under his breath and counted to ten. Then he shoved his feet into the sneakers that lay askew on the mat and jogged out the door, slamming it behind him so that even Mari in her repose with her labored or feigned breathing would be sure to hear him leave.

NICO

New York City
December 2002

The changes in Stella's son were striking, not subtle. His face
had clearly changed: more angles, fewer instinctive smiles.
Even his writing seemed more blasé, as though he couldn't
be bothered to form a complete sentence. It was strange how
dramatic changes seemed when you couldn't see them happening in front of you, the way you didn't notice a plant
growing when it was in your own living room, but when
you came back after a vacation, it had suddenly sprouted six
inches. Stella couldn't pinpoint it, but Nicholas seemed different somehow, including his name.

"Nicholas," Stella had called as soon as his face turned the
corner from the arrivals ramp and he made his way to the
baggage carousels. She'd leaped up and run toward him in
a manner she might have scoffed at had she been watching
another parent. She couldn't help it. She wanted to drink in
her son, remember what his hair smelled like, what his body

felt like in her embrace. But everything was off somehow—
even his name.

"Hi, Mom," he'd said, slightly breathless after she'd released him from the hug. "Can you call me Nico now?"

"Oh," she'd said. She could feel her face flushing as though
someone had pointed out that her zipper had been down.
"Why?"

"It's just what everyone called me over there," he said. He
shrugged and straightened his shoulders, his eyes focused on
the conveyor belt.

"I guess I could try that," Stella said. She observed her son
as though he were behind a glass case, the way his fingers
flexed and his jaw tensed.

"I can't place what's different about you," she said on the
drive home. "Was it the fact that you maneuvered your way
around a foreign country? Were you popular? I bet everyone
wanted to be friends with you. I bet you were a total star,
the cool American kid. It was a girl, wasn't it, some pretty
Russian doll? Sorry." She'd caught herself. "STD."

"That's not technically an STD, Mom," Nico said. "A doll
is what you call a pretty girl, so that's not wrong."

"So, was it?"

He shook his head and went back to staring out the window. Even though she could reach out and touch him, she
sensed a deep schism between the two of them, as though
Tallinn had been planted between them and was growing
subterranean roots that would eventually strangle them from
below. Her son had been swapped in a KGB maneuver; the
real Nico had been left behind and a stand-in had been sent
in his stead. *STD*.

"So what *is* it?" she asked. Perhaps being straightforward
was the best approach.

"What's what?" Nico asked, leaning his head against the window and looking up at the sky.

"What's different?"

"Nothing. I don't know—maybe I'm worldlier or something."

"That's not a word."

"I don't know what you're looking for, Mom."

"I'm not looking for anything." Stella blanched and looked back at the road. "I guess I just missed you. Look, I took the whole afternoon off. Do you want to head over to City Bakery when we get home? They have this new chocolate-caramel-doughnut-cookie thing that absolutely must be shared."

"I thought I'd meet Toby and the guys this afternoon. I haven't really talked to them since I left. I only have like, a week before Paavo gets here." Nico hadn't turned his head from the window the entire time. It was as though he was taking in all the sights whizzing by for the first time.

"Oh, okay," Stella said, turning on her left blinker. "Well, I'd like to spend some time with you, too. Hear some stories, just catch up."

"Maybe this weekend," Nico said. "I missed a whole semester of wrestling. I want to catch up, too." Stella pursed her lips. She'd formed this child, his very flesh and bones within the caverns and contours of her own body. She'd been responsible for creating the curls and synapses of his brain matter, for stacking the sinews of his musculature within her womb. She knew it was silly to feel proprietary toward him after all these years, but when she reminded herself of the pure and simple biology of Nico's existence, it was difficult to let him go when he'd just arrived. Stella longed to grasp Nico and squeeze him like a sponge in order to learn everything he'd seen, thought and experienced since he'd been gone.

★ ★ ★

Nico wished he could preserve the encounter with Mari in much the same way. But when he began to realize that the occasion was over and done with, he began to distance himself from the encounter in stages.

Immediately afterward, standing in the pale twilight of the Sokolovs' den, the act had felt nefarious. *He* was culpable for having stained Mari's sheets with his sweat, for having bitten her top lip until it was pink and swollen, for leaving little crescents in her skin from his fingernails. What's more, Mari was Paavo's sister, a sister who may as well have been his own for the four months he'd spent in Tallinn. As skittish and timid as Paavo was, Nico had no idea how he might respond if he ever found out. He found himself lurking around the house almost as anxiously as Paavo himself; slipping in and out of the bathroom like a thief, and trying his ultimate best to be quiet when he was in his own room.

The next week, as Nico packed up the vodka, the dolls and the tablecloth for his family, he remembered that he'd only gone up to Mari's room because she'd said she had a gift for him. The guilt dropped off him like a cloak and he felt suddenly duped and naive. *Mari* had been the seducer, luring Nico up to her dimly lit lair when the entire family was absent from the house. It was Mari who had lined her eyes with kohl so she resembled that cat stalking him on his very first night, a wild feline who would ultimately get what she wanted. It was Mari who had begun touching him, in a way she had never touched him before; in fact, except for when she'd fallen asleep on his shoulder in the car or when she'd changed his vodka socks, he didn't think that she had ever touched him at all. Over time, he began to feel like the victim; Mari had taken advantage of *him*. She had initiated every touch, every breath, each flicker of her tongue. She'd known exactly what she was doing from the start. Nico wanted to feel indignant, but he knew exactly what his friends would say if he complained: "So what?"

So he let himself shift to the next step. He accepted it, embracing the action fully as Barbara would have wanted him to experience everything he was exposed to in Tallinn. He relived it. He recalled all the actions, the touches and the shivers. For those twenty-two minutes, Mari was a star that he had reached out to with his bare hands and caught as it sailed across a crystal clear sky. She sparkled, stretching her taut calves, presenting him with her elegant but accessible breasts and a belly button chasm that Nico hadn't realized was an irresistible body part until he was lost in it.

He began to wonder if sex upon returning home would be completely different. There hadn't been any expectations in that cloistered room in Tallinn. There had been hand placements that had prompted soft coos. There had been awkward tracings over skin, kissing in unerogenous areas, crevices explored with tentative fingers, soft blowing in an ear, which had been subtly turned down by a shake and a turn of the head so the ear was out of reach. There had been guidance, as though the entire act had been planned out from the start. There had been unease at the start, which had quickly translated into hunger, a brave recourse for the seduced, he who had scarcely been expecting such an invitation. High school sex was sex for sex's sake. It was sex for bragging rights, for the ability to cross over from one side of a deep divide to the other, entirely for the intention of feeling smug. No one was experienced or possessed a skill set that made sex worthwhile, meaningful or even pleasurable. High school sex was a deed that was done so that it could never be undone. But of course, once the act was over between Mari and Nico, it was as though nothing had happened, and the two retreated to their own quarters, much like mating lions that had completed their biological business and now would embark on the matter of pretending the other one didn't exist.

The fact was that he hadn't seen much of Mari in his last few days with the Sokolovs. She had been out of the house before he awoke, and came home late in the night. Vera reported that she was out on calls and auditions; Viktor had redeemed himself and business was really picking up for her. On Nico's last day, as Leo was about to return him to the airport from which he'd collected him four months before, she sauntered casually into the kitchen.

"Just wanted to say goodbye," she said, her hands deep in her pockets. "All the best." Nico felt a pang in his side. His body was responding physically to her nonchalance. Mari's hair was tied back in one of her signature knots, but her fringe spread across her forehead like a windshield wiper, clearing her face of emotional clutter. Her dungarees were frayed and pale from washing and her T-shirt rode over the rise of her pelvic bones as she loitered in the doorway.

"Thanks," he said. He slid his chair back opportunely, hoping it might encourage her to come and touch him. He would welcome even a chaste exchange now: a hug, even a handshake. But Mari remained loitering by the doorway and finally leaned against it, establishing her station there. "Come visit us in New York sometime. Maybe they'll send you out there for a job."

She smiled. "Maybe. Keep in touch. And good luck with wrestling."

He ducked his face behind his mug of steaming tea. There didn't seem as if there was anything else to say, and simultaneously as if there was everything to say. But none of it could be said with the audience of Paavo, Vera and Leo. With the lengthening of the silence, Mari stepped backward into the hall. And then she was gone.

Nico wondered if he'd played everything all wrong. That perhaps Mari's nonchalance and standoffishness had been the foreplay, the dance she had choreographed in order for Nico to step up his game and try to seduce her again. But it was too late. It was time for him to leave Estonia. Resigned, as Paavo and Leo packed the car, Nico had stolen into her empty bedroom and helped himself to one of her head shots and a handful of comp cards. He knew no one, not any of the team or even Toby would believe him unless he brought physical evidence.

It wasn't that Nico was unattractive or undesirable. He had heard that girls thought he was cute; he had even dated the preppy Charlotte James, in the first few months of sophomore year. After a few weeks of dating, she'd told Nico that she liked him because she could imagine him turning out very handsome when he was older. He'd been rather startled by her declaration. Did that mean he wasn't handsome now? Did she mean that she would stay with him until he was adequately handsome? Or that she wanted to stay with him until they grew old? In the juvenile fashion that serves all high school students, Nico broke up with her at the end of the fourth week without asking her what she had meant. She stood opposite him in the empty hallway that had been cleared out instantaneously by the last bell of the day, her large eyes quavering and rolling around in their sockets in an attempt to avoid eye contact with him and not spill the tears that had gathered. He'd been surprised at the pinching feeling he felt between his own eyes when he saw her holding hands with Wilson—his own teammate!—later on that month, but he didn't mind because he was a stronger wrestler than Wilson anyway. But Charlotte James was no Mari Sokolov.

Before that afternoon with Mari, Nico had been looking forward to his return home, to his bed that held his body's indentation, to a room with an actual door that closed, to the brutish camaraderie of his teammates and the wise tutelage and gruff bark of Coach's orders. He'd found himself trying to remember the scent of the laundry detergent that Stella used, the slip of a MetroCard through a turnstile, the heady aroma of the hot chocolate at City Bakery. He'd even missed squat thrusts during wrestling practice.

But now the desire to return to all that was familiar seemed to disappear as he found himself only yearning to be with Mari. He pictured the two of them walking down a street but whether they were in Manhattan or Tallinn was unclear; the only sharp edges to this daydream were the two of them together, fingers linked, inhabiting the comfortable silence that only lovers can maintain. He imagined the faces of other men in a restaurant as he pulled a chair out for her to fit her slim body into, faces filled with abject jealousy and remorse that this stunning woman had chosen this ordinary man. He imagined the hours that they would lose simply just lying in bed side by side, because their connection had to be more than sex; it was kinetic, set in motion from the moment Mari happened upon him in the early morning of his first few hours in Estonia. The daydreams were harmless, or so he thought. When he realized that Mari and thoughts of being together were occupying his every waking moment, and sometimes his subconscious when he slept at night, he told himself to get a grip. He was turning into a needy, desperate being, pining over a woman who lived on a completely different plane than him. What was that hormone that was released during sex—oxytocin, was it? The intimacy hormone, they had called it in biology, that bonds you to your mate. He shook his body, as though he could rid himself of it. Maybe Mari's body hadn't produced enough to make her feel the same way. It appeared that the seduction had really just been all about the sex.

In the mirror in his childhood bedroom, he looked the same, now with a slight hangdog expression from thinking unrequitedly about Mari. He had to snap out of it and move on. He couldn't pine after her in his bedroom like a brooding teenager in a John Hughes movie. But it felt disingenuous to return to his world without a nod to what had happened. After a while, he began to wonder if their tryst had accomplished the opposite of what he'd felt initially. Had she actually succeeded in setting him free? One thing was for sure: he'd been changed. Mari had changed him.

NICO

New York City
January 2003

The final stage of Nico's metamorphosis had been empowerment. A slightly different person exited the lobby doors of
his apartment building with Paavo by his side on that first
day of the spring semester in New York City. Nico had developed a slight swagger in his walk. He'd spiked his hair
gently, he tucked his shirt jauntily in on the side but not
the front, the way he'd seen in the magazines Mari brought
home from her fashion shoots. He felt a great deal of confidence in the way he spoke to people. He felt like addressing
the whole of Fifth Avenue as they walked down the street.
He was even able to keep up with Paavo's strides as the boys
walked toward the subway.

"Check this out," Nico said, pointing overhead. "There
are these random seagulls that nest in the floral crest of that
building over there. It's so weird."

"Why is it weird?" Paavo asked, craning his neck without
breaking his stride. Four screaming gulls circled and dove

from overhead, while one kept watch from the edge of the building. "Don't the birds need a place to build a nest?"

"Yeah, but you'd expect like, a pigeon or a sparrow. This is Fifth Avenue, right smack in the middle. It's the farthest you can get from water on either side, so why would seagulls hang out here? They're just...out of place. It's like a polar bear hanging out on a patch of sand."

"It's warmer here than Estonia," Paavo said, popping his top button and opening his chest to the wind that whipped down the street.

"Dude, everywhere is warmer than Estonia," Nico said. The boys smiled and Nico felt relaxed about being around Paavo for the first time in weeks. He'd already been worried about Paavo's comfort once he'd arrived in New York City, coupled with what he might or might not have found out before he'd left Tallinn. Nico, on the other hand, had smiled enough for the both of them, mostly out of nervousness. He wasn't sure what Mari had shared with her brother after Nico's departure. Did Paavo know about the afternoon? Was he incensed with Nico's behavior, or was he just being his usual stoic self? It seemed that Paavo remained ignorant to all that had transpired. He hadn't mentioned his sister once. As calm as Paavo seemed, Nico was the opposite inside. He perversely brought her up time after time.

"How's Mari doing? Her modeling going okay?"

"Yes," Paavo said. He pulled the straps of his backpack away from his armpits. "She's counting down the days until she leaves for Moscow."

"I bet she's going to make it big over there."

"She wants me to leave after graduation, too. She says there's no future for either of us in Estonia."

"How come?"

"Jobs are scarce."

Nico nodded. "Times are tough. Here, too."

"Yes, but here it's a trend. It'll change next quarter or the one after that. In Estonia, that's how it is all the time."

"Do you think you'll leave?"

"We'll see."

At the registrar's office, a thin sheen of sweat overtook Paavo's forehead as they waited their turn. When he removed his backpack and placed it on the floor, two strips of moisture lined his armpits over his green T-shirt, turning it a darker shade.

"You okay?" Nico asked.

"I told you—it's warm here compared to back home," Paavo said.

A thickly built woman with mannish features approached. Nico greeted her as she extended one hand toward Paavo.

"Hallström kid? Welcome," she said. "Come with me. I'll hook you up with your schedule for the semester. Nicholas, go on ahead to homeroom. I'll make sure he gets to where he needs to go." Paavo looked as though he were about to be devoured, his eyes darting wildly from side to side.

"You'll be okay?" Nicholas asked. Paavo nodded.

"Yes, of course. You must not be late, Nico."

Nicholas sighed. "It's really not a big deal if I'm a little late. All my teachers know I'm in the program. They'll cut me some slack this week while you get adjusted."

Nico's classmates not only cut him some slack, they wanted to hear all about it. Nico had spent the past week thinking about his return to school. Hallström was an opportunity that most students were never granted. He had the chance to make the most of himself, to reintroduce his peers to a new Nico, one who was potentially more popular and charismatic. He'd had a slight internal conflict over whether he should return to wrestling, but he figured that since Mari was clearly into his body and wrestling had made it this way, there was no reason to give it up. Band, however, had to go. There had been no playing, or hardly any practicing while he had been abroad, but there had also been a realization that the flute was really a pussy instrument.

In homeroom, a girl turned around in her seat to talk to him. "Nicholas, heard you just came back from Russia."

Nico glanced up from his notebook. He could hardly believe it. He had sat behind Cassidy Simon for three years, and this was the first conversation they'd ever had. She was certainly pretty, but it was more than that. It was that she was unattainable. Nearly every guy in Nico's class wanted to date her, but she hadn't shown interest in anyone since the first day of high school. Her father was a big-shot music producer, and she had backstage passes to practically any rock concert she wanted.

"It was Estonia, actually. And it's Nico. It's what they called me in Tallinn. Sorta stuck." Nico winked at Cassidy and was immediately horrified. He'd never winked in his life. In fact, the few times he'd tried, he had felt so self-conscious that he had tried to pass it off as though an eyelash had fallen in and he needed to blink it out rapidly. Cassidy didn't skip a beat.

"I like it." Cassidy turned her entire body around to face him. "Very Velvet Underground."

Soon, Nico and Cassidy would spend much of their time together, platonically at first. She would invite him to attend a Weezer concert, and then to hang out with the band in their trailer where it was parked outside the stage door exit on West Fifty-Second Street, and it would only be around three in the morning when they descended the trailer steps that he would attempt to kiss her as she turned her head toward him under a streetlight. She would lean into the kiss

but then pull away, deciding on the spot that they were better off as friends than as lovers, but make a promise to him
right then and there that this incident wouldn't affect their
friendship. Fairly soon after that, Cassidy would prove to
be right, as she nominated him for student union president.
Then it wouldn't be long before Nico found himself giving
a speech in front of the whole class, denouncing ninth period and vowing to do away with it altogether. He would
pledge to start an anti-bullying initiative—at this he made
eye contact with Paavo, who was sitting in the first row in
the auditorium during the student debate—and would follow
through in his senior year to work with the dean of students
to create a no-tolerance policy that would result in black
marks on students' permanent records if they were caught
participating in any bullying-related activities.

Nico would eventually be elevated into a new spotlight
cast by his newfound friendship, by the speeches he had to
deliver as the president of the student union, by getting voted
captain of the wrestling team by the rest of his teammates. It
was only natural that the girls would follow at some point.
But until then, Nico would settle easily into the glow that
that December afternoon had left upon him.

At the end of that first day back at the Manhattan School
of Science, Nico had exhausted so much energy in creating his new persona that he could barely envision getting to
wrestling practice. He stood in front of the registrar's office,
leaning against the doorway, watching the building empty as
if a magnet were drawing students out. From time to time,
people waved at him, or stopped to chat, but Nico kept his
eyes keenly peeled for the bowl cut of Paavo's head. There
he was, standing near the wall, erect as an arrow as he kept
his distance from the flow of students exiting the building.

"Nico," Paavo called, his face relaxing at the sight of him. "Well? How was it?"

"Good," Paavo said. "Interesting. There are so many students from Europe here. Many who moved recently from Russia, did you know? It was nice to speak to them in the language. And Sabine is in my English class, so it was nice to have a familiar face."

"That's good. I hope people are being nice to you, or I'm going to have to knock some heads."

"No need, Nico. Everyone is very nice."

"You ready to go? Wrestling practice starts in fifteen minutes."

Nico and Paavo were the first inside the locker room, which held the lingering odor of bleach. Nico's friends generally gathered by the water fountain toward the exit, but Nico wanted to avoid any attempts his friends might make at sabotaging his secret. There would be a thousand questions for Paavo—they might imitate his accent, ask about KGB ties, but mostly, Nico was nervous that they would ask about his sister.

The day Nico had returned from the airport, he had tucked Mari's head shot and a comp card within the pages of his calculus textbook and slid them out in front of his friends at their usual corner table at the diner. The booth was windowed on each side overlooking the skate park across the street. The cold hadn't deterred the skaters from rolling their boards over the undulating parabolas, and the sound of wheels scraping against the concrete accented the boys' conversation as they pored over Mari's photos.

"She's a knockout," Chen said.

"Definitely *Maxim*-worthy," Toby said. "What did I tell you?"

"*She* came after you?" Carmine asked. Nico nodded. He'd

thought that bragging about Mari would have puffed him up with pride, but he felt strangely territorial. He reached for the photos but Carmine held them out of his reach.

"What's the rush?" Carmine's long arm held the comp card over his head and scrutinized it like an X-ray. "I could stare at her all day."

Now Nico could hear his teammates filter into the locker room, and he hoped they would remember what he'd told them about being discreet about her in front of Paavo. Nico got dressed in record time as Paavo loitered on the bench, opening and closing lockers. Nico knotted a bandanna around his neck and nodded to Paavo as they let themselves into the gym.

Coach was at the far corner, scrutinizing a clipboard. Nico jogged out toward him.

"Looking good, Coach," he called. He could see the sinews in the man's legs even from the three-point line and the arrow-like muscles in the backs of his calves pointing down toward his narrow ankles as he bounced on his toes.

Coach looked up. "Lefty! I missed you, man." They exchanged fist bumps.

"That nickname has even more meaning now that I've lived in a formerly communist country for four months." After the four months in Tallinn as Nico, he'd nearly forgotten about his wrestling nickname and he smiled fondly at the mention.

"Hey, there's no shame in it. In fact, I hear Magnet High School has a left-hander now. In your weight class, too."

"Finally, some apples to apples," Nico said.

Coach chuckled. "Oh, please. You've done fine even with your handicap, no pun intended. So, how was it? The formerly communist country?"

"It was good."

"That's it?"

"What else are you looking for?"

"More than teenage code. Give me some details, Lefty."

"I didn't do any wrestling, if that's what you're wondering. They do have this thing called Wife Carrying, though, which is exactly what it sounds like. You carry your wife through this obstacle course. People are really serious about it."

"Crazy. What's the point?"

"I guess way back robbers used to literally steal people's wives and forcibly marry them. But now it's all friendly. The wives *volunteer* to participate."

"I don't even know what to do with that information. The people must be interesting, to say the least. Speaking of which, where's your friend?"

Nico pointed at Paavo, who was settling himself in the bleachers.

"Lefty, you know I don't run a day care," Coach said to Nico. He raised his voice and called to Paavo. "Hey—Paavo? Welcome. Go throw on a jersey and some shorts. I have some extra kits in my office. There's no watching on this team." Paavo stood up uncertainly, and Nico nodded to him and pointed toward the office.

With Coach's face having narrowed down so much as well, the pads on his glasses couldn't grip his nose, which looked more like a beak now. The glasses slipped down. Coach pushed them up with his forefinger. They slipped down again. Watching him made Nico sympathetic for Coach, and he looked away in embarrassment. Coach was hairy; *hirsute* was the appropriate SAT word for it. Little succulents of growth sprouted from his ears, and vines of hair snaked down his still-muscular quads in mossy clumps.

"Anyway, you're different somehow. What changed?" Coach asked.

"My mom said the same thing. I don't know, I'm a man of the world," Nico said, bowing deeply.

"You're a man about to do five suicides. Get to it, suck-up." Coach grinned.

Nico jogged over to the red line. He felt suddenly energized by his teammates' voices echoing through the locker room, pounding their fists into empty lockers in glee, happy to see one another. A rush of air filled his chest and he smiled, happy to be considered one of them, happy to be part of a team, happy to have a foundation.

"Sucking up to Coach already, Lefty?" Carmine hollered. He jogged up and slapped the side of Paavo's head lightly. Paavo flinched. "Ooh, sorry, guy. Didn't mean to scare you. Who're you anyway?"

"This is Paavo. From Tallinn?" Nico had found that saying that someone was from somewhere specific made it seem less ignorant.

"Paavo! Oh, right, the one with the hot—" Nico shot Carmine a glance and shook his head. "P-Train. How long are you going to be here? You gonna wrestle with us?"

Paavo didn't seem sure how to proceed. He'd thought he might watch from the bleachers but now that he was in shorts and a jersey, he felt more on display than ever.

"I will try."

Carmine's face became very still and he recited, "Do. Or do not. There is no try." He guffawed and slapped Paavo with his huge bear paw. He whooped and ran back to the rest of the team, who were filtering into the gym. "P-Train's joining the team."

Nico was about to say that Paavo was going to mostly observe, when Paavo spoke up in a Yoda-like voice.

"Yes, help you I will," he said, his voice gravelly as he bowed down. "But I must warn you that I am leaving in a few months so I won't be able to win the championship for you."

Carmine's laugh was deep and throaty. "Oh, I like you all right," he said. He grabbed Paavo in a gentle side headlock and rubbed his head.

"All right, boys, suicides all around. Let's go," Coach called.

Along with the gentle ribbing that accompanied all athletic camaraderie, Nico was grateful for these practices. For those two hours, he didn't have to think, because Coach thought for him—how much weight to lift onto his shoulders, how many push-ups to do, how far and fast to run—the banter was easy, too. His teammates were all easygoing boys. There wasn't much to their conversations: sports, girls, breasts and weight—their own. Except this time he would have to babysit Paavo, make sure he was comfortable, that the other boys didn't overwhelm him. The fact was, Coach barely allowed him time to think about Paavo, or Mari for that matter.

By the end of the session, Nicholas was spent. Every single tendon in his body hurt. Every joint, every muscle. He flexed and relaxed his fingers, which were singing after he'd gripped the bench press with all his might. It didn't help that he hadn't been lifting all the previous semester. He felt the flesh where his fingers connected with his palms; the calluses had softened since last year but would harden with a few more sessions, as reliably as weeds.

His lips curved into a smile. These were the signs of a wrestler, that he was dedicated to his craft. And now he could go home, attack his homework with the same intensity, inhale dinner before he fell into the pillows of his privileged lifestyle and pass the fuck out. That was another reason he loved it. Coach helped you forget everything you had on your mind—whether you were failing precalculus, the girl you'd been seeing started seeing one of your teammates, or your parents were being dicks. Coach overrode your troubles with core work, intense drills and so many turns of the jump rope that whatever was plaguing you before practice became a warm, fuzzy memory at the end.

Paavo, on the other hand, wasn't sure he believed that his fears could be sweated out. Throughout that first session, he jogged alongside the rest of the team, falling back and leaning over his knees as though his laces constantly needed retying. Nico shot him quick glances to ensure he'd be okay as he traversed the track. But Nico was impressed by how hard Paavo pushed himself. The long wet stain that started at his neckline was nearly at his navel by the end of that first practice.

On the train ride home, both Nico and Paavo were wrung out like dishcloths, damp and weak. They rattled home side by side, slight smiles on both their faces as their heads bobbed in rhythm to the cars over the rails, lulling them into silence and sleep.

PAAVO

New York City
January 2003

Paavo had to take a proper nap when he got home. He'd
spent the first morning at Nico's school in a haze, wandering
hallways to figure out where classrooms were. The school
was about four times the size of Eesti High School, and he'd
gotten lost a few times before finding the class and slipping
into the back and finally realizing that seats were assigned in
each one. And then there was wrestling. Without a base to
start such intense exercise, he felt like an impostor amongst
the boys who all knew which weights to lift, to only wear
wrestling shoes on the mat because your street shoes were
dirty, to pull the deltoid bar in back of your body not in front.

By the end of the semester, Paavo would lift, stretch, push
himself harder than he'd ever done before. He'd learn to
mirror Chen and Carmine and even Nico on the mats. His
nimbleness would prove to be an asset to his wrestling; before
anyone knew how, he would wriggle out of a clutch and have
his opponent in a hold. He would become Coach's assistant,

keeping track of points at meets, once catching a referee error that would otherwise have lost MSS a title. His body would fill out as though a balloon had been completely filled with air, and long, vine-like muscles would attach themselves to his bones. His deltoids would come into existence. But that would be at the very end, just before Paavo returned to Tallinn with a new physique that would inflate his confidence and keep the gang at bay.

But right now, he felt like those seagulls on Fifth Avenue; wearing another costume, in another era. He needed to be more like a pigeon, blending into his surroundings, silently floating from one class to another, taking care not to draw attention to himself. As good as his English was, Paavo made sure to think each time he spoke. In class, he was deliberate with his sentences, shaping them like pastry, delicately, lest they fall apart from too much handling. Estonian spewed forth from him more naturally; for that matter, so did Russian. He used his English with his friends at school, or at times with his sister, Mari. Part of him felt a little defeated; he'd boasted to Nico about his English skills, but it was exhausting trying to think in the language. It was a different exhaustion than the one that had followed him around Tallinn. In Tallinn, he'd been constantly trying to escape the threats, the prospect of the gang of boys waiting for him around corners. But no one was after him here. He didn't have to avoid anyone.

He fell into his nap as if he was sinking into a warm bath, sleeping intensely for two hours. When he awoke, he could hear clattering from the kitchen and the dull, metronomic clunk of a knife against a cutting board. He had a crick in his neck. He reached behind his head to massage his nape, and his fingers hit something. A notebook. He turned on the bedside lamp and opened it to the bookmarked page.

Paavo Sokolov
Dirty blond
Crooked incisors
Bowl haircut
Skittish; scared rabbit expression

He flipped to the first pages.

Nicholas Grand
Stella Grand
Arthur Grand

It continued on from there. Names and features filled the pages, notes on hair and eye color. It seemed like a catalog of everyone Nico's sister Nora knew. He pushed himself off the bed and walked down the hall toward her room. The door was slightly ajar and Paavo could see Nora lying on her stomach, pawing at a small black device.

"Hi," Paavo said through the slit in the door. Nora looked up. She had been scrolling through her MP3 player in an attempt to create a good, throbbing, beat-forward playlist for the gym, one that she liked enough to keep her moving through the music and wouldn't allow her to jump off the moving conveyor of the treadmill as it raced beneath her. She turned her head and assessed quickly in her mind—bowl hair, crooked incisors, chapped lips. She felt something click in her mind, like a slot machine aligning three screens of cherries, and she smiled.

"Hey, Paavo. Come in," she said, sitting up and folding her legs underneath her.

Paavo took a few tentative steps into the room, as though approaching a wild animal.

"How was your first day?"

"Good. Wrestling was difficult. But I am glad that I went. It is good to feel…alive."

Nora smiled. "I know what you mean."

"So you are in college?"

"Taking some time off."

"Do you not like your university? Nico said it's beautiful in Vermont."

"It is."

"Nico said you're taking some time off."

"That's right."

Paavo waited as Nora looked off into the distance. When it seemed clear she wasn't going to speak anymore, he reached into his pocket and withdrew the black notebook. "In any case, I found this, and I think it belongs to you." Nora's eyes widened and she gasped as she practically pounced upon Paavo, tearing the notebook from his hands. "I… I thought I lost it for good. I've been running around like a crazy person… thank you."

"You're welcome." Paavo stood and walked toward the door.

"Hang on. You have to let me explain."

"It doesn't matter, Nora," Paavo said. "It is your own business."

"Paavo…wait."

He froze at the door, pivoting slowly as he turned back toward her.

"I have a condition."

"A condition?"

"Yes, it's…it's hard to explain, because it's so…esoteric."

Paavo furrowed his brow.

"So…strange," she said.

"It is okay. I am also a bit strange."

Nora smiled and looked down at her hands. "I was in a

car accident last year. I hit my head, damaging the part of the brain that's responsible for facial recognition. I have trouble identifying people's faces. Even people I've known my whole life: my parents, Nicholas, my best friends. God, it sounds like some *Onion* story or something."

"Onion?"

"Forget it. I just mean that it sounds ridiculous."

"No," Paavo said. "It's not ridiculous. Does it hurt?"

"It did. I was in the hospital for a few weeks. But the condition doesn't *hurt*, per se. Well, not unless you count the constant bruising of my ego, or the fact that I can't be sure that I will recognize my own family when I wake up in the morning, or my closest friends. And sometimes I'm not even sure I know my own face. And so...well, yeah, I guess you could say that it hurts." Nora looked down at her hands again.

"And so the notebook," Paavo said. "It's a..."

"A cheat sheet," Nora finished. "A reference guide."

Paavo nodded. He looked around the room, as though searching for something. He sat back down on the bed. "Does it help?"

"Sometimes. But you probably don't even realize it, but when you see someone your mind makes a split-second decision about their identity. It gets clumsy to constantly have to check a handbook before deciding whether to say hi to a colleague or a classmate."

"Yes, I can see this. Is this why you don't want to return? To Vermont?"

Nora nodded. "I'm scared to see people I know but not know them. But I feel so uncomfortable all the time. I guess the best way to put it is that I'm scared of making friends and seeing old ones."

"Why is that something you would feel badly telling me?"

"I don't know. You're new here. I can't imagine life has

been easy since you landed off that plane. I can't imagine you have stepped into MSS and made dozens of friends."

"It isn't so bad," Paavo said. "To be honest, I'm not as alone as I was when I was back home."

"Really?" Nora said. "How's that?"

"That, too, is a long story." Paavo grinned.

"Fair enough." There was a knock at the door before Nico popped his head in.

"Mom called dinner a while ago."

"Sorry. I didn't realize it was so late."

Nora and Paavo exchanged glances and tight smiles as they rose from the bed.

"I have only one more question," Paavo said as he halted at the door frame. "Is that really how you see me? What you wrote? That I am a scared rabbit?"

Nora colored. "No, I mean, it's just…like first impressions, you know? It's just a stupid thing I keep for myself."

"Nora—" Paavo lowered his voice and leaned in toward her "—I'm not offended. It is interesting to literally see yourself mirrored in someone else's eyes. It can be…an awakening."

NICO

New York City
February 2003

Looking back, Nico was embarrassed that the trip to Ellis Island during the second semester of the Hallström year had been an awakening. America had always been the center of his world, and the fact that he hadn't realized it until now made him feel insulated and ashamed. Years later, when Nico ran for office, he would understand that this had been the pivotal moment when he recognized that there was more to this country than world domination. He would look back on this day as he listened to an immigration council present a package that would support education for new immigrants to New York. He'd support that package, explaining that this country was so great because of the people that came to it from outside its borders.

But during that program trip, the group huddled together at the tip of the city, a gate preventing them from falling into the waters of the Hudson below. Even though the temperature was unseasonably mild for February, the wind whipped back and forth and Malaysia and Anika held on to the spiny metal posts to keep from gusting over. Barbara was counting them in pairs, and then by countries and then by boys and then girls when Nico and Paavo raced to join them.

"Boys, when I say nine fifteen, I expect you to be here at nine fifteen," Barbara admonished. She began her count over again. Paavo shot Nico a look, which Nico ignored.

"Tickets," she exclaimed brightly, satisfied with her tally. She walked down the row as the students had obediently lined themselves up by partner. Nico was tempted to call Pyotr *Peter* to see what would happen. Evan stood apart from Pyotr, as though he didn't want to be associated with him. He clutched his ticket in his hand as the group filed toward the ferry terminal.

"This is the place, right, where all the immigrants from all over the world came to this country? Ellis Island? It seems inspiring," Paavo said.

"I guess," Nico said, yawning loudly. "I've never been."

"Really? Why not?"

"It's for tourists."

"So? It's an important place. You don't think it's worth visiting?"

"I guess you take these kinds of places for granted. You get used to them. Real New Yorkers have never been to, say, the Empire State Building."

"That's silly. You're missing out on so much of your own country."

"Why don't you let me be the judge of that?"

"Suit yourself," Paavo said. "I think you're being silly."

As they waited for the ferry to arrive, Nico felt his anger build up toward Paavo. He was tired of being nice to him all the time. He was tired of tiptoeing around him as if he was walking on thin ice. He didn't want to take him to wrestling practice anymore. He felt like arguing, starting a roaring fight so they might not speak for the rest of the day. He wondered if Barbara might break them apart and partner him with Pyotr instead.

"I certainly hope you didn't feel that way about the Twin Towers," Paavo continued, jerking his chin toward the gaping hole a few blocks from where they waited. "Because that's a shame if you never saw the view from the top before they fell."

"I used to hang out in the mall at the bottom of the World Trade Center during my lunch period. I felt no need to ride to the top and gawk at the city like a seagull," Nico said.

"You never went up the Twin Towers? That's so sad. What kind of New Yorker are you?" Pyotr asked, sidling up to them. "And what's with the faggot hats?"

Nico's patience was thinning. It was one thing to be upset with his exchange partner, but now this Russian goon was clearly starting something. He felt as if the whistle had just been blown on the mats and he had to be the first to pin his opponent, the air pushing through his nose like a bull's. It was all he could do not to paw the ground with his feet. "I'm a born and raised New Yorker. Even though I never went to the top of the World Trade Center, I miss the hell out of those towers every day. I miss glancing downtown— I miss the dependability of seeing those two buildings rising up out of the skyline. My country, no, my city was attacked that day. And you can never take that away from me. What do you know about it anyway?"

"I know the rest of the world has been feeling and going through this shit for years, centuries even. So for you to sit there telling me that your country is going through so much pain is bullshit," Pyotr said. The Czech girl—the pretty, brazen one in Paavo's English class—had joined them.

"What are you guys talking about?"

"*You* tell them, Sabine. Tell them how fucked-up it is that Americans think they're immune from it all, that they haven't had to deal with the hell of terrorism when the rest of us are pretty much sidestepping it and praying each day that we don't have to lose someone."

"Aren't you from St. Petersburg?" Nico asked. "What kind of terrorism are you dealing with on a daily basis?"

"Are you sure you want to get into this conversation?" Pyotr asked. "Be very sure. Because it's going to be a long, messy debate, and you're going to lose. I don't care whether or not you are on the wrestling team or whatever it is, because this is an actual political discussion and you need to get *your* facts straight." Nico could see Barbara out of the corner of his eye, poised to jump into the circle, but also wanting them to handle it on their own.

"What facts? What terrorism have you had to deal with?" Nico challenged him.

"Do you mean to say that just because I wasn't there to witness bomb blasts and mass murders in person that they haven't had an effect on me or my family?" Pyotr narrowed his eyes incredulously. "That being an eyewitness is the only thing that matters? Because there's a fair amount of trauma associated with secondhand war. Paavo, come on, man. Tell him. Tell him about Siberia. Tell him about your grandparents."

Nico swiveled toward him. "What is he talking about? What about your grandparents?"

"It's nothing. Guys, let's just drop it. It's a nice trip. Come on, be civil."

Nico pushed on. "What *about* Siberia, dude? Tell me."

Paavo sighed. "It's not something we *like* to talk about. My father's parents are Russian, as you know. They moved to

Estonia during the Soviet occupation, when the Red Army was trying to get Russians to be the majority in the Baltic States. And my mother's parents, well, they were Estonian nationals. And during the Communist times, during the culling, the NKVD tore into their home, arrested them and sent them to the work camps in Siberia. Where they died. I never met them. Luckily, Mama was visiting a cousin in Germany at the time. Otherwise, I would never be here."

Nico felt heat spreading across his face. He swallowed hard and put his hand on Paavo's shoulder. "I didn't know, man. I'm sorry."

"So, see? You aren't the only ones that ever suffered." Pyotr spit the words out.

"There's no need to be so harsh about it, Pyotr," Paavo said. "Nico didn't know. Aren't we here to teach one another?"

"There's no need to protect him, Paavo," Pyotr said. "Our entitled all-American hero could stand to learn a thing or two. After all, that's what this whole *experience* is for."

Oh, irony of ironies, Nico thought to himself. *If only Pyotr knew the truth about who was protecting whom.* He took a breath and quelled the anger that was rising in the pit of his stomach. "Dude," Nico said, measuredly, as he glanced toward Barbara. "Pyotr or Peter or whatever the hell your name is. I don't know what you think you know about me, or what you've decided is true. I'm not entitled. My parents—both of them—work hard and pay taxes. They deserve the home they have built for us. Just because they haven't had to fight in wars or flee the country doesn't make them any less deserving citizens."

"It's not your family who makes you entitled. It's your country," Pyotr said. He turned up the collar to his jacket, worn leather with deep creases and cracks running across it like arteries and veins. He moved away then, grumbling in Russian under his breath. Although the wind continued to whip through the slotted gate and blew litter in tidy little circles around their feet, Nico could sense the tension hovering over them like a rain cloud. He looked at Paavo and smiled tightly.

On the train ride home, the boys were silent as they sat shoulder to shoulder, swaying as the train car pitched and yawed. Just as Paavo's drowsy eyes were about to succumb to the soothing rhythms, Nico spoke, his throat raw from being silent for so long.

"Does the rest of the world feel like we got what was coming to us?"

Paavo opened his eyes as if remembering suddenly where he was. "I won't say 9/11 was justified. But your country doesn't have a good history of being a nice guy on the campus."

"You mean we're the big man on campus."

"Yes, of course, but also not so nice. There is much resentment toward your country, Nico, because your troops come in, do what they want, take what they want, no questions asked, no consequences. And after 9/11, all we hear from the US is revenge, revenge, revenge. 9/11 was a terrible day. I won't contest this. But I am in agreement with Pyotr when he says that the United States conveniently ignores the fact that this sort of behavior has been going on each day, for decades, for centuries, in other countries. But from an American perspective, it's new."

Nico nodded, chewing on his bottom lip.

"I hope I haven't offended you. I just want to be honest with you, and help you understand where Pyotr and a lot of the rest of the world is coming from."

"You haven't offended me," Nico said. "I'm feeling schooled. Enlightened. And incredibly embarrassed."

Nico would go home and begin fervent research on America's foreign policies. Of course, all he'd learned in school had cast his country in a favorable light, but for the first time, the students in the Hallström program had made Nico understand that his country had a long way to go in order to make things right in the world. When he entered the political world in a few years, America's public image and everything he wanted to do in order to right it would become one of his personal hot buttons on every campaign he would ever work on. But for now, it was time for him to make up for lost time and educate himself on how little he knew about the way the rest of the world viewed him.

NORA

Nora had thought long and hard about how her best friend would view their friendship once she had made her decision. After hemming and mulling and hawing and stewing, Nora decided to attend Claire's wedding as a regular guest instead of as a member of her wedding party. Claire had hugged Nora, and promised her that it didn't change anything between them. Nora watched from an aisle seat as Claire's sister stood at the altar, beaming in her promotion to maid of honor. Nora clutched her black notebook in her hand until it began to perspire and ink bled onto her palms. She put the notebook into her purse at that point; she couldn't risk anything happening to it. She hadn't allowed it out of her sight since Paavo had returned it to her. But as much of a disappointment as it had been to not participate in Claire's wedding party, she had to admit that she'd come a long way. The support group had been great for her. She'd put her self-consciousness aside and asked her friends to start wearing things that might help her to identify them. She'd started to post some of her photo portraits online and had been receiving some positive feedback about her use of lighting and angles. And then she'd had a breakthrough.

Nora had been attending the group for six months when she and her father made a trip to the grocery store together. The two walked down Twenty-Sixth Street in silence until Nora stopped to point at a bus stop movie poster.

"Ugh," she said. "He's such a dirty old man, don't you think?"

"Nora—" Arthur stopped walking "—you recognize that actor?" Arthur was unabashedly ignorant of celebrity faces, names and gossip. He'd pawed through an issue or two of *People* while waiting at the dentist, but tossed the magazines aside when he didn't know anyone in the photos, and more importantly, when he didn't care.

"Come on, Dad, you have to know Jack Nicholson."

"That's not the point. *You* know him, Nora. That's all that matters."

A quiet but fierce smile crept across Nora's face as she recognized the importance of this potential truth, not allowing herself to fully believe it yet. Nora and Arthur picked up their pace as they neared the grocery store with its wide paneled windows plastered with neon posters for luminously colored fruit and triple-liter bottles of cola. Instead of grabbing a cart and consulting Stella's list, they veered left toward the cashiers where Arthur grabbed a battered *People* magazine and flipped through its pages. He opened it at random and turned it around to face Nora, covering the type with his palm.

"Who is that?" he demanded.

"Ricky Martin."

Arthur moved his hand and nodded, his eyes flitting from the page to Nora's face like fireflies. "And this?"

"Britney Spears."

"That."

"Hillary Clinton."

It appeared that celebrities hadn't been spliced from the recesses of Nora's mind.

"Nor, we can use this to help you," Arthur said. His voice traveled up a scale as his excitement mounted. "You can use people that you recognize to remember other people. You know—I look like that hunk, that guy you and your pals are always going on about. That Brad Pitt fellow."

Nora let out what could only be described as a guffaw. The first guffaw in fact, since before her accident. "Hardly."

But he'd been right. Her father had been onto something. She could use celebrities to help her place people; it could be her prop, which she'd been asked to identify at her first group session. The notebook that Nicholas had given her was filled with notes on bone structure, moles and facial hair. But this was easier, Nora realized, to liken people to celebrities. She rewrote her book, thinking long and hard about the people in her life and who they resembled. Her father couldn't have been further from Brad Pitt; he was more like a young Sam Waterston, with his heavy brow and his patrician nose. Her mother was a perfect marriage of Elizabeth Taylor's delicate elegance and Christiane Amanpour's all-knowing onyx eyes. Nicholas was like that boy on the Campbell's Soup commercials, the one who races home in the rain with his dog to be comforted with a steaming bowl of soup in his mother's kitchen. Claire was, without a doubt, the epitome of the lead singer of Stardust, the teenage band that seemed to be overtaking MTV each time she turned it on.

But when Nora met Paavo on the evening of his arrival,

she was stumped. He wasn't unattractive, but he wasn't particularly memorable, either. He was toothy like a boyish Ted Kennedy, but almost as pale as Edward Scissorhands. She scribbled a few notes into her notebook and hoped they would suffice.

When she'd misplaced her notebook, she'd felt completely lost and then completely embarrassed when Paavo returned it to her. But then she'd started talking to him. He just seemed to get it. The cool thing about Paavo was that he didn't carry any emotion on his face. He neither smiled nor sneered. He was a blank slate, and she didn't have to worry about being herself around him. She began to run into him on purpose, in the kitchen, in the living room. He began to seek her out after he'd returned home from school and finished his homework. She began to crave his strange little riddles because they were so silly and thoughtful and unique.

A few weeks before Paavo was due to head back to Tallinn, Nora stuck her head in the doorway of the guest room, where he was sitting on the bed fiddling with a Rubik's Cube.

"Hit me," she said.

"I've been saving this one all day for you," Paavo said, turning the grids of the cube. "I don't have teeth, but I bite."

"A comb? No wait, that has teeth." Nora came and sank down into the chair next to Paavo's bed. "Okay, I give."

"The cold."

"I've been meaning to ask you why you like riddles so much."

"I don't know," Paavo said, looking down into his lap.

"Yes you do. Tell me."

"I suppose because they make you think. They're never really what they appear to be. When you think it's one thing, it's really another. When your brain can't fathom that there could be an answer to a clue, there always is one. And when

a riddle makes you feel completely useless, completely ridiculous, that this combination of words has baffled you, that
the world is falling down around you, somehow the pieces of
your mind come together like the plates of the earth under
our feet, and you come up with this answer that makes total
and complete sense and all is right again."

"That's deep, Paavo," Nora said. "You think differently
than I do. Because try as I might, I'm not as quick as you are."

"You have to approach them from another angle, the one
you don't think of at first," Paavo said. "It's sort of how I
think you should maybe approach your condition."

"What do you mean?"

"Well, the prosopagnosia. You feel stifled and limited by
it."

"Obviously. How else am I supposed to feel?" Nora stiff-
ened, taking her legs out from underneath her and hugging
herself.

"That's instinctual. I don't blame you. But what if you
conquered it? Like I have been doing with wrestling with
Nico. What if you got to understand it from the inside out?"

"How am I supposed to do that? I'm already going to this
group and reading everything I possibly can about the subject, which, I've gotta tell you is difficult to find."

"So you have an opportunity to add to a missing dialogue.
You can study it. You can take classes that help you understand, and you can write a memoir or a paper to help others
that feel as lost as you do."

"I guess so…" Nora said, chewing on a fingernail.

"Nora," Paavo said. "It can become something you own
instead of something that owns you."

"Well, what about you?" Nora asked.

"What about me?"

"What are you going to do about the neo-Nazis?"

"How do you know about them?" Paavo asked. He leaned back against the headboard on his bed. Nora pulled her chair forward.

"Nico. Don't be mad at him. He's worried about you. He just wants to help. And so do I."

"It's just so embarrassing," Paavo said, picking up the Rubik's Cube again and rotating the sections around. "Like I'm some baby or something."

"Bullying has nothing to do with being babied," Nora said. "Bullying is a cowardly thing to do, and ganging up on one person isn't right or fair."

"Well, it's a tough time in Estonia right now, identity-wise. Somehow these boys found out that my grandparents are Russian, so they're making my life miserable. After years of oppression, once Estonia claimed its sovereignty, a lot of Russians ended up staying here. There's still a huge divide. And the more conservative Estonians, like them, believe they should leave the country altogether. It's a conflict we'll be dealing with for years to come."

"But why should you have to deal with it? It's not your cross to bear."

"It is, Nora," Paavo said, flicking the last row of colors into place as he solved the Rubik's Cube. He tossed it onto the bed, where Nora picked it up and turned it around in wonder. "I'm the next generation. And it's turned me into this scared little person who stays inside all day long reading books on coding like a nerd. I'm such an STD."

Nora snorted. "You know what that means?"

"Come on, it's so obvious. Your whole family mumbles it whenever anyone else says anything remotely European-sounding."

"The Grands *are* pretty transparent," Nora said, shrugging. "Why don't you take your own advice?"

"Which is?"

"So you're a self-proclaimed nerd now. But you like cod-ing, right? You like computers?"

"I do. They are like one big riddle."

"So what's wrong with that? Go with it. Computers, cod-ing, that can be your thing. Who says you have to play sports? It's not a prerequisite for life."

"I just don't want to be scared anymore."

"You don't have to be. Do you know how intimidating that was just watching you solve that puzzle? Dive headfirst into what you love. Don't let this situation own you. Own it yourself."

MARI

Tallinn
March 2003

That winter, the silence had seemed to own Mari. In the lead-up to her departure for Moscow, it felt as if her career had come to a screeching halt. The calls had stopped. The stack of glossy magazines that Mari bought before her auditions lay stunted. Vera had considered going out to buy the latest issues, and clearing away the ones that she and Mari had read and reread until they'd memorized how to make an exfoliation mask from the contents of your fridge, or how to form a perfect French twist. But that felt disloyal to her daughter, who now ghosted about the house like a mirage, her face drawn and dismal.

Estonian winter had seemed to mirror her demeanor; the sun rose glumly in the mornings to its apex in the frigid sky. Mari usually lived for the short daylight hours in the winter, spending as much time as possible outdoors. But she'd shrunk from the sun like a vampire, avoiding the elegant columns of light that filtered in through the windows as though they were sipping softly at her strength. She poured herself like a puddle in a chair and spent her time drinking tea and flipping through the same pile of magazines that seemed to taunt her.

Vera tiptoed around her daughter as though she were an active volcano, behaving as though the slightest movement might set off cascading streams of molten lava. She replenished Mari's teacups and made her sandwiches. She tried hiding the stack of magazines, but Mari discovered them and ferried them up to her room, at which point she began staying there throughout the day.

When Leo had appeared at the table for lunch alone one day, Vera headed upstairs. She knocked softly at the door. "Lunchtime," she called. There was a soft moan from the other side of the wood and Vera pushed the door in.

Mari was lying on her side toward the wall, her face contorted in agony. Her fringe was plastered to her forehead and her blouse stuck to her back, slack with sweat. Vera sat beside her. "Are you ill? What's happened?" Mari had a hand curled over her body while her other one signaled for her mother to leave the room.

"I won't go," Vera retorted. "Tell me what's the matter." Mari pushed at her mother's shoulder urgently, and Vera sprang up just in time to have Mari roll over onto her side and deposit a stream of clear liquid from deep within her body into her wastepaper basket.

"You need to eat something," Vera said. "Come downstairs and I'll make you a light broth. It's probably just a virus."

Mari shook her head and squeezed her eyes shut. "I'm too tired," she whispered.

"Well, then, you're going to the doctor," Vera said, squeezing her shoulder. "Get your shoes." Vera watched as Mari pushed herself off the bed in slow motion, her eyes sunken into her head, deep purple clouds of exhaustion puffing around the sockets. When she removed a piece of stray hair from her mouth, Vera saw her fingers, swollen and pink like the tiny blood sausages in the glass case at the market. Mari's normally full lips were chapped and deflated. An alarming thought sprang into Vera's mind but she flicked it away as though it were a tiresome gnat. She created a buttress of pillows and leaned her daughter against it.

"Levya," she called. She heard his footsteps, and Leo appeared, huffing. His barrel chest protruded over his towel as he clutched it around his only slightly thinner waist.

"I'm about to sauna," he said. "What is it?"

"Mari isn't well. Can you drive us to the doctor?"

It was confirmed: five weeks in. The fetus was the size of a peppercorn. There were small indentations in a pin-sized head that would become a nose, eyes and ears.

Vera felt her lungs collapse. She gripped the back of the chair to feel herself hold something, to feel her arm muscles engage, to feel as if she had power over something, anything. In that small, sterile room, Mari and Vera both felt the space getting smaller and smaller by the moment, closing in on them, capturing them like a cage. Vera looked at her daughter. While her body quavered like a leaf, Mari's face was clear and undisturbed; if it had been a pond, Vera could have skipped a stone effortlessly across it. Mari hadn't spoken since they'd arrived at the office, but Vera answered all the questions the doctor had asked of her, at least when she knew the answers. She didn't know a few things—did she smoke, did she drink, the date of her last period. She didn't know when it had happened, with whom or, for goodness' sakes, why. There were a thousand questions to ask her daughter, but Vera found herself asking only one: "What do you want to do?"

Mari held herself upright and looked at her mother for the first time. "I want to go home," she whispered. Vera held her hand out and Mari put hers in it.

Leo could tell precisely what was wrong with his daughter. Mari had returned from the doctor weeks earlier hanging from her mother's arm. Vera had shuttled her upstairs and told him that she was under the weather. A slight flu. But he was no fool. He wanted to know, how had it happened? Where? And with whom? He wondered if it had been some sleazy, sweaty Ukranian model; he tried to shudder the thought away, but flashes of strange overbronzed skin against Mari's porcelain body kept rising in his mind. He didn't ask Mari that first afternoon as Vera had requested, taking care not to voice the very questions that were plaguing his mind. Mari spent most of her time in bed now, languishing like a flower that badly needed watering, pushing herself up to sit when Vera arrived with a tray or a glass. Her face had become withdrawn and pale. The stack of magazines that had littered the perimeter of her bedside had been cleared away and replaced with a trail of Hematogen wrappers that whispered in the breeze of the open window like the carcasses of dried leaves. How ironic that Hematogen, the Russian candy bars constituted of cow's blood enriched with iron and vitamins, were what Mari craved these days when both she and Paavo had resisted them so obstinately as children.

"How are you?" Leo asked, opening the door and indicating the wrappers on the floor. "Ema said you wanted more. I can get some this afternoon."

"Thank you, Papa. That would be great. They seem to be the only things I can keep down."

"Are you okay, Mari?" Leo asked cautiously. His daughter seemed too weak to snap back at him, but he knew that her rage could build and erupt when she had the ability to do so. "What can I do, my baby?"

It turned out that Leo, despite his constant nagging that Mari's beauty, and certainly now her modeling, were sure to get her in trouble, fell over himself in kindness toward his daughter. Upon his return from work, he dampened washcloths and peeled open more Hematogen bars. He cleaned out her trash bin after she heaved into it. He smoothed the hair away from her face while she was sleeping, murmuring over her lithe body that finally quieted after being rocked by waves of nausea.

Neither Leo nor Vera demanded to know the father's identity. There was an unspoken rule in the house not to worry Mari with such details, to stress her out any more than her body already was. At times Leo yearned to close the door to her bedroom and withhold any more Hematogen bars until she disclosed the information. But his concern for her well-being and that of his unborn grandchild's was stronger than his curiosity.

The season had passed fitfully; Vera and Leo fretted over their daughter. In her ninth week, Mari braved the stairs. She held the banister with both hands, edging sideways as though the staircase were a ship and would cant with the next rising swell. She sat at the table opposite her parents and told them her plan. She would leave. She would go to Moscow; Viktor had told her that was where her future lay. She has exhausted everything she can in Estonia. There is nothing more for her here.

"But what about the baby?" Vera asked, her fingers gripping the edge of the table.

"What about it?" Mari said. "I will have it there. I want to start new. I want to do this, Ema. I've thought it through."

"Mari, you have no idea what difficulty a baby will bring," Vera said. "How will you support yourself?"

"What else? I'll model."

"But you haven't told Viktor about your condition, Mari. How can he say that your future is in Moscow when your future has been completely rewritten?"

Mari stuck her chin out. "I'm not showing yet. Plus, Viktor said I'd make more in one week in Moscow than I would in a month here. It's true—those insipid Tartu boys make double what I make when I am working triple as hard. This country is completely backward. I can't stay here if I want a future for myself and for the baby. I'll put it away. I'll save. But I have to leave, Ema. If I don't, I'll be stuck here forever. Papa, tell her."

There were two single mothers in Leo's office that each left at five thirty on the dot every day. Neither of them went for a drink at the bar around the corner. Neither of them attended the office outing each summer or the Christmas party in the winter. Now that he thought about them, he realized that it wasn't necessarily their home lives that made them look harried when he arrived at the office; they had already been there working for hours. He made a mental note to be kinder to them, to ask after their children. "Mari, I'm not sure," Leo said. "You're so young. To be balancing a career and a baby in a new town... I'm not sure you're thinking this through."

"It's not a new town," Mari said, her eyes flashing. "We have been there before. I can do this. I need you to believe in me." Vera and Leo exchanged glances.

"Let us think about it," Vera said, placing her hand over Mari's.

But that wasn't good enough for Mari. The next morning after Leo returned from work, he found his wife standing in the kitchen, clutching a piece of paper to her chest, her face shifting like the early tremors of an earthquake. Leo had the foresight to ask in Estonian, *"Mis viga?"* Vera snapped out of the trance—whether from shock of the language or from realizing that someone else was home with her—to show the note to Leo.

Mari's letter had requested her family to give her space. She was going to Moscow, to have the baby there. She was going to live off the savings that her previous year of successful modeling had brought in until she gave birth, at which point she was going to find another agent, who would bring in more jobs. She would coax her body back into modeling shape—Cindy Crawford had done it, Laetitia Casta and Elle MacPherson. Mari had the same drive, the same resolve when she put her mind to something. She would take care of herself, go on long walks in order to maintain her lean, long legs. She would rub her belly furiously with shea butter and later, with a vile concoction of stewed herbs and roots that she'd wrap and press against her stomach even once it was small and taut again in an effort to avoid stretch marks.

It doesn't matter who the father is. He's not involved and I don't want him to be. I ask that you respect my decision to do so. This is my path, and I am going to follow it through.

Leo read and reread the letter and then took the stairs two at a time to his daughter's room where he saw her closet emptied and half her bookshelf bare grinning like a toothless old crone. Mari was gone.

NORA

New York City
June 2003

It wasn't that the fear of her condition was gone. But it was getting easier to talk about it. Talking to Paavo was easy, even though he had been the first person outside of her small circle of doctors, her family or the group she'd felt comfortable confiding in. With Paavo, it had felt almost normal, as if she was sharing that she was nearsighted or had needed orthodontic treatment as a child. Paavo never judged her or pretended to understand something she knew he never would unless he, too, experienced a sharp blow to his own fusiform gyrus.

Sometimes she wasn't sure that she had experienced it herself, but from time to time, she forced herself to remember her reentry into her new life, the one where she had to work extra hard at everything—faces, contours, hairstyles. Somehow it reminded her that she used to be a different person before; that she used to be normal. And that now, after the accident, everything had changed.

Nora and Paavo should never have met in real life, but the Hallström program helped them identify the kindred spirits in one another that they hadn't encountered before. After that first awkward interaction over Nora's notebook, Paavo began to understand something innate in Nora. Perhaps it was because she didn't judge him on his skittishness, but instead used it as a device to remember him.

After the first conversation opened the gates of understanding between the two, Paavo began greeting Nora each afternoon on his return from school with a riddle, which quickly evolved into a conversation. Between her biweekly group sessions, Nora visited the library, returning home with stacks of books. It was Paavo who had sparked her interest in understanding her condition better, after he'd suggested that she return to school to take a few psychology courses to get into her own mind, understanding exactly what was happening when it perceived faces. She had started sitting in on some classes at the New School after Arthur had called in a favor from an old colleague. They revved her brain more than philosophy ever had. She felt herself gravitating toward a different calling in life. She wondered if it might be too late. She'd even gone to the bookstore and bought two of the required books for her Psychology in the Meditative State class, underlining passages and reading ferociously when she should have been writing the proposal for her own thesis on Kant. She felt the knowledge she was absorbing unlatch a caged door to her head for the first time in a year, allowing her heart to sing.

Friendship with Nora came easily for Paavo. Maybe it was because she was a girl, maybe because she was older, maybe it was because she didn't know the history of his downturn into meekness. By the time Paavo returned to Tallinn at the end of the semester, he had helped Nora forge a new path for herself. And she had succeeded in helping him realize that he didn't have to stay scared forever.

June 26, 2003
Nora—

I want to thank you for your hospitality and openness while I was in New York City. It is a difficult thing to come to a new country, but you were welcoming from the start.

I had this thought and I didn't want to forget it. I was thinking about you and your condition and I wondered if the situation was that your brain was just weeding out the important people in your life. For example, when you need to know someone, you just know him or her and when you don't really need them in your life, your mind has a difficult time grasping their identity. Does that make sense? It's like your mind is a sieve that's only holding the really essential people close to your heart. It's why I think you've never had a problem recognizing Nico or your parents.

In Russian literature, there is something called *dusha*. At the heart of it, it means soul. To have *dusha* is to do something from the bottom of your heart, with love and passion. I think anyone can have *dusha*, from pianists to politicians. When we go out to eat in restaurants in Tallinn, my family, we rate places on *dusha*. It can be some of the finest food we have ever eaten, but if it's not made with intention, with love, by someone who truly cares about others enjoying their food wholeheartedly, well, you can taste it with every bite. I'm sure you have had similar such meals.

Anyway, I was thinking about *dusha* and in light of the idea, I don't think your situation is necessarily a bad thing. I think it's that you're able to see people's souls; that you're able to see into them, past their faces and into their hearts. I think you are seeing their *dusha*, that if they are worth having their souls seen by you, then you remember their face. I think you should no longer think of your condition as a bad thing, but as something that helps you find the difference between the meaningful and those you have to see, like the people in front of you. I think once those people make themselves important to you, or you find the meaning in them, that's when you will begin to recognize them for who they truly are. Maybe it's a romantic notion, but I think it explains a lot. For now, I hope it helps. And for now, I hope you're feeling better.

Warmly,

Paavo

MARI

Moscow
September 2003

Mari had first felt the baby kick when she was on a go-see
for a new clothing catalog geared toward university students.
The briefing packet included a description of the line: "schol-
arly and cheeky." She'd pondered what this might mean as
she stood in front of the mirror in profile, scrutinizing her
usually taut torso which now had a slight overhang of flesh
protruding over the rim of her jeans. She chose a blousy
wrap dress with strategically placed ruffles across her abdo-
men, hoping she looked every bit the fashionable academic.
As she kicked off her heels at the doorway as requested so
that the casting agents could see her at her true height, she
hesitated ever so slightly. The makeshift runway, composed
of a long roll of white contact paper, scratched the soles of
her bare feet. She found herself praying that the ruffles had
masked the bloat; if asked, she would tell them she was on her
cycle and that the bloat would dissolve. But she wasn't sure
what she'd do if she were cast. At the end of the runway, she

turned this way and that so the casting directors could view her from all angles. It was then that she nearly fell over from the tiny but certainly perceptible jab just beneath her belly button. She steadied her composure by flipping her fringe out of her eyes and flashing a broad smile at the row of men that sat behind folding tables, observing her every move.

In a corner of the hallway amongst the other models waiting their turns to be assessed, she found a spare patch of wall where she leaned back and caught her breath. She placed her palms flat against the base of her gut. Had she imagined it? No, there it was again. The tiniest flutter within, as though a butterfly was trapped within her organs. She closed her eyes for a moment. When she opened them, another model was staring at her. Mari had seen her before. She was a leggy brunette with toned biceps and thin lips. Since Mari's arrival in Moscow, the two had been orbiting the same circuit of casting calls. On a number of them, the girl had been clutching a child's hand, whispering to her in Russian that she had to behave and sit quietly while Mama went into the room. The model nodded toward Mari's hands enveloped over her stomach.

"How far?" she asked.

"Sorry?" Mari asked, letting her hands drop to her sides.

"How far along are you? I'd say twelve, thirteen weeks?"

"I don't know what you're talking about." Mari flushed and looked down to the ground.

"It's not me you need to worry about," the girl said, moving closer to Mari so her shoulder blocked the other girls. "It's them." She nodded toward the room from which Mari had exited.

"Shit," Mari hissed. "You can tell? That means they..."

"Please—" the girl sighed "—men are clueless when it's this early. Trust me. It's the middle of your second trimester that you need to worry about. That's when I had to come clean. I'm Ginevre."

"Mari."

"I know. I've seen you around."

Mari nodded. "Same. So you kept doing this, huh? Even after? I've seen you with your little girl."

Ginevre snorted. "If you could call it that. My stomach is tighter now than it ever was—you sell your soul to Pilates, but trust me, it works. Yet there's still a stigma that I'm a mother. My agent tried to get me to put it on my résumé, saying it would get me onto a whole other tier, but it's *das vidanya* to the twentysomething world. I am eking my way through, hoping I still pass."

"Oh, you do," Mari said. She wasn't lying; Ginevre was pert and lithe.

"We have a little model mothers group. You should join us," Ginevre said. "A friend owns a tearoom where we meet every other week. We watch one another's kids when we have calls. It's great support, and we share stories, give advice, that kind of thing."

"Thanks," Mari said. "I'll definitely think about it."

"Well, whatever you do," Ginevre said, "just don't breastfeed. It makes your tits sag, and then you're pretty much done for good. No bra, no matter what they say about lift and defying gravity, can correct that."

Mari thanked her and left the go-see, worried that one of the other models had overheard their conversation and passed it on to the casting directors. She figured she still had a few more weeks of modeling left in her before she really began to show. She approached calls now with a newfound zeal, attending up to three auditions a day, throwing herself into modeling with a fervor she hadn't thought possible, until she finally admitted that she herself could no longer mask her

ever-expanding stomach and chose to hole herself up in her
small apartment to ripen like a fleshy peach.

Months later, the nurse in the Moscow hospital told Mari
that the memory of the pain from the birth would soon sub-
side so that she'd be willing to do it again. *It's true*, she'd said,
her white orthopedic shoes squeaking against the shiny li-
noleum over which faint, crimson streaks were still visible
from where Mari's blood had been mopped up. *Otherwise
the human race would die away.* Mari scoffed when the nurse
turned away to adjust the IV line. Mari would remember
every single grasp within her innards as they wrenched her
apart, every sucking in of her breath as she had been forced
open like a juicy pomegranate. She would remember the
purple light that seemed to emanate from the corners of her
delivery room even though the lights had been turned out
in an effort to calm her. She would remember the glow from
the heart rate monitor that was tracking the tiny heart that
beat inside her; she had to wheel the whole contraption into
the bathroom each time she wanted to sit on the toilet. And
after being jolted and racked by contractions that seemed as
if they wanted to rip her apart, she remembered sitting on
the toilet for hours, the endless urge of wanting to shit and
shit and shit until the seismic forces cooled inside her. She
would remember the weary nurse who rubbed her haunches
methodically as she knelt on the floor, braying like a farm
animal until the doctor helped her onto her back in the bed
and told her to push like hell.

Mari remembered, and as a result, Claudia would be the
end; she was sure of it. And when that same nurse came in
after it was all over to check her vitals, she patted her hand
and said, "What a short labor, lucky girl." Mari didn't have
the energy to say anything. She lifted her arm weakly so the

nurse could strap the blood pressure cuff onto it and turned her head the other way so she didn't have to look at her face. What the hell did she know? The ten-hour ordeal had felt like eternity.

When she'd felt well enough, Mari asked for her daughter to be brought to her room. A different nurse wheeled in a box with transparent plastic sides, like a jewelry case. Mari had stared at the tiny wrapped package nestled into the bassinet with suspicion. She'd been in a fog after she'd released the tiny body from her own. It wasn't until one of the nurses brought the baby to her breast that she remembered Ginevre's advice. She'd looked at Claudia, her *daughter*, mewling with all her might, her tiny pink mouth gasping for her nipple like a guppy, and Mari hadn't had the strength to resist, saggy tits be damned.

Mari would never admit that her daughter was named after a model; that was far too gauche. But that goldi-locked face with the perfectly horsey teeth had adorned her walls in her Tallinn bedroom, a role model in the truest sense of the word.

Once she had regained the strength she needed to return home, and Claudia was blessed with a clean bill of health, Mari returned to her tiny apartment with her tiny daughter in her arms. It had been alarming how needy her cries were, how incessant, how little Mari could get done for herself and around the house even though it felt as if all Claudia did was sleep and nurse and cry. If not for the crying, Mari thought, perhaps she might have survived. But she was startled by the way that Claudia would bawl for what seemed like hours on end, and then gasp, her face turning red and then violet. After the harsh realization that she hadn't spoken to another adult in two weeks, and a cursory glance at her dwindling bank account, Mari enrolled herself in a series of Pilates classes and tracked down Ginevre's number.

Ginevre was true to her word; models who barely looked as though they had birthed one or two children—in Sabrina's case, three—clustered around a table in the back of the coffee shop where they assembled on Wednesday evenings. Mari tugged her stroller toward the circle, making sure to give each of them a quick once-over before she mentally committed. Luckily none of them resembled her in the least, a good sign that boded well for the future of their friendships. Model friends should never look alike, Mari had learned. You didn't want to tempt the fates of competition, tears or cattiness. Ginevre had clearly spoken about her before, because they all fell upon her, holding their children on their hips, one brazenly breast-feeding her child under Ginevre's critical eye as they welcomed her into the fold. It was the first time during her modeling career that Mari finally felt part of something. *This* was the community she'd been yearning for, not the snarling clutches of girls all vying for the same roles that she'd encountered so far. The group, composed of seven model mothers, was an eclectic bunch; Sasha, Yulia and Sabrina had founded the group three years earlier; Ginevre and Fleur had both left the ultracompetitive modeling world of Paris for Moscow since then, and Aisha and Jasmine had recently relocated from Cairo and Tehran, respectively, along with their daughters.

Almost immediately, they began to teach Mari the ropes. In order to survive in Moscow as a model mother, you had to work under a few select agents. Ginevre advised Mari to dump Viktor as soon as possible and gave her the names of three acceptable agents who would make her rich, if not famous. Mari clutched the list so intensely within her fingers that the sweat made the numbers bleed into one another, so

Ginevre wrote them down again. The other breast-feeding mother, Yulia, tutored Mari on how to protect herself from leaking when she went on go-sees. She instructed Mari not to think about her daughter while she was at calls lest her breasts seep dark clusters onto her dress. She showed her how to pad her bras with half a maxi pad in each cup, giving her the illusion of a woman more naturally endowed than she was.

An unspoken rule of the group was that none of the models referred to or asked after the fathers. Mari didn't even know if the fathers were in the picture unless one of the girls volunteered the information. Sabrina, with her brood of three, mentioned her boyfriend from time to time, much to the chagrin of the other mothers, whose mouths turned down in response to the mention of a man. It seemed that all the other girls were just as alone as Mari.

In truth, Mari tried not to think about Nico. But frustratingly, Claudia was a constant visual reminder of her father. She had his short, stubby fingers and a mole at the side of her neck that Nico had on the back of his. She had his elfin ears and his pointy nose. Mari had read that babies biologically resemble their fathers upon birth; it was a natural instinct built into the birthing process so that male mammals wouldn't eat their own kind, or abandon them in their time of need. But Claudia didn't need her father. He wasn't even in the picture. Why couldn't her own daughter resemble her mother when she was all she had?

She couldn't help but wonder what Nico was doing over there on the other side of the world, not longingly but rather matter-of-factly. She was curious about that life, the one that if everything had moved more traditionally, she might be living. She wondered if she would ever crave the desire to pack Claudia up so she could see the foreign land that was technically partly her daughter's.

September 2004

EESTIRIDDLER723: Nico, hello!

HEADLOCK12: P-Train! Haven't talked to you in forever.

EESTIRIDDLER723: I know. It's been a while.

HEADLOCK12: I'm at college. Got here yesterday.

EESTIRIDDLER723: Wow, college already. How is it?

HEADLOCK12: New, different, overwhelming. All the things it's supposed to be. Have you left for training yet?

EESTIRIDDLER723: I leave on the first of October. Why is it overwhelming?

HEADLOCK12: Just massive, and everyone is always amped. It's like they're all on something. Who knows, maybe they are. I met my wrestling team at dinner. They were welcoming, which was nice, but you know, just a lot to take in.

HEADLOCK12: By the way, Chen and Carmine say hi. Carmine is at Reed in Oregon, and Chen, the mama's boy, is at NYU. :)

HEADLOCK12: I haven't seen you on here in a few weeks. Are you nervous about the service? I can't believe Estonia has mandatory service. Haven't you guys not been in a war in like, 40 years?

EESTIRIDDLER723: It's only for eight months. Peacetime training. But they're taking volunteers for the Multi-National Force to Iraq.

HEADLOCK12: Promise me you won't even consider that. You'll enroll in college, right? For next year?

EESTIRIDDLER723: Perhaps. That is still to be determined.

HEADLOCK12: Wait, why?

EESTIRIDDLER723: I was working at this IT company called CallMe over the summer, helping them run subset analyses and simulations. It was really interesting work, and they asked me to stay on.

HEADLOCK12: English, please! What does that even mean?

EESTIRIDDLER723: They're trying to bridge the gap between people across the world. Make the world a smaller place.

HEADLOCK12: How are you going to do that?

EESTIRIDDLER723: It's a communications initiative. It's in beta testing. I'm not at liberty to talk about it.

HEADLOCK12: I see.

EESTIRIDDLER723: I'll let you know about it when I can. But between you and me, I think it's going to be important.

HEADLOCK12: That's awesome, as long as you're happy. And you can always go to college next year.

EESTIRIDDLER723: Perhaps.

HEADLOCK12: What does that mean?

EESTIRIDDLER723: Only that there are many variables. I will be a reservist once I leave the military. I might be called up. Or I might just join CallMe full-time. My number got called in the army during a crucial few months within the company. I have received special governmental permission to continue work while I am here, during my free time, of course.

HEADLOCK12: Wow, sounds like these people have some sway.

EESTIRIDDLER723: As I said, I think the technology will change things.

HEADLOCK12: Wave of the future and all, huh? Well done, P-Train.

HEADLOCK12: How's the family? I know your dad took the make-up test a few weeks ago, but I didn't want to email him in case...

EESTIRIDDLER723: Yeah, good you didn't. He failed it. Again. It was a rough month, but nothing that couldn't be salved with a bottle of Viru Valge. Mama promised him that he would only have to take it one more time, but he says they have already taken his dignity and refuses to re-enroll. Mama's at her wit's end with him. She's not sure what to do.

HEADLOCK12: Poor guy. I feel his pain. Estonian was the hardest class I've taken in my life.

HEADLOCK12: So, how's Mari?

EESTIRIDDLER723: Still in Moscow.

HEADLOCK12: Wow, she must have hit it big.

EESTIRIDDLER723: She said being closer to the action would increase her chances of getting booked. She always says she's *so busy*, which I think is *such bullshit*.

HEADLOCK12: Well if you talk to her, tell her I say hi.

EESTIRIDDLER723: When is your first wrestling meet?

HEADLOCK12: Next week.

EESTIRIDDLER723: Good luck.

HEADLOCK12: Ha thanks. I'm probably going to get creamed. If you thought I was big, man... I'll have to send you a picture of the guys on my team. They're massive.

EESTIRIDDLER723: I am sure you exaggerate.

HEADLOCK12: Maybe a little. :) But for real, drop me a line from time to time, ok?

EESTIRIDDLER723: I will.

HEADLOCK12: Speak to you soon. Night, bud.

EESTIRIDDLER723: Good night. All the best.

PAAVO

Northeast Defense District, Tapa, Estonia
October 2004

The rumor spread during Paavo's orientation at basic training that the previous year, a trainee had shot himself and died instantly. His entire troop had been given emergency leave and excused from the remainder of training due to trauma. But as Paavo entered the entry hall that led toward the barracks, it no longer appeared to be a rumor. As his troop marched forward, they passed a square portrait of a young man with the ghostly fuzz of a mustache perched atop his thin upper lip. The olive-green soldier's cap on his head was slightly askew and his eyes were so piercing and luminous that Paavo felt as though he were being watched. *In Memoriam*, the plaque below read. *Urmas Kul, 1987–2003*. He would be certain to pay careful attention in Ammunitions, though they wouldn't be handling weapons until more than halfway through their service. Paavo felt a sharp poke between his shoulder blades, and he straightened his posture mechanically.

"That guy," Priit whispered hurriedly from behind. "That

guy offed himself last year. Remember hearing about it?" Paavo kept his eyes trained forward.

"It was an accident," Paavo said, murmuring out of the sides of his mouth like a ventriloquist. "He didn't know the gun was loaded."

"That's what they want us to think," Priit said. "Think they'd have all these conscripts if word was that *Eesti Kaitsevagi* made you suicidal?" Paavo concentrated on following the shoulders of the recruit in front of him. The rough edges of the material of his jacket were scuffed and worn, probably passed down through the years. The group came to a halt as they allowed a man dressed in a Facilities jumpsuit to push a cart holding a large, bulky item covered in burlap through the hall ahead of them.

"Wonder what's in there," Priit said. "Ammo, perhaps? Bodies?" In the introductory exercises, Priit had tried to partner with Paavo at every opportunity, but luckily they had been paired off alphabetically by last name so Paavo never had to deal with him. Priit was needy and desperate for attention, attaching himself like a leech to anyone he thought might be willing to listen. Perhaps if Priit were ignored, he would get the hint and fall back. Instead, goaded on by a silent and captive audience, Priit prattled on, unbeknownst to their captain, who was conferring with his senior at a heavy wooden desk in the middle of the long hall.

Paavo had attended the mandatory physical checkup over the summer without a fuss. It had been Vera who had been a mess, wringing her hands and reminding him again and again that he had special skills that would likely exempt him from having to enlist.

"It says here, Paavo," she said, waving the sheet he'd received from the Defense Forces the previous week. "Look. I'm not making it up. It says, due to any exemplary displays in IT, commerce/business and technology. IT. That's you. Just take them all your CallMe work from the summer."

"That stuff is confidential, Mama," Paavo said, pushing his foot into a sneaker. "You're not to tell anyone about it, and I certainly can't be taking work out of that office. Honestly, it's fine. Reservists have never actually been called up. Who knows—I might fail the physical altogether. They'll probably think I'm too weak or out of shape and then I'll be back behind my desk at CallMe, letting my muscles atrophy." But Paavo's senior year on the soccer pitch had strengthened his legs and toughened his core. His quads were like the thunderous ham thighs that hung in the butcher's window in Raekoja plats, and when he wore shorts, his calf muscles bounced as though there were Ping-Pong balls encased within them. He was certainly fit to enlist in the Estonian Compulsory Military Service for the eight months of required stay. As their captain walked back to them, Paavo could tell he'd only recently been promoted, as he held his head high, but walked on the tentative, spindly legs of a newborn calf.

"Recruits," he yelped; it was unfortunate that his voice hadn't been upgraded along with his status. Sometime in the past year, Paavo's thin, reedy pitch had been replaced with the deep rumble of a bass drum, making Vera jump the first time she'd realized that it was her son and not an intruder answering her from his bedroom. "You'll now be receiving your bunking orders. Step forward as I call your names and claim your sleeping kits."

Paavo's bunk was underneath Ragnar's, a hulking man with gray-fringed sideburns, and opposite Toomas, one of the hairiest Estonians Paavo had ever seen. His entire body was covered in a blond pelt; his cheeks were furry and thin, fine strands peeked out from the cuffs of his jacket onto the backs of his hands. Priit, luckily, was assigned to the far end

of the tunnel-like barrack, where he would have to befriend
an adjacent bunkmate to bother. Paavo tucked the sheets onto
the insubstantial mattress and unfurled the thin brown blanket over it. He sat down over his work, wondering how many
bodies had sat in this very spot over the years. The reservists had only been reestablished once Estonia had established
its independence in 1991. Paavo could barely remember the
day. There had been a celebration that remained rather fuzzy
in his memory. The family had paraded to Toompea, to a
crest on a hill overlooking their tiny, medieval city. Paavo
remembered his father feeling grumpy about attending, but
Leo had allowed Mari to stick a small flag with those three
solid blocks of color into his cap and had walked down the
path holding onto Paavo's small hand. Vera had painted three
stripes of color onto each of the children's cheeks and Paavo
had swiped at his nervously as they walked, leaving a big
black-and-blue smudge down the side of his jaw. As they
neared Toompea, the hill was already pulsating with people.

"I thought we might have been early," Vera said, aston-
ished at the masses milling about, kissing one another, painting the ubiquitous three stripes of color on exposed skin,
waving flags, cheering, shouting, and above all, mostly
drunk.

"I'm not sure about this, Vera," Leo said.

"Nonsense," Vera scoffed. "This is history. We have to
stay and be a part of it." They settled against the metal fence,
feeling invigorated by the parade that trailed beneath their
feet and the hum of the crowd surrounding them. Bottles of
communal vodka were being passed around, and Leo found
himself holding one and then another.

"In the spirit of the day," he shrugged, and took two large
swigs from each of them. Vera shook her head and concentrated on the crowds below, where majorettes were twirling

batons and there was even a man shooting fire from a cone. She tried not to notice when another pair of vodka bottles made their way back around their way, and instead grasped Paavo's and Mari's hands with fierce focus.

Sometime in the afternoon, Paavo recalled peeling himself off the fence upon which he'd draped himself when his legs were too tired. They were commemorating the extinguishing of the eternal flame that had been lit in front of the Bronze Soldier Statue during the time of Soviet power. The speeches had droned on; ancient women were being honored for having survived the dark trenches of Siberian labor camps and returning to their homeland to tell the tale. Dozens of garlands and bouquet after bouquet of marigolds were bestowed upon them, the stark orange of the petals searing bright against the black sea of their dresses. Paavo remembered wondering where the little old men were. He must have gone to Vera to ask her this when he found her standing, watching the masses of people below. Her cheeks were wet and she swabbed at her eyes before grasping Paavo's hand in hers.

"Maybe it's time to go," she'd said. "Let's find your father and Mari."

They found Leo leaning against a stately birch tree, his eyes at half-mast. Mari was asleep on his shoulder. The rubble from the celebration surrounded them, including empty Vana Tallinn bottles, discarded Estonian flags that had lost their stems and confetti that would eventually seek new life as mulch. Paavo didn't remember much more, other than the fact that when he went to stand next to his father to wake him, his breath puffed out with the sour smell of vodka.

"Come on," Vera said, standing over her family. "We've all had enough." Paavo hoped that a celebration of that stature would turn his father's glum demeanor into something upbeat. He didn't understand why Papa had been so down since

Estonia had announced their independence, but he hoped that things would settle at home, that a dove from the dule that had been released into the air—"Commemorating peace for our people," Vera had whispered into his ear during the solemn ceremony—might come to roost in the eaves of their house, bestowing calmness and serenity on the family over-all. But Paavo's room shared a wall with his parents' room, and each night, hours after he'd been tucked in to sleep, their conversations rose in an arc, the timbre of their voices piercing the veiled nights. Papa was upset—he was afraid about something, and Mama was constantly comforting him in her gentle, honey-filled voice that everything would be okay.

That had been almost fifteen years ago. Now Paavo concentrated on the two knots in the wooden slat of the bunk above him. Ragnar shifted and the knots on the board dipped dangerously low. Paavo closed his eyes. During those awful nights when his father would drink and his parents would fight, he remembered wishing he could have been a twin, so that one Paavo could have been Russian with Papa and the other Paavo could be Estonian, so that both parents could be happy. One could brandish his Estonian passport proudly and the other could hold on to his gray passport that allowed his legal status in the country, but not his ability to vote or become a true, accepted citizen. Those things didn't matter to the second Paavo. He just wanted his father to stop feeling like an alien in an independent world; he wanted to show his support to this man who had always felt like an outsider. And now, he thought, if there were two Paavos, one could complete the mandatory military service and the other could continue the work he'd already set into place at CallMe.

NORA

Ann Arbor
November 2004

Just as Paavo had suggested, as soon as she began to under-stand her condition, Nora left the version of herself that was frustrated, angry and bitter behind. After the spate of psy-chology classes she took to finish her degree in that sum-mer after Paavo had left New York City, she was shedding that version of herself, leaving the anxious, worried Nora behind to try to understand herself better. She applied to a number of combined master's/PhD courses in psychology and the following year, packed herself up and headed off to Ann Arbor. The University of Michigan had offered her a scholarship as well as a teaching stipend, and she'd already begun correspondence with some of the professors over the summer. She found a quaint apartment in a walk-up build-ing off campus in downtown Ann Arbor that had a court-yard and a twin building facing it.

On her first night in the apartment, she wandered down Main Street clutching her black notebook, browsing in used bookstores, ducking into breweries and cafés before ordering a take-out sandwich to eat in the privacy of her new home. The living room was brimming with suitcases she hadn't unpacked, boxes of cheap furniture from IKEA that she'd had delivered straight to her apartment but hadn't yet constructed, psych textbooks that she'd brought from the courses she'd taken in college. Her bed was the only furniture in the apartment, and she spread a towel over the naked mattress and opened her sandwich. From the window, she could see through the window of the adjacent apartment. Solid blue curtains were drawn across them, but there was still a narrow slip of space between where they met. She hadn't noticed how close the other apartment had been before. There was movement behind the curtains and suddenly the curtains whipped back to reveal a man framed in the window. He was dressed in a blazer and jeans, resembling a darker-complexioned John Cusack.

He waved and Nora jumped. She smiled nervously and made to grab her sandwich and move off the bed, but he had anticipated her flight and rapped on the glass sharply and shook his head, petitioning her to stay. She looked at his face. It looked smart, well-read. He must have been in his late twenties, and his skin was the color of very milky coffee. She liked that he had a slight underbite. She waved back, feeling very conscious of herself. He mouthed something, but she shook her head in confusion. He held a finger up and disappeared out of sight.

When he returned a few minutes later, he held a piece of white paper with the words, "What's your name?" written in black marker. Nora smiled, embarrassed, looking down at the floor. She shook her head. He knelt briefly, and then stood back up, holding another piece of paper. "Shahid. That's me."

She smiled. He pointed back at her. She shook her head, and he pointed to his head and shrugged.

He scribbled, "Rumpelstiltskin?" Nora giggled and shook her head. She mimed looking at her watch, tapping it and pointing at herself and then away. She waved again. The man pouted, sticking his lower lip out.

She cursed herself for not having put up curtains yet. She waved at him, turned away and ate on the living room floor. She hoped that they wouldn't run into one another on the street. It would be embarrassing and would remove the allure of communicating with him across the way.

But the next night, she sensed movement again. It was like clockwork. Each evening she would return from the Psych building, toss her bag on the bed and stretch out. Each evening, she would hear the sounds of life coming from other apartments—chopping, chatting, singing, but she would lie on her bed with a book between her hands and wait for the curtains to part. She still wasn't sure she recognized him each time, but the underbite helped, as well as his aquiline nose with its high bridge. She wasn't close enough to see, but she thought he might be showing the early tracings of a goatee. He parted the curtains as though he expected her, and she glanced up from her book, pretending not to care, pretending not really to see until he gestured toward her, waving spasmodically until she had to laugh.

Now he held up a piece of paper. "I know you can see me. Don't play hard to get."

Nora looked away. She wasn't sure what she was supposed to expect from him; what were they supposed to do? Become friends? She watched him across the alleyway. His face fell when he realized she wasn't going to respond, so he walked away, letting the curtains fall behind him. She waited there with her book on the bed until the room darkened and she dared to leave the apartment to hunt down some dinner.

But though she'd been reluctant to communicate, she missed his presence. She went back to her bedroom each evening, waiting for the curtains to pull back. On the fourth night when he still hadn't shown up, Nora gave herself a talking-to and went to meet some of the psychology graduate students at a happy hour she'd originally declined.

But then, early the next morning, Shahid parted the curtains, seemingly to let whatever thin light trickled down from the sky and entered the partition between their windows into his room. Nora had been organizing her jewelry tree on her dresser when she perceived movement out of the corner of her eye. She moved toward the window and frantically waved. Shahid nodded knowingly and smiled. "Want what you can't have?" he wrote.

Nora shook her head, frowning. She held up a finger and looked around her room, grabbing a Sharpie and a dismantled cardboard moving box. On it, she wrote, "Where have you been?"

"Open the window."

Nora shook her head furiously. It was imperative that they keep up this charade, or everything would fall to pieces. It was silly and maybe a little romantic, but she wanted to keep things in their places until the world shuffled and she could no longer have control over them. "Better this way."

Shahid smiled at her.

"Student?"

Shahid shook his head. "Professor. Physics."

Nora raised her eyebrows, impressed. "Young professor. Your students must love you."

Shahid laughed. "You?"

"Grad student. Psych."

"Am I the star of some social experiment?"

Nora laughed and shook her head. She was running out of room on her cardboard box. She held a finger up and disappeared from the window. In the living room, she frantically tore open boxes, sorting through them until she found her dry erase board and markers.

When she got back to the window, he had turned away and was fiddling with something on his phone. His face lit up when he saw her again. She held up the whiteboard. "Typical. Indian physics teacher."

"Don't generalize. I'm Pakistani." He smirked at her and nodded at the whiteboard. "Environmentalist. I dig. :)"

She giggled. She liked this back-and-forth. It was so much easier than remembering a face, knowing that his would always be the one on the other side of the glass. But she wanted to keep things fresh. "Gotta go," Nora wrote. "See you later."

On the sixth day, Shahid wrote, "Let's meet." Nora grimaced. "One meeting?" Shahid's smile was earnest, reflecting the intensity of his scribbling.

She had been tossing this idea around in her head for a few days now, usually just before she went to sleep. Meeting him in person meant that she would have to conjure up the face she saw from across the way. This way was easy—he would always be there. From across the way, he would always be Shahid. On the street, in a coffee shop, in a bar…who knew what he would look like? Who knew if she would recognize him? Her secret would be out, and that was more shameful than flirting with a complete stranger from across an alleyway. She shook her head.

"So you're just a tease."

Nora smiled, biting her lip. She knew that was her signature move. That meant she was in it. She waved at him before lowering the shades she had finally installed. Then she shut off the light and left the room.

Once the school year began, it turned out that Nora's grad school schedule and Shahid's teaching one were in sync. On the third day of classes, she nearly bumped into him while he sorted his mail in the foyer. He was shorter than he'd appeared across the alleyway. She ran her quick assessment.

Gold earring
Latte skin
Pressed button-down shirts
Groove in his forehead
Slight underbite
Early 90s–style goatee

"Shahid?" she ventured.

Cheeky smile

"Rumpelstiltskin!" he cried. His voice was deep and flecked with the hint of a British accent as he rolled his *R*s. "At long last we meet."

"It's Nora," she confessed.

"Thank goodness," he said. "I was starting to feel like we were in some Italian neorealism film, all that schoolyard back-and-forth."

"I'm not sure what that means," Nora said. "But it's nice to finally meet you."

"It really is," he said, taking her hand in his. She looked down at her feet and back up at his face, bracing herself as though it might rearrange into a jigsaw puzzle as faces usually did. But nothing at all had moved; his features were exactly where she'd left them within the curled sections of her fusiform. She sucked in her breath, shocked by the normalcy of it all. She closed her eyes and reopened them. *This is how it used to be*, she reminded herself, blinking back tears. *This is how it used to feel to meet people and remember. To recognize.*

"Are you—are you okay?" Shahid asked her. "You look a little pale."

Nora nodded vehemently. "I'm absolutely fine."

From: EESTIRIDDLER723
To: Noreaster
February 5, 2005

Hi Nora,
Are you married yet? Don't forget to send me an invitation! All your emails are all about Shahid. Are you getting any work done while you're there? Only kidding, of course.

Things here in the army haven't been bad, though I am grateful for all the training I had with the wrestling team back in New York. It set me up for a good athletic regimen. I have completed all the obstacle course drills as well as the running and lifting. But I just found out last night that I am getting a reprieve from army training. CallMe petitioned the government and I am being pulled out in order to return to the implementation work I had been working on for the past year. Jaak and Riki, the founders, said we are getting state funding to complete the initial stages of our research and to implement the pioneer program of CallMe within Estonia! I'm really looking forward to it.

I know you can't ever be "healed," but you have come such a long way, Nora. You should be proud of yourself. I am very proud of you for turning your "condition" into something you have begun to understand and that you are turning into a career. Remember what I first told you about *dusha*? I don't want to get ahead of myself, but perhaps Shahid has it, and this is why you can see him for who he is. Maybe your soul has sought his, and determined that it is worth recognizing.

I have one for you: I touch someone once and last a lifetime.

Hugs,

Paavo

P.S. Give up? It's LOVE. :)

NICO

New York City
June 2007

It wasn't that Nico went looking for love; it was more that it seemed to find him. In his first year of college, the charisma he'd cultivated in high school seemed to attract girls almost as soon as he set foot on campus. Two different women in his semantics seminar vied for his attention—a risky situation, as the class size was only twelve. There was something alluring about him, about the way he focused mostly on his studies, his collegiate wrestling career and student government. His charm extended to everyone. Between classes and while lounging on the grassy knoll in front of his dorm, he almost always found himself deep within a scrum of students, all vying for his attention. It was no surprise that he ran for and won class office every year he was nominated.

"So what's wrong with Middleton?" Nico asked Toby. The boys were on the phone in their sophomore year of college. Nico wound the phone cord around his wrist as he pushed off the floor with the other hand. He puffed and grunted into the receiver.

"I think I made a mistake coming here. I think I might want to transfer," Toby said.

"Where to?"

"Anywhere else. Dude, are you working out?"

"Just some push-ups."

"Could you be here, in this phone call, for maybe five minutes?" Toby took a deep breath in.

"Sorry, man. The coach here makes Coach back home seem like my grandma. He kicks my ass like you wouldn't even imagine. And I went down a weight class, so I need to make sure I'm at the top of it." Nico rolled over onto his back and started a set of crunches, breathing through his mouth so Toby might not hear. "So tell me about Middleton."

"I just don't feel like I fit in. People are so different here."

Nico snorted some air out of his nose. "Well, go join some stuff. Do some Ultimate Frisbee. That's a good way to make friends."

"It's not a question of making friends. It's more than that."

"Hey listen, Tobes, I'm so sorry. There's a class board meeting I have to attend. Can I call you back tomorrow?"

Nico started writing a few articles for the *Varsity V* that year, claiming his own masthead and column in the second semester. When his classmates all started applying to study abroad programs in their junior years, Nico declined the opportunity.

"Been there, done that," he told them. "I was in Estonia for half a year. Not sure I need to repeat the experience." Instead, he stayed behind at school, heading up the school paper and taking the train into the city in the evenings to intern at the Francis Foley for Staten Island City Council District 52 campaign office. It was a makeshift office, run out of a storefront next to a sandwich shop in St. George, so that salami and mortadella wafted through the shared vent and circulated in the air above the phones where volunteers made cold calls for donations. Francis Foley was a client of Arthur's, and once Nico had mentioned his desire to work on an electoral campaign before graduation, Arthur secured all the details for the introduction, including the fact that the headquarters were within walking distance of the ferry.

On his first day, while he was disappointed to be greeted by stacks of fund-raising letters, envelopes and stamps, Nico finished the job in a few hours. Martin Foley, Francis's nephew and campaign manager, told him to sit tight until the copy shop down the block completed the next round of envelope stuffers. In the meantime, Nico wandered around the office. He read through the press binder stationed by the door, aligning himself with Foley's policies and points of view. He read articles the staff had printed out and pinned to bulletin boards. He found some stray papers that had been abandoned by the printer and began reading through them. It was a speech—one that Foley was scheduled to deliver that evening at a fund-raising dinner that cost four hundred dollars a plate. It was good, but it could be better. There was no arc to the oratory, no pluck to the heartstrings. Nico took a pen and highlighter to the pages, writing notes in the margins and scoring through redundant sentences, reforming and redefining passages. He retyped the whole thing, printed it and left it there.

He couldn't have orchestrated it better himself. Just as he sat back down at his desk, Francis Foley opened the door to his office and strode out toward the printer. He collected the pages, his eyes scanning the words.

"Martin," he called, "this isn't what we talked about."

Martin took the pages from Foley. "That's because this isn't it. Where'd you get this?"

Nico stepped forward. "That's my take. Here's your original. I thought there were some facets of civil liberties that could have been brought to the forefront. Also, it kind of glossed over the whole police truancy situation, which is top of mind right now, don't you think? And the first draft danced around minimum wage, so I addressed it head-on."

"Who the fuck are you?" Foley asked the question almost tenderly.

"The new intern," Martin said. "I did not give him access to this. Sorry, Uncle Frank."

"Are you shittin' me? An intern?" Foley perched on the edge of Nico's desk. "Where are you from?"

"Here. New York," Nico said. "I'm in my senior year of college."

"Thank God for that," Foley said. "You're coming to work for me after you graduate."

Martin looked at the papers. "It's good?"

"It's fucking brilliant. What else you got?"

"What do you mean?" Nico asked.

"I have a press con tomorrow afternoon on the transportation hike. Are you up on the issue?"

"I can be."

"You sure you want to go back to school? If you can write like this, I'll hire you full-time right now."

"I have to finish college, sir," Nico said. "But I can work remotely if you want."

Within the first month of his time with the Francis Foley campaign, Nico graduated to deputy campaign manager, much to Martin's chagrin. Between term papers and putting the paper to bed on Sunday nights, Nico wrote speeches and press releases, helping Foley transition from potty-mouthed politico to silver-tongued Staten Island council member. And when Nico graduated, Foley stayed true to his word, hiring Nico as his chief of staff and head speechwriter.

Nico Grand was the youngest chief of staff ever appointed in the history of New York City politics, though one would never have known it. His voice—both literal, behind the scenes, and literary, as it was translated through countless communications—was mature in its intonation and intent. Nico brought a lyricism, an empathetic consideration to his words that hadn't been heard in the political arena before. Constituents were astounded when he stepped onto the stage from the wings after Foley delivered one of Nico's speeches in order to clear away any detritus or notes that Foley had left behind. And Foley gave Nico a lot of leeway when it came to Nico's own agenda, insofar as it aligned with Foley's own policies. Nico headlined at the weekly city council meetings, opining on issues that held a personal stake for him: the cleanup of the piers at Arlington, an investigation into the clean water habits of a renowned pizza parlor in Battery Weed, whether a halfway house in Sunnyside was operating up to code.

After two years in the Foley administration, Nico's fame had spread, not only across borough borders, but also specifically into the heart of the city. Just as legislation was passed for reclamation of the borough's landfill—a major coup and one of Nico's initiatives—the city comptroller's office called in a favor. His chief of staff had absconded over a petty disagreement and was now working in the public sector. The office needed someone almost immediately to smooth over the backlash, and was Nico interested?

From: EESTIRIDDLER723
To: HEADLOCK12
September 17, 2007

Nora has been keeping me updated with all your news (since I don't receive it from you!). I am so proud. You're making great things happen. And now she tells me that you are going to City Hall? What will you do for the comptroller?

I'm writing to you from Prague, where I am setting up CallMe's first remote office. Tallinn headquarters hit capacity at the same time that I hit a programming wall. I've been feeling pretty bored, so Jaak and Riki found funding for me to learn new code from a bunch of guys they know while I'm setting things up. And (ssh!) I've heard rumors that we're about to receive some major funding from the Danish government, which could really help us expand across Europe at some point, and then eventually the world. I contacted Sabine, and we are meeting for a drink this afternoon. She's taking me to try Prague's famous black beer. I hear it packs a punch. Send a search party if you don't hear from me.

From: HEADLOCK12
To: EESTIRIDDLER723
December 15, 2007

P-Train, sorry it's taken me so long to write back. I feel like the last two months have been two years. I moved to Tribeca. I have my own apartment now, which feels like a huge sigh of relief after living with three other guys in that cramped place in Murray Hill. I finally feel like a grown-up. It's easier to get to work, and the apartment has a great view of the river. Are you going to come visit sometime soon, or has CallMe completely consumed you? How was Prague, or are you still there? How's Sabine?

Speaking of Hallström people, I saw Evan on the train the other day. The poor guy has gone completely bald. He's working in finance and he said to say hi. I asked him about Pyotr and he looked at me like I was crazy. Guess they haven't been in touch!

Work is exhausting, but awesome. I don't ever really sign off. I work when I get home and I work as soon as I get up. But it's a good time for me. There's a chance I might transition over to the mayor's office, so I am trying to keep my energy up and my eye on the prize. I'm dating around, no one particularly exciting, but it's not like I have time for that either. I'll try to write again soon, but I don't really have any news other than work, work, work. Tell me some news from your end. Nora's good, but I know you guys are in touch. She's nearly done with her PhD. And, as you know, she's totally in love.

How's Mari?

From: EESTIRIDDLER723
To: HEADLOCK12
January 15, 2008

I'm scheduled to return to Tallinn in two weeks, but I don't think I ever want to move back home again. Prague is spectacular. It's such an ancient city, unlike Tallinn, which feels like it was built a few decades ago. Prague has so much history. Tallinn does too, I guess, but it's so disjointed that it's hard to follow it. We were Danish and then Swedish and then Russian. At the end of the day, we're all mutts.

I've been taking on a great deal more coding work, and I'm feeling really good that CallMe will be going global—beyond Europe—in a few short months, so you and I can talk for free over the internet, and you will also be able to share files, photos, work on documents simultaneously with a colleague. I know you will be discreet, but please don't share this information with anyone, as it's top secret. We heard that one of our biggest competitors was trying to launch some similar items, so we need to be sure that we are ahead of the game.

I've been spending a lot of time with Sabine. She has been a good friend to me, and has made me feel at home in her city. While she's in medical school and barely has any free time, she has introduced me to her friends so that I always have something to do on Friday nights and she always takes the time to send me a message and ask how I am doing. I bring dinner to her flat a few nights a week and we catch up over one of her study breaks. I know what you'll say, but it's not like that. At least, I don't think it is.

Nora said Shahid got a tenure track position at Columbia and that they're going to move back to New York together. She's going to set up her own private practice? He sounds like he's really good for her. Have you met him? What do you think?

Mari is doing well. I receive intermittent information about her from Papa and Ema from time to time and occasionally she remembers to respond to me. I'm going to visit her in Moscow on my way back to Tallinn after this trip. She's had some interest from Victoria's Secret, all very under the radar for now, but her agent is trying to sell them on the idea of a Dark Angel or something like that. I've never understood that world. What the hell is a Dark Angel?

From: HEADLOCK12
To: EESTIRIDDLER723
June 12, 2008

P-Train, I am the worst. I owe you a thousand emails. I'm so sorry. Things have been absolutely insane over here. I wish I could be like one of those Hindu gods with a hundred arms so I could get things done. I'm not complaining, of course. It's all been really good. This might be the first non-work email I've written in almost a year.

Okay, I have to come clean. I haven't only been working. I started seeing this girl. You know me—I dated around during college, after college. I didn't really have time to commit to anyone or a relationship in general. But that's what's so great about Ivy. She's in politics too, and she's tenacious. She started as a page in the mayor's office when she was in middle school, and now she's working her way up in the attorney general's office. The great thing is that she's really committed to her career too, so she's not interested in moving fast or settling down or anything. She gets the whole political thing, and how there's a right time for everything. So that's good.

My other big news is that I'm going on the campaign trail this season. This is sort of the last box I want to check on my career goals. Shelley Dale has been congresswoman for a few terms, but she's upping the ante to Senate this year. This is really high profile for me. She hired me as her campaign advisor so we're hitting the road starting this weekend. I spent the last few weeks writing a bunch for her, so I'm ready to hit the ground running. Ivy is staying behind in the city, but she'll come out a few weekends as things pick up.

Are you going to visit Mari in Moscow, or did that already happen? Say hi for me.

PAAVO

Moscow
May 2009

As far back as Paavo could remember into their childhood growing up together, Mari had never shown any maternal sensitivities. She'd never pretended to feed a doll, or tucked them into bed, had never thrown a pillowcase over the circumference of her head and marched solemnly down the hallway toward an invisible husband at a make-believe wedding. Vera had once told a story about how Mari had taken her first look at her little brother, proclaimed that he smelled funny, and then turned back to a set of LEGO blocks that she snapped together with the newfound aggression of a jealous older sibling.

But what Paavo didn't know was that Mari approached Claudia's entry into her life as she might step into a pair of high heels: poised, confident, assured. She accepted the little wrapped bundle into her arms, her face slack from the exertion of birth, but beatific with the presentation of her efforts. She had mentally prepared for this day—not just the physicality of her delivery, but shifting everything in her life to accommodate this small, pink, suckling little thing.

For those nine months of Mari's pregnancy, Vera and Leo visited Mari as much as she would allow. She had tried to keep them at arm's length, feeling fiercely independent and assuring her parents that while she was incredibly busy, she had the full support of her friends in the model mothers group. Vera insisted on visiting her daughter and granddaughter along with Leo twice a year, for Midsummer's and on St. Catherine's Day in November to celebrate the women in her life. For years, army training and then intensive weeks with CallMe had occupied Paavo's time while his parents journeyed to Moscow. Mari's schedule hadn't brought her back to Tallinn, so he'd had to make do with quick stopovers en route to Riga and Prague while Claudia was very small. So when Jaak and Riki asked Paavo to set up the Moscow office, Paavo welcomed the few weeks to finally get to know his niece.

Paavo's modest hotel was around the corner from Red Square, but he decided to walk the five kilometers to Mari and Claudia's loft apartment opposite Gorky Park. The wind rustled the trees as he neared the blinking lights of the carousel, and Paavo found himself bracing for the visit. He wasn't sure how he should interact with this little girl. Would he introduce himself as Onu? He should have brought her something—a doll, some chocolates, some clothes. What did little girls like these days? He pressed the buzzer for their apartment feeling sheepishly empty-handed.

Mari opened their door, smiling broadly. "Little brother!" she exclaimed before she enveloped him in her arms. It felt strange to admit it, but his sister had always been attractive, and the years had been good to her. Her cheeks were pink and flushed, her hair swept back from her face, and her body held no trace that she'd carried a child within it. "Took you long enough to come see us."

"I'm sorry," he said. "But it's not as though you've come home to visit, either."

"I know," she said, closing the door behind him. "Ever since Victoria's Secret, things have just exploded. I've barely had a weekend off in weeks. And Tallinn isn't really where the action is anymore."

Paavo stepped into the entryway. Large black-and-white prints were mounted on the walls. But everything else was white: the chairs, table, the walls, the floor. The place had the look of a corporate apartment or a real estate staging space. There was no clutter or toys or indication that a young girl lived here.

"It's...nice," Paavo ventured. "When did you move in?"

"Oh—" Mari dismissed the comment with a wave of her hand "—we're barely here. Last week was Prague and Venice and next we're hitting São Paolo. Claudia will have seen more of the world by her tenth birthday than I'd seen before I left home."

"Where is she?" Paavo asked.

Mari pointed toward the sofa. Paavo pushed his shoes off but walked into the living room wearing his coat. A slim girl sat on the very end of a beige sofa, leafing through a book. Paavo sat on the sofa opposite her and crossed his feet at the ankles. The girl looked up.

"Onu Paavo," she said in Estonian.

Paavo smiled and nodded. "You remember me."

"*Rad vas videt,*" she said with perfect intonation. *Nice to see you.*

"You speak Russian, too," Paavo said.

"*Et français aussi.*" *And French, too.* Claudia looked back down at the open book on her lap.

"Wow," Paavo said, looking up at Mari. "She's quite an accomplished young lady."

"Yes, so will you please tell Ema that she wants for nothing?" Mari sighed, sinking down on the sofa next to her daughter. "Claudia has a better education than she would have ever received in Tallinn."

"Do *you* live in Tallinn?" Claudia asked.

"I do," Paavo said. "But I travel quite a bit. Just like you."

"Do you have a tutor, as well?" Claudia asked.

Paavo smiled. "I work. Just like your mother."

"Oh," Claudia said. Paavo found himself studying his niece intensely, wanting to drink in all her details, as though memorizing her face might make up for lost time. He took in her perfectly arched eyebrows, her snub nose and the mole at the base of her neck as she collected her hair in a bunch and braided it deftly to hang over one shoulder. He took in her squat fingers that didn't seem to quite fit with the rest of her lithe body as she turned the pages of the book. This child was half his sister, and therefore nearly half of him. It was fascinating to see the result. He could feel the question building up inside him, but he had promised his mother that during this trip he wouldn't pry; he wouldn't do anything to drive Mari further away than she had already gone. But he knew Mari better than that; it couldn't have been a male model. She had scoffed at their idiocy, their constant peacock-like preening. Throughout her auditions in her teenage years, she hadn't found a single male model that could carry on an intelligent conversation.

Later, after Mari had boiled pierogis, sliced up a loaf of crusty bread and tossed a vibrant green salad, after they'd eaten in the pristine kitchen, which looked as though it had never been used before, after Claudia and Paavo cleared the table and stacked the dishes in the dishwasher and after Claudia had said good-night without being asked and scurried off down a long hallway and disappeared behind a door with a click, the siblings nestled into opposite ends of the white couch with large globes of brandy in their hands, their feet poking one another familiarly.

"I don't know how you did it," Paavo ventured. "You raised that little girl. You did it all by yourself."

"Never underestimate the power of single mothers who model," Mari said, raising her snifter. "Seriously, it took a village. I couldn't have done it without them."

"I'm really glad you had them, Mari. I'm relieved that you did." The loud, insistent second hand of an unseen clock ticked away in the silence. Paavo looked around, searching for the source of the sound and found nothing. "I'm sorry. Ema made me promise not to ask, but I have to. Why did you do it, Mari? Why did you run away?"

Mari sighed and looked up at the ceiling as though for strength. "Not bad, little brother. You lasted a whole two hours."

"Ema and Papa would have helped you. Ema got pregnant with you when she was twenty. They know what it was like to be young parents. They would have understood."

"Who says they didn't?" Mari asked, pulling her legs toward her.

"They were so down when you left the way you did. You should have seen them moping around the house. It was like I was living with ghosts."

Mari snorted, smiling down at the ground. "Wow. He's a better actor than I would have given him credit for."

"Who? Who's a better actor?"

"Papa. You really didn't know?"

"Know *what*, Mari?" Paavo could hear his voice climbing, and he willed it down, though he felt vulnerable and exposed.

"It was his idea, Paavo. Papa suggested I leave Tallinn. He orchestrated my whole move to Moscow. He all but *handed* me the keys to our place in Petrovka." Mari swirled her brandy and sipped it.

"But why?" Paavo put his glass down and sat up straight.

"He never said as much, but I think it was because he was hoping to join me. I think he was hoping that me being here would persuade Ema to move to Moscow. So he wouldn't have to feel like an outsider in his own land, as he always said."

Paavo frowned. "But that doesn't make any sense. As much as Papa grumbles, he's happy in Tallinn, in Estonia, isn't he? He's lived there for more than half his life. He has his job, and Ema and Deda and Babu and us. I don't understand why he would drive you away."

"He didn't drive me away. When I knew I was pregnant, I made up my mind that I wanted to leave. It was a nearly immediate decision. I saw how my life was going in Tallinn. I'd have this baby, live with Papa and Ema and have some thankless job that I would soon learn to despise. This way, I could write my own future. I went to Papa and told him as much. He didn't send me away. He helped me." Mari watched Paavo as he picked up his brandy again and drank it steadily until the glass was empty.

"Refill?"

"Yes. I think I need one," Paavo said.

"Will you come back to see us while you're in town? Claudia needs to get to know her Onu." Mari reached over and grasped Paavo's hand with an urgency she hadn't seemed capable of all evening before letting go to refill his glass.

Paavo visited Mari and Claudia three more times that week. Each visit was like the careful peeling back of an

onion; Paavo made sure to inquire delicately, lest he inter-
rogate Mari into silence. Unlike her mother, Claudia presented herself to her uncle as an open book, inviting him
back into her room to look at all her dolls, her books and her
clothes. Claudia's room, at least, had the trappings of a five-
year-old. Multicolored crates held assorted toys, bookshelves
were stocked and overflowing, and Paavo was grateful for
the great bursts of color in Claudia's domain, from the curtains to the rug to her bedclothes. Paavo loved every moment he spent with his niece, and he mentally documented
each piece of information that he learned about her. Claudia
loved colors. Claudia was fluent in four languages. Claudia's
favorite book was *Pushkin's Fairy Tales.*

On Paavo's fourth evening at their home, Mari poked
her head into the kitchen, where he and Claudia were im-
mersed in the opposite pages of an underwater-themed coloring book. Claudia was shading the shell of a turtle in a
light purple color as Paavo gave a blue hue to a coral reef.

"Will it be all right if I run a few errands while you're
here? I won't be long." Paavo glanced at Mari as he reached
for a turquoise crayon.

"Of course. Take your time. We'll be fine."

"Onu, I've never heard of blue coral before," Claudia said,
pointing to his side of the book.

"Well, who has ever heard of a purple turtle?" he asked.
"Onus can have an imagination, too."

"But you're an adult." Claudia cackled.

"And so?" he asked, feigning shock. "I'm not allowed to
be creative?"

"Not as creative as me," Claudia said.

"Fair enough," he said. "I will probably never be as creative as you, even if I tried."

"Onu, I want to be an artist," Claudia said.

"Very good," Paavo said. "We will add that to the list. So now, you'll be a model slash conductor slash inventor slash artist?" Claudia had ambition.

Claudia nodded. "I like it," Paavo said. "I think you'll be the first of your kind." He sat back and watched her. During the few days he'd spent with Mari and Claudia, he had almost forgotten himself and his desire to uncover the cloak-and-dagger operation that Mari had pulled off almost six years prior. That his father had colluded with Mari to send his only daughter and the grandchild inside her away had baffled him; he had returned to the hotel room and to work the following morning with his head in a cloud. He went through the motions of directing employees at the Moscow office of CallMe but could barely wrap his head around the recent developments. But when he returned to his sister's apartment that evening, the haze in his head dissipated as he became enchanted with Claudia. He mused at how trusting children were when you gave them the slightest bit of attention; they were all yours whether or not you'd been a stranger mere hours before. Claudia melted into him, giving him her possessions at first, then herself slowly and then quickly and then all at once. He found himself falling in love with his newly recovered niece, this inquisitive, forthright, charming young girl, who was a likeness of Mari in each of her forms, both physical and behavioral. Claudia was so innocent yet simultaneously self-assured, so gracious in her acceptance of her new Onu into her life.

Paavo watched as she exchanged the lavender crayon for an inky eggplant color. She was so sure of herself at such a young age; Paavo hadn't carried himself with half as much poise until after he'd returned from New York with the skills and wrestling savvy he'd learned from the team, as well as the confident way the rest of Nico's teammates had wel-

PIA PADUKONE

comed him into the fold, no questions asked. He watched as Claudia tilted her head to the side, the apex of her tongue sticking out of her mouth as she directed her full concentration to the page.

"Onu, you have to sign your page," Claudia said. "That's how I'll remember that you did that one. Like this." He watched as she scribbled her name in the lower corner, below a rainbow-colored crab. Claudia was left-handed.

Paavo remembered how teachers in grade school had always tried to correct the left-handed students, silently but constantly transferring pencils to their right hands as they completed math problems or wrote sentences. Even the words in Estonian, *pahem* meaning left and worse and *parem* meaning right and better, exacerbated the cultural preference. Even Nico's nickname on the wrestling team—Lefty—called out his handedness.

At first, the thought bypassed Paavo like a breeze. So many people are left-handed. But as he watched Claudia fill in an octopus's arm with varying shades of red, he stared hard at her face. Claudia wasn't a spitting image of Mari, not really. She had a ski-bump nose. She had stubby digits in contrast to Mari's graceful piano fingers. She had a heart-shaped hairline. He did some quick math in his head. Claudia had been born exactly nine months after Nico left Tallinn. It couldn't be. Could it?

The questions nearly tumbled out of his mouth to Claudia, who wouldn't have known the first place to begin. When had it happened? Where had Paavo been? Why, when Mari hadn't shown the slightest interest toward Nico during his four months with the Sokolovs? Did Nico know? Did *Claudia* know?

By the time Mari came in the door, Paavo had worked his brain into such a state that he was impressed with his ability to settle Claudia on the couch with a DVD and a snack without arousing her suspicions. The inner workings of his mind were frenetic with pulses, synapses firing rapidly one after the other in quick succession. He was pacing in the foyer as Mari came back in, holding several bags, her cheeks rosy from the chilled air.

"How was it?" he asked. He couldn't keep the sneer out of his voice. "Did you get everything you needed?"

Mari looked taken aback. "Yes. Thank you for staying with her," she said. "What's with the attitude?"

"Claudia. She's left-handed."

"Yes, so?" Mari said, setting her bags down. "Don't tell me you believe in all that handed mumbo jumbo."

"Nope. That's not it at all," Paavo said, continuing to pace back and forth across the perimeter of the foyer. "You know who else is left-handed? Do you?"

"Well, lots of people, I'd imagine," Mari said. "What's this about, Paavo? Stop pacing—you're making me nervous."

"Nico." Paavo stopped in front of her. "Nico Grand is left-handed. Who is Claudia's father, Mari? Enough of this impossible secrecy."

Mari looked down at the floor, pushing her shoes off with her toes.

"I thought I was the one who was obsessed with riddles. But I solved this one, didn't I? What prize do I win?"

"Okay, enough, Paavo. Yes. It's him."

"Obviously, it's him. Claudia has his nose, his fingers, his brow... Did you think I was stupid, the two of you? All those years ago just because I was so timid, you decided to parade around my back together and get, well, pregnant?"

"It wasn't like that, Paavo," Mari said. "It's a lot more complicated." She reached her hands out toward Paavo but he shrugged away.

"Please, Mari," Paavo said, rolling his eyes. "I may be inexperienced with women, but I know how some things work. The crazy thing is, he was *my* exchange student. You barely showed the slightest interest in him while he was there. I can't believe you hid this from me."

"I don't know what to say," Mari said, looking down at the ground. "This is the whole reason I didn't want to tell you."

"What, because I would get upset? Damned right I would. At the very least," Paavo said. "Does *she* know?" He nodded toward the living room. Mari shook her head. "Are you going to tell her?"

She put her hands on Paavo's to calm him, but he shrugged them off. "Maybe someday I'll tell her," Mari said. "But right now, it isn't relevant. We don't need anyone else. We have each other."

"That's so far beside the point, Mari," Paavo said. "I feel like a complete moron. You've completely duped me. And Ema, Papa, and Nico—"

"They know," Mari interrupted. "But Nico doesn't. You can't tell him."

"What, Nico doesn't know that he slept with my sister? Did you drug him? Was he unaware of having had sex with you?"

"Paavo! No, of course not. I meant that he doesn't know about Claudia."

Paavo shook his head. "This is too much. I can't believe this, Mari. I can't believe that had CallMe not sent me here, I'd never have seen you. I'd never have figured this out. What if Claudia hadn't wanted to color? I'd still be left in the dark. I need to clear my head. I'll see you later." He pushed past Mari and walked out the door into the chilled night air.

"Don't go like this, Paavo. Claudia really loves you. And you're my brother."

"Exactly my point."

Paavo stalked the five kilometers back to his hotel, muttering and exploding in anger every so often. By the time he let himself into his room, he had worked himself into such a state that he fell into the bed and fell fast asleep. He dreamed of little Claudia taking a position on a padded wrestling mat in a purple singlet, and Nico, stepping forward to show her how to take down an opponent.

NICO

When Nico was in Buffalo, he dreamed of Mari for the first time in years. He hadn't thought of her since college, when each night before a wrestling match, he would picture her face with its electric-blue eyes and tight lips and masturbate silently, his roommate asleep in the bed a few feet from his. The first time he'd done it, he'd felt so ashamed, staring at his reflection in the dorm room bathroom, his face flushed from the exertion. But it had helped him wrestle so well the following day, that it became his routine. His college coach had clapped him on the back after he had stepped off the mat and removed his headgear. "Grand—that was fantastic. Where did that come from?" Nico had shrugged humbly, but he knew the exact origin of his strength and focus and he'd grinned to himself. Conjuring Mari became his good luck charm, one that he would never share with his teammates because he was embarrassed, and because he felt proprietary over her, over his ability to perform because of her.

It was a little pathetic; he knew that. But it worked. And at the end of the day, winners weren't pathetic.

On that first day on the campaign trail in St. Louis, he awoke in the middle of the night, his throat parched and his knees aching. He felt inadequate; as the youngest chief campaign advisor on any senatorial ticket, there were constant reminders of his youth and inexperience. It seemed that every other staffer was a campaign veteran who all seemed to start their conversations with, "Back on the Dukakis trail…" or "When we were working the Mondale polls…" It didn't seem that Nico could ever catch up. But the congresswoman was using Nico's speech in the morning, to address a convention hall filled with ironworkers who were losing faith in the ability of their union. Nico hoped that his words would renew and reinforce the bonds between unions and the congresswoman's campaign, and had industriously peppered the speech with metaphors like "forging ties," "welding us together," "soldering our best parts to create a stronger union." He felt sick; was there time to rewrite the whole speech? Nico flipped through channels and scrolled through his cell phone in an effort to distract himself. Just as he was about to call the front desk to see if he could score some NyQuil, Mari's face flashed across the screen. There she was, stalking the runway, wearing oversize fluffy white wings and a barely there black lace bra and matching underwear. She walked on sky-high heels, moving forward with poise and ease, with the slightest smirk on her face. She'd made it across the Atlantic divide. There she was, on national television. Did that mean she'd made it here, as well? He felt momentarily betrayed. She'd promised to get in touch if her career brought her stateside. But perhaps the commercial had been filmed in Europe. As soon as she'd been there, she was gone.

He quieted his indignation and focused on the task at

hand. Muting the television, awash in the flickering lights of a late-night talk show, he performed his ritual and was asleep in no time. He knew it was shameful, imagining the woman who had taken his virginity six years ago.

"It's just this once," he told himself that evening. But then the following night, after a treacherous Q-and-A session with a dozen degenerate journalists who poked holes in his responses and bullied him into near submission, he begged out of drinks with the rest of the staff and retreated to his hotel room, flipping channels for that ad again, and when he failed to find it, he Googled her. He'd had no idea she had hit it so big; there were pages and pages filled with her, scantily clad, or zoomed in to her perfect features. He clicked and scrolled for hours, reintroducing himself to her adult self. Her cheekbones had become more angular and her lips soft and pillowy. He remembered how she held her body erect, posture being of utmost importance above all, the slant of her tweezed eyebrows, her nervous habit of drumming her long fingers against her thighs.

At breakfast each morning, where he disciplined himself to have two cups of black coffee, a banana and a small bowl of yogurt while on the campaign trail, his fellow staff members would eat warily, their faces down to their meals, but their eyes alert toward everything happening around them. Nico couldn't help but smile into his coffee with each sip and think of all the goodness that Mari had brought him. He was sure she had no idea what that afternoon had meant to his life's trajectory. Unknowingly, she had charged his confidence levels, increasing his ability to speak up for himself, and in turn, pushing him into the spotlight. Nico was no longer timid about what he wanted; he saw and went after it. And when he felt the slightest weakness or doubt, he would remember how strong he'd felt in those weeks after he'd returned from Tallinn, how capable and assured, helping him to ultimately retrain his eye on the prize.

The days were getting longer and longer, each one feeling as though there were five or six of them packed into a single one. Nico wrote each speech as though he were delivering them. He sat in his hotel room, estranged and removed from the rest of the team, composing sentences and ideologies in his head before committing them to paper. He imagined the roar of the crowd upon the oration of a paragraph, the tension and the voice mounting over and over again. The drama was what engaged him, the excitement of the enormous host of people looking over the room or the hall or the arena. Nico longed to be behind the podium for longer than just sound check. He wanted to feel the charge of it, but most of all, he wanted the people to know that they were his words. He'd thought that having his words aired and applauded might be enough, but instead, each speech made him increasingly bitter that someone else was passing off his own work. Watching the congresswoman deliver his work was proof that Nico could turn a phrase beautifully, that he was insightful and thoughtful. He knew he could bring a crowd to its feet, even if the intonation and the elocution weren't his. His desire to conjure Mari each evening turned from a pure and simple need to a fulfillment of frustration. He knew he was getting complacent by imagining her each night, but by the sixth week on the trail, he had dug himself into a hole so deep, there was no getting out.

The next morning's speech was of the greatest magnitude; the teacher vote was the widest margin they had of that election year, and to be able to clinch them would mean a certain win for their team. The speech was to be given to a hall filled with educators, and the congresswoman was going to discuss her devotion and commitment to the future of education, to the sense of self that had been lost in the power of teaching young people recently. The idea was fueled by the one that all teachers should take a huge sense of pride in teaching because they were the ones that would be remembered above all else, above the lessons and the exams and the final papers. It would be their style, their voices, their presences that students would ultimately recall years later. Nico had written it as a lecture in a school hall, with audience participation, modeled after a TED talk, complete with slides and clicker that he would control as the congresswoman would stroll across the deep stage, offering Nico's words, accepting Nico's applause.

But the congresswoman hadn't emerged at breakfast that morning and after a few urgent calls to her room, which were answered and met with dead silence, Nico found himself rapping on her door with one hand while he held his cell phone in the other, with the congresswoman's chief of staff on speakerphone. Mike Raimi's wife had delivered their third son the morning before, and Mike was taking the call from the waiting room of the hospital on the Upper East Side in New York City. The congresswoman opened the door wrapped in a hotel blanket, sniffling and hacking into a tissue. She held up a hotel memo pad, upon which she'd scribbled, "Lost my voice. Can't talk."

"Shit," Nico had muttered. "Shit, shit, shit. Mike, she lost her voice."

"Shit. Fuck." The words lost their gravitas through the tinny quality of the speakers. "I'll get on the next train."

"Absolutely not, Mike. Your wife will kill you. You can't leave your family. Let's think, let's think. What if...what if we just do a meet and greet instead of the speech?" Nico asked, stepping into the room. "A handshake op or a...a press conference? I could field the questions."

"No way, Nico," Mike said. "This one is way too important. We can't lose this opportunity. Figuera already deposited the remainder of his campaign fund into the Board of Ed. We have to make our mark. That speech is our only hope. It has to be delivered." The congresswoman nodded vehemently, before collapsing into a round of hacking coughs, and pointed at Nico.

"No. No way, Shelley."

"What? What's she saying?" Mike asked.

"That I should give the speech."

"You know, it's not a terrible idea, Nico," Mike said.

"Me?" Nico said, his voice rising higher. "I'm just behind the scenes."

"Look, we're going to lose them unless we deliver with gusto. If it were anyone else, I'd be on the next train there, but you can handle this. You've got presence, charisma. Just add a prologue explaining the circumstances and who you are. They're your words—you might as well deliver them."

Nico couldn't deny it: he'd imagined this day from the moment he had set foot inside Francis Foley's ad hoc campaign office. Each sentence he crafted on behalf of another person was another layer of proof of how much he desired for the people to truly pay attention to the man behind the curtain. But other than reading his words aloud to ensure rhythm and cadence, he hadn't practiced at all. Just like that first day when he'd learned he had two days to apply for the Hallström program or miss his chance altogether, he seized it.

"Okay," Nico said, looking at the congresswoman, lying supine and camouflaged amongst a barricade of plush white pillows. "I'll do it."

From: EESTIRIDDLER723
To: HEADLOCK12
July 27, 2009

Dear Nico,
Circumstances unite us, but they don't make us stay together. Circumstances and complete folly, complete coincidence have brought us together, but no glue exists that forces us to stick by one another.

There are a million reasons why we should have revolved out of one another's orbits, but one major one as to why we haven't. Did you ever wonder? Did you ever consider that every action has a reaction? Lest you mistake this for one of my riddles, I'll just say that on a recent trip to Moscow, I learned something—presumably by accident—that hasn't been sitting well with me at all. I'll let you figure out the punch line.

From: HEADLOCK12
To: EESTIRIDDLER723
August 16, 2009

P-Train,
I'm sorry we haven't been able to connect in a while. Things have been

busy and frenetic, but I have called you a few times. Have you not received my voicemails? I got your email, and I have spent the last few
weeks puzzling over it. I read it over and over, even printed it out and
carried it around with me, staring at it like one of those Magic Eye posters, as though the answer would miraculously appear in front of me. I'm
honestly stumped. Clearly I did something to offend you or your family, but I'm at a loss. I've never even been to Moscow, so I can't imagine
what you're talking about.

Can you give me a hint? Are you okay? Do you need anything? Money?
Do you want to come visit? I'd love to have you. You can meet Ivy and
travel with me. I'd come see you guys, but it's just not the right time.
We're working toward the election next year, and they've packed my
schedule pretty tightly. I have a lot of work to do if I'm going to step it
up and take it to the next level. I've never felt so responsible in my life.
It's sort of an overwhelming feeling, like I'm walking on ice; any minute
I'm going to eff up. Anyway, I want to talk about your letter, so please
give me a call.

From: HEADLOCK12
To: EESTIRIDDLER723
September 4, 2009

I haven't heard from you, but I am going to chalk it up to how busy you
are with CallMe. By now, you must be back in Tallinn. How are things
with CallMe? Any updates? I can't wait to try it out. When are you guys
going global?

I'm still feeling really weird about your last email. I'm going to keep
writing to you until you write back. I'm going to keep sending you flowers
and throwing stones at your window. And if that doesn't work, I'm going
to stand outside your house wearing a trench coat and a giant 80s style
boom box. (Did you ever see that movie?)

Paavo, man, talk to me.

From: HEADLOCK12
To: EESTIRIDDLER723
October 12, 2009

I'm really starting to feel like a needy boyfriend here. What did I do? Send me a riddle, anything. I'm desperate.

NICO

Tallinn
April 2010

It was the same and it was completely different. The air smelled the same—chilly, unassuming and somehow mysterious. But this time, Nico could pinpoint the mystery: fear. When he'd arrived in 2002, the fear was of the unknown, of this family, of the people who might or might not welcome him into their lives. This time, the fear was of what this country had become in the past eight years since he'd been here. His contact with the Sokolovs had been intermittent at best; he'd emailed with Leo for a few months after he returned home, but after a while, his own responses had petered out once he got on the campaign trail. But it was unlike *Paavo* to drop all contact. Paavo, with his puppy-dog loyalty to respond and to initiate conversations. Paavo, who has set up a multimillion-dollar organization in the back room of a two-bedroom apartment in Lasnamäe, a corporation that went public last year. A corporation that was sure to bring Estonia—and the Sokolovs— a great deal of esteem and fanfare. *Perhaps the fame has changed him,* Nico thought to himself. Not that he blamed him. Nico knew that he had changed—his temperature had cooled. He had less time for trivial matters. He returned phone calls and emails rather discriminatorily, with an unspoken underlay of *What's in it for me?*

There was still no direct route to Tallinn from New York, so Nico flew once again through Stockholm, purchasing an overpriced cup of coffee at Arlanda and watching the flow of people as they settled into the gate to await the connection to Tallinn. This time, the plane was full. This time, the passengers came in assorted flavors and colors: Japanese businesspeople carrying slim laptops; tall, statuesque women who resembled models; techies wearing wrinkled cargo pants with headphones wrapped around their heads; polished, Scandinavian designers. Nico's mission was twofold. First, to find Paavo and ask him what gives regarding his cryptic emails to which he'd left no reply thereafter, and second, to have a vacation of some sort for the first time in five years.

After that first speech that Nico had delivered on the congresswoman's behalf, events had tumbled forward in great succession. The Teachers Union had responded so positively to his words that Nico was promoted to chief of communications, the congresswoman's second in command for public appearances. Nico began fielding questions for open press hour single-handedly, delivering speeches when there was a clash in scheduling, and generally providing the campaign with a great burst of youth, energy and bravado. Nico's reputation in turning the congresswoman's campaign attracted the attention of Mark Strong, the leading contender for New York Senate, and he was poached quietly and neatly out from under the congresswoman's nose to be Strong's chief of staff. People had never met anyone like Nico. He walked into a room and owned it, his confidence blooming out in front of him, owning topics that he had no background in, sometimes making things up as he went along. His ability to weave oratory was keen, skilled, patient. His voice had a calm timbre that attracted listeners, whether or not you were a believer in the agenda he was pushing.

During his time in Albany, he received multiple side requests to pen speeches—from CEOs of corporations, from figureheads asked to deliver commencement addresses; once even a hopeful Oscar Award nominee, who had heard of Nico's unique ability to sculpt words and wanted them in her clutch for the evening. He took them all on, charging exorbitant fees for his time but churning out pages and pages of inspiring text for all manner of clients.

But when Paavo's puzzling email came through, and there was no response, Nico realized that he could use a vacation. Why not Tallinn? It was where it had all started. Nico owed a lot to Tallinn for crafting him into the force he was today.

The terminal seemed to have tripled in size since he'd first landed in 2002, but then again, he felt larger, too. Not in weight or appearance, but in mentality. He'd gotten skilled. Wrestling was a lot like politics. He'd learned to use his brain the same way he used his body on the wrestling mat—negotiating releases, anticipating moves. Wrestling wasn't just about your own ability; it was about being able to read your opponent, gauging how his mind worked to be one step ahead of him to see where he wanted to go.

As Nico's heels clicked against the parquet, he noticed a huge reading space near a café. *Take a book, leave a book.* There were sections in Estonian, Swedish, Finnish. In the English section, Nico plucked *Riddle-Me-This: Brainteasers Not for the Faint of Heart* off the shelf and stuffed it into the side pocket of his messenger bag. Next to the library was a charging area where you could charge practically any device for free. And Nico's phone picked up a wireless signal almost immediately. For free. There really had been a technology revolution in this country; Paavo hadn't been wrong.

He stood on the threshold of the Sokolovs' kitchen door. He could hear movement inside and Vera's steely voice speaking in rapid-fire Estonian. Nico found himself yearning to burst through the door, but another voice responded almost immediately. That was Leo's gravelly timbre, responding in long elegant sentences. Nico could barely remember Leo speaking more than a few words at a time, much less in this language, this new language that appeared more foreign to Nico than ever before.

Nico tapped at the door. The conversation continued— rolling vowels, staccato consonants striking against the others. He tapped again, a little louder this time. Footsteps neared and the door flung open.

"*Tere,*" Nico said. "Surprise!"

"Nico?" Vera stepped back. "You are here. What is it? Is everything all right?"

"Everything's fine," Nico said, stepping into the house. It smelled comfortingly the same as it had eight years ago, like rye bread, yeast-filled and hoppy. Leo was sitting at the round table with the flower-patterned cloth in the middle of the kitchen, which looked exactly and comfortingly the same. It was as though he'd stepped back in time to 2002. "I just wanted to come for a visit. I haven't seen you guys in, well, eight years. Can you believe it?"

"Sit, sit," Vera said, pulling a chair out. "But why didn't you call?"

"The looks on your faces were worth it," Nico said, sinking into the chair. "I didn't mean to scare you. I'm really sorry."

"Where you are staying?" Leo asked, reaching across the table to shake his hand. His eyebrows were up, but he hadn't smiled. Not yet.

"What are you talking about, Levya? He's staying here," Vera said, kneading her hands into Nico's shoulders.

"No, no," Nico said. "I've already checked in to my hotel in Old Town. I am just here to visit you guys." He turned to Leo. "Was that you speaking Estonian?"

Leo's face broke open, and Nico nearly staggered back from the effect it had on him. Leo's smile was like a meteor shower; if you missed it, you might have to wait for days, even years to see it again. It hit Nico just then how inured to smiling he had become. It was like second nature to him. He smiled automatically, in line for coffee, on the subway, sitting behind his desk when he picked up the phone. In the public eye, if you didn't smile, it meant you were hiding something of which you were ashamed. Nico smiled so much sometimes that at the end of the day, his face hurt.

"*Jah,*" Leo said. "I passed the test. I am legal now."

"You have been legal," Vera said. She clutched the hairs at the scruff of his neck and tugged them gently. "But yes, Leo is finally an official citizen. With a red passport to prove it."

"Congratulations," Nico said. "That's amazing news. How'd you do it?"

"Study, study, study," Leo said.

"Good for you," Nico said. "That's just incredible news. Where is Paavo?"

"Oh, no, Nico," Vera said, her voice dropping an octave. "He did not tell you? He has moved to Prague permanently. It was supposed to be only for a short while, but CallMe asked him to stay on and use Prague as the base to open other satellite offices. He's the—what is his exact job, Leo?"

"Chief programming officer."

"Wow. That's quite a title."

"But you! Paavo said some time ago that you are in politics. Are you going to be president? Can we say we know you?" Vera asked. She poured a cup of coffee and slid it across the table to Nico.

Nico felt himself turning on his smile. "One step at a time. I've been pretty active in city politics, trying to work my way up to an elected seat one day. Not a big deal. But CallMe went public. *That's* huge."

"Yes, okay." Leo waved the comment away. "It is easy to become famous in Estonia. It is so small. But to stand out in a city like New York, in a country like America, this is truly great."

"Right now, it is not so easy to find work in Estonia. So for Paavo to be so busy is lucky. Finding work is difficult these days, so if young people can afford it, they go abroad. Paavo was smart to take an interest in computers," Vera said. "I don't truly understand what it is that he does for CallMe, but he has money and he is happy and that is all that matters."

"I guess I…we haven't talked in a while." Nico felt suddenly foolish. What had he been thinking, coming to Estonia on a whim? He took the book that he'd found in the airport out of his bag. "Will you give him this when you see him next?"

"Of course, Nico." Vera looked at the title and smiled.

"Anyway, I want to hear about everything. The test, Paavo, Mari. I've seen the Victoria's Secret ads. She's really taken off. Is she still living in Moscow? Can I take you to dinner?" Why was he acting so desperate? It felt as if he'd run into mutual friends of an ex and was trying to glean any information he could without showing that he cared about this person he was supposed to have completely extricated from his life. He had Ivy now. It didn't matter. It shouldn't matter.

"That will be nice, Nico," Vera said. "I can put the *sult* away for another day. Unless you would want some?"

"No, no," Nico said, rising from the table. "Save the *sult*. Come on, my treat."

There hadn't been a restaurant like this eight years ago. When Nico first visited Tallinn, the few times the Sokolovs had eaten out together had been to a restaurant that served more of the same kind of food that Vera made at home, so he hardly saw the point in going out in the first place. It was all Estonian missionary food, heavy roasts and potatoes, sweet and tangy jams and globs of mayonnaise. All the restaurants looked similar: wooden and oppressive, with chairs that shook the room when you pulled them out, sometimes with long, communal picnic-like tables at which you were forced to rub elbows with the party seated next to yours. But the restaurant that Leo and Vera and Nico had walked to—walked to!—in the newly built Kumu Art Museum seemed as if it could have been constructed on the Lower East Side, all light and air and minimalistic design. The food was presented in delicate portions, with ingredients leaning against one another intricately like the modern art Nico never understood.

Their stainless steel table overlooked the entryway to the museum and Nico noticed as tourists meandered up the path, clutching guidebooks in different languages. He didn't have a recollection of much tourism, even though Eesti High School was in Old Town. In the summers, Paavo had told him, the streets were filled with people from the cruise liners pulled into the seaplane harbor, spilling people onto the narrow twisty streets as they negotiated cobblestones on their wobbly sea legs. The restaurant was full; some tourists, but also smartly dressed locals and a few raucous businessmen and women were seated around a large oval table where there was clearly a lot of Viru Valge being passed around. Leo turned down the offer of a cocktail and instead chose a glass of red wine, which he proceeded to sip throughout the evening.

"So tell me," Nico said, once their orders had been placed. "I'm sorry I've been so bad about keeping in touch. Paavo and I traded emails for ages, so I got all your news from him. But I guess with work and everything, we sort of lost contact. Tell me about the test."

"He did very well," Vera said, patting Leo's hand. "I was so proud of him."

"After four tries," Leo scoffed. "At some point, they were bound to run out of questions."

"They make it very difficult for you," Vera said. "It's not right. It's not fair." Leo put his hand over Vera's and gave it a gentle squeeze.

"Well, better late than never." Nico raised his tumbler of vodka and clinked it against Leo's wineglass. "Does it feel different?"

"Yes and no," Leo said. "I can vote now. And I can travel without feeling like I am being denied entry to my own country."

"You didn't tell him the biggest news of all," Vera said. "Go on. Don't be shy."

"What?" Nico asked. He found himself hoping it was some news about Mari.

"The chickens," Vera said. "Say it, Leo."

"You finally got rid of them?" Nico asked. "God, you hated those things."

Vera laughed. "Guess again. He got his own."

"You didn't," Nico said. "You're a changed man, Leo Sokolov."

After a small tussle over the check—Nico insisted on paying—they walked out. The food had been excellent— Scandinavian in its preparation and arrangement, and plentiful, but Nico got up from the table feeling hollow. What was Paavo's word? *Dusha.* Soul. The food had been bereft of it. He rubbed his stomach. He hadn't thought he might miss all that soporific meat, the leaden way his head and stomach felt after a classic Estonian meal. He didn't want to go back to his hotel room after this meal. He would feel even emptier. Why hadn't he insisted that Ivy join him on this trip? He wished he'd known that Paavo wasn't going to be here.

As he held the door open for Vera, someone grabbed his arm. "Nico?"

Nico answered "Yes?" before he turned to see the man's face. As soon as he did, he was unsure. The man was tall, dirty blond, pale. A scar stretched across his jaw like a threat, and his clear blue eyes were reminiscent of a bottle of Bombay Sapphire gin, a gentle reminder that Nico shouldn't drink anymore. It was important to remain clear, levelheaded. That just because he wasn't in a New York City restaurant didn't mean that his behavior couldn't get back to constituents back home.

The man's face burst into a smile. "I thought it was you. What are you doing here?"

Nico plastered his public smile across his face. He could already feel his vocal cords calibrating before he launched into his politic spiel.

"I'm visiting…" Nico faltered. He held his hand out. "I'm sorry. I'm very sorry, I don't remember…"

"Heigi." The man grasped Nico's hand in his own and

pumped it up and down furiously. "From Eesti. You sat in front of me in Estonian Literature."

"Heigi," Nico said, even though he wasn't sure at all. "Yes, of course. Do you remember Paavo? These are his parents."

"The famous Paavo," Heigi said. "*Tere*, it is good to meet you all. You must be so proud. What luck running into you. I'm having a party this evening. You must come, all of you. Come."

At ten thirty, Nico found himself walking from his hotel down the one long street of Old Town that didn't have a dead end. Walking through these quaint, cobblestone streets didn't dredge up any memories as he thought it might. In fact, he couldn't remember half of the squat yellow buildings that surrounded him; he was sure that most of the shops didn't exist when he went to school a few streets over. Or was Eesti High School that way? Every which way he turned, there were bookstores and restaurants and souvenir shops, which even at that hour of night were open and lively. There were entire stores devoted to Baltic amber, and window fronts glowed from the golden stones embedded in necklaces, key chains and charms. He felt disoriented and lost from the pallor of jet lag that was starting to cast its dreary shadow over him.

He found himself grateful for the multiple—free—wireless signals that his phone picked up during the walk from his hotel to the address that Heigi gave him, and the little blue dot that stood for his location was starting to blink closer and closer to his destination.

Nico marveled at Europe. He had forgotten how the streets in this continent were built hundreds of years ago, that there had been countless wars, political battles and social revolutions that had taken place right where he stood. The grandeur of New York City didn't stand up to this kind

of history, however electric the vibe was at any given hour.
It reminded Nico of how in high school, they'd spent one
year on world history, one on European and two years on
American history, a country with a fraction of the history of
the rest of the world. He thought back to his apartment, to
his parents' apartment, to the art galleries and hot-dog carts
and the trees rich with color in Central Park and of how he
wouldn't trade it for the world, for any other history than
the one his city had made for itself in its short life. But he
had to admit that the Old World was certainly charming.

The narrow street took a slight uphill, and his legs began
dragging. The street was lit on either side by gauzy, yellow
streetlamps, and the click of his heels reverberated across the
buildings on either side of the street. A fleeting but vivid
memory skittered across his mind of dashing across these very
cobblestones with Paavo. Why were they running? The GPS
on his phone confirmed that he was at his destination and
he looked up. He could hardly believe it. He hadn't put the
two together when Heigi scribbled down the address, but
he was standing in front of Pikk 59, the exact place that he
and Paavo had scrambled into after they had been running
from someone. Paavo told him to run, so he'd run. And then
Paavo showed him the structure, and they walked around
to the courtyard, found a broken window and crawled inside. The windows that led to the basement were bricked
and silent, but the face of the building was still regal with its
arched windows and terraced promontories. He could hear
the party from the ground floor, lots of laughing, talking,
and he was sure he'd heard three champagne corks open in
rapid succession.

Nico rode the gilded cage elevator up to the top floor. The
door opened before he'd even had a chance to ring the bell.

"Nico!" A woman put her glass of wine on the ground

and leaned forward to press her cheek against his. "I thought we'd never see you again." *This must be how Nora feels all the time,* Nico thought. Why does everyone recognize me, but I can't place them? He slipped his shoes off next to the pile in the entryway and examined the slim woman with long, dark lashes and blond hair with dark roots, a style that looked regal on her rather than trashy. *The European advantage,* he thought.

"Katrin," Nico said, suddenly recalling her name. "I thought you'd be living in Paris or something."

"Ah, that was a childhood dream," she said. "But I have a new one. Well, I suppose he's more of a reality. Tim, come meet Nico. Tim, Nico spent a few months on an exchange program here when we were in high school. Tim is a pilot. He's based in Toronto."

"Katrin, let him through the door," Heigi called. "Then you can show off your new arm candy."

"He's not my arm candy. He's my fiancé." Katrin glowered at Heigi, but she stepped aside to let Nico into the living room. There were at least a dozen people milling about, but the space was so large it hardly appeared full.

"Come, let's get you a drink," Heigi said.

"This is huge," Nico said, following Heigi around the curve of the living room that led to the kitchen. "Does my memory serve me right? Isn't this—"

"The former home of the KGB?" Heigi smiled. "Sure is. Second only to the Bat Cave. How cool is that? My company just finished the work, and I moved in a few months ago."

Heigi's real estate company focused on buildings with histories. They sought out architectural commodities, gutted the insides, gave the facades a face-lift and resold individual lots inside at what, Nico figured, judging by the scotch collection clustered on the bar, must be an abhorrent price.

"People are dying to live here," Heigi said. Nico thought

about the irony of Heigi's statement. People had been dying in here long before Estonia had been declared independent. They'd been tortured in the building's very basement and the windows were still bricked up in a nod to the attempt to stifle their screams. He thought about Vera's parents. Had they been brought to this building before being sentenced to work themselves to death in a Siberian work camp? Nico wanted so badly to ask Heigi what the plans were for the basement. He pictured a finished game room or a communal bar area where residents could gather, immune and ignorant of all that had occurred around them.

"Are you sure you don't want something stronger?" Heigi asked, passing Nico a glass of wine.

"I'm sure," Nico said.

"So, have you been doing this for a while?" Nico asked, taking dainty sips.

"Real estate? Nah. It's something new. I started out in construction after Eesti, and then a few years later, I met Magnus." He nodded toward a broad man in a deep blue suit who was talking animatedly to a woman whose face Nico couldn't see. "He's Finnish, you see. He was just starting out with the Linna Group when we met. They take over some of the most pivotal structures in major European cities. People are clamoring for these addresses. It's incredible what they will pay in order to say that they live on the site of the Führerbunker in Berlin. It's like, the more notorious, the higher the price. It's quite disgusting, really." Heigi laughed, and poured himself another few fingers of scotch.

"Who are all these people?"

"Actually, I don't know most of them. Friends of friends and so on. The girls in that corner you know. They went to Eesti. You know Katrin, and there's Made and Urve. And their boyfriends," he whispered. "All rich. All foreign."

"I guess those are the circles you run in now," Nico said. He was starting to feel a bit nauseous and wished he'd taken Vera and Leo up on their offer of a nightcap at their home instead. "You have to go after the big fish, right?"

"Oh, they're not my clients. They're the golden ticket out for those gals."

"What do you mean?"

"They've had it with this country. They'd be out of here by now if they could. But they can't, so they do the next best thing. Marry up and out."

"That seems sort of harsh. I thought they all work."

"I'm not accusing them of being gold diggers. Maybe the word I'm looking for is *opportunist*."

Nico definitely felt sick. "What's so wrong with Estonia anyway?"

"Absolutely nothing, so long as you're in the right business. We're a tiny little country, but tech-wise, Estonia is at the forefront. We're going to be unbeatable one day. TIT is really heating up."

"Excuse me?" Nico nearly spit out a mouthful of wine.

Heigi chortled. "I'm surprised you're not well versed with the name by now. It's practically Paavo's second home. Tallinn Institute of Technology? It's where he started CallMe with those two guys from Mustamäe?"

Nico shifted his weight and took a long draught of wine. "I, er, haven't talked to Paavo in a while."

"Man, what a bright guy. He really played his cards right."

"It certainly seems so. But it seems he escaped, too, to Prague."

"Sure, for now. But he knows what he's doing. He'll be back. He's one of the leaders of the e-revolution. One of his mentees helped to reinvigorate the electronic voting system for the last election. We had more than sixty percent voter turnout."

"That's way more than the States could dream," Nico breathed. "Incredible."

"I know." Heigi smirked. "But of course, we're not perfect. We still have things to work on. If you're not in tech, or something related, there's a huge perception that life is greener outside our humble borders, so lots of people are leaving. For example, you know our generous maternity leave?"

"More than a year, right?"

"One hundred percent paid in full. You know why? We're hemorrhaging people. Losing them to other countries, other sectors all the time. That maternity policy is an incentive to get people to stay here. But I think it's only a matter of time before things begin to right themselves. You couldn't pay me enough to leave right now."

Nico smiled at Heigi's enthusiasm. It conjured Leo's fond love for this little country when they'd gone foraging for mushrooms all those years ago, even though he'd been denied an Estonian passport for most of his adult life.

"What about people like him?" Nico gestured toward Magnus, whose arm was around the woman he was speaking to, while the other was gesturing so wildly that the vodka in his glass sloshed over the side. Magnus's smile was all teeth and grimace, a shark circling its prey. "People are leaving, but he's coming in?" Nico felt suddenly protective of Estonia.

"The ones who see opportunity are in the right place at the right time," Heigi said. "While others are impatient to change their lives overnight."

Nico moved on to speak with Katrin and Urve, though Made didn't appear to remember him and disappeared onto the terrace with her boyfriend. But as the evening rode on—

ward into the early hours of morning, he felt really ill. Trendy food didn't necessarily mean better food, though he was fairly certain that the feeling in the pit of his stomach was despondency rather than food poisoning. What had happened to the innocence of this little fairy-tale country, with its Gothic steeples and cobblestone streets? With its electronic voting and omnipresent wireless connections, and its experimental tech labs into which neighboring countries were funneling money, its position at the forefront of the future seemed secure. Estonia had grown up. As Heigi rounded up the remaining guests to down shots of vodka on the roof, Nico thanked his host, bade a quick goodbye to the girls, took the winding stairs down to the street, where he could still hear the party echoing, and vomited against a bricked-up window of the former KGB headquarters of Tallinn.

Nico felt instantly sobered, though still confused and disoriented. He felt as if he'd just stepped off the plane in Tallinn for the first time back in September almost a decade ago. And just like that day in September, he felt completely displaced. He could identify the feeling now. It wasn't an upset stomach. He felt alone, completely alone in a city that was never truly his to begin with. Nico in Estonia without Paavo felt illegitimate; he had no reason to be there. He wasn't sure what happened between him and Paavo, but he was sure that he didn't belong here. He wasn't really sure who did.

NORA

New York City
March 2012

Nora had never felt more at home than she did in her office, the SafeSpace headquarters. And she was busier than
ever; her schedule was in overdrive. She'd gone from having
great gaps of time in her days with which to while away the
hours doing endless, interminable Google searches, having
long romantic lunches with Shahid in the student haunts near
Columbia, where he'd been hired as a tenure track professor, splitting apart the frayed ends of her hair, or when the
weather changed for the better, taking long, luxurious walks
along the lengths of New York City avenues. But then the
article in *New York* magazine had been published and the
ringer on her phone seemed as if it was broken—as soon as
she placed the receiver in its cradle, it would ring again; as
soon as she answered there would be the telltale beep of another caller waiting to get in touch with the psychoanalyst
Dr. Grand, whose name and reputation preceded her. She

had to hire a secretary to manage her calendar. She hadn't realized that there had been so many people who might need her, who needed the strength of her abilities. It was her creation—patent pending—that would allow her this sort of fame. That one published essay had reached all five boroughs, even parts of New Jersey and Westchester, pulling out all those disbelievers, all those skeptics who worried about their images, what they'd appear to be if they stared someone in the face and told them their problems. Pure humiliation could sometimes drive people away before they even had a chance to consider therapy. So Nora had created SafeSpace. This was like no other safe space in any other therapy session she'd monitored or observed. While technically, all therapy sessions were supposed to be safe, or you had no right to be holding one, SafeSpace was a darkened room with dim lighting where patients could sit or lie or stand erect, however it pleased them. When they were settled, they pressed the glowing green button and a screen would open on the other side whereupon Dr. Nora Grand would emerge and begin. She never saw them; they never saw her, much like a confessional in a Catholic church. But unlike those chiseled wooden screens, decorated with weeping angels and exuding the pungent aroma of a swinging metallic thurible, SafeSpace separated patients with a state-of-the-art slate slider with soundproofing when they just needed a moment—to cry, to talk out loud, to curse.

Throughout her schooling, Nora had scoffed at all the fads—the sleep therapy, the hypnosis—but during psych lab one day, on a particularly difficult run when she wasn't able to identify anyone, not her lab mates or even her advisor, she'd had a brain wave. She had to recognize her returning patients; she couldn't label a disorder or background with the wrong face. She would come across as unprofessional, undedicated, and her condition would undermine the hard work she'd put into everything she'd worked toward.

So she'd blindfolded her subjects, talking to them through microphones one at a time from the other side of a screen, her voice muffled and her body invisible, and realized the power of physical division. People didn't like admitting their feelings, their failings or shortcomings, especially not to a stranger. This was the inherent weakness in therapy in general, that you could always feel judged. Therapists were human, after all, and if someone kept returning to an abusive relationship, or couldn't extricate him- or herself from a deep-rooted gambling addiction, they sat smugly next to you, thinking they were better. They would never make those decisions; they would never stoop quite so low. Nora considered this idea for a long time. She thought first about using masks, but they were frightening to her. She thought about sleep masks, but that was dangerous, too, because patients couldn't see her but she could see them. Finally, she settled upon the dark partitioned room—a dark space, a *truly* safe space.

Between her nine and ten-fifteen appointments, she took a few minutes to unwind in her office. On her desk was the old black notebook that Nico had given her, though at the time he had been Nicholas. She had filled it up completely, but kept it on her desk as a constant reminder of how hard she had struggled in those early days. The notebook was next to a pile of the same issue of *New York* magazine. She grabbed a pair of scissors and cut the article out of one of the copies and folded it into an envelope to send to Paavo. The article was titled "Speak into the Dark" and reported Nora's evolution in creating SafeSpace in a wry but unchallenging tone.

She credited Paavo with her success. Talking through her fears had helped her realize her interests and motivations. If it hadn't been for his suggestion to take a few psych classes, she would have ended up a sad philosophy major with no direction, no employment opportunities and a rather unhealthy obsession with wanting to talk about Kierkegaard at dinner parties. Those few psychology classes had transformed her completely. In those final months when Paavo was living with the Grands, Nora was no closer to being able to identify faces than she was when she was first released from the hospital. But she could see one thing extremely clearly: her future in psychology. It had been from learning and studying herself that she'd felt herself transitioning toward the desire to study others. Her prosopagnosia morphed from a crutch to a catalyst.

Now, with her schedule book overflowing with new patients, she knew she'd made the right choice. It was clear that she wasn't alone in her fear of talking to complete strangers, and in her case, even friends and family. At its core, the inherent beauty of therapy was sharing your most intimate thoughts with a stranger, one who didn't know your background or what might be best for you in the long run. But the added benefit of SafeSpace was that you were truly talking to a stranger—someone who didn't even have to lay eyes upon you if you didn't want them to.

SafeSpace was opening up two more centers across the country; Nora's lab mate Stephan was the head of one of them in Chicago. He'd scorned her research at first, but ultimately came around when he saw the immediate results she received from participants who were previously unwilling to talk about their pasts. And she'd received interest from a psychiatrist in Lincoln, Nebraska, whose patient population consisted mostly of geriatrics, a group of baby boomers that seemed morally opposed to the idea of telling a stranger anything at all. She visited each of these offices, ensuring that

the screens were within her standards, that the soundproofing had been installed, and felt pretty darned smug about
her life's work thus far.

There was a knock at her office door and her new secretary poked her head in. "You have a new patient. Should I
send her in?"

"Give me three minutes, Sari," Nora said, gathering a
sheaf of fresh papers and scribbling with one of her pens to
make sure it worked. She clicked her glow light on and off
so she could see her notes while in the session. "Fresh tape?
We ran out just before lunch."

"Installed it before I stepped out."

"Background?"

"Just emailed it to you."

"Let me see." Nora double-clicked on the email. "No
name?"

"Opted out. She's F78A for the files." Nora smiled. This
secretary was already a good investment.

"Okay. Give me five instead. Thanks." A long, loping
scrawl filled the screen. Nora preferred Sari to scan in the
files directly so she could glean additional information from
patients' handwriting. So much of therapy was based on body
language and facial cues and tics; if she had to cut those out
in order to provide SafeSpace, she needed as much insight as
she could get. She scanned the paragraph, jotting down tidbits and buzzwords that she could refer to if conversation ran
dry during their time together, but silence was rare. While
this new patient had written quite a bit, it was all fluff; there
didn't appear to be much background to her story. Nora
frowned. The patient was a career woman whose past was
coming back to haunt her and she needed guidance to move
forward. Well, if that wasn't vague... Hopefully the woman
would say all she needed to say during her session. Nora made

sure the red light above her door was on, indicating that her patient was in place and that the session was already being recorded so that Nora could refer to it along with her notes when she debriefed in the evening. She gathered her pad, pen and glow light and pushed gently on the hidden door.

She blinked; it always took a moment for her eyes to adjust to the dark, but the track lighting she'd installed helped guide her to her chair. She could sense a body on the other side of the screen; the patient was seated and was jiggling her leg up and down. Nora settled into her chair. She extended her glow light. Her fingers holding the pen cast a long, eerie shadow against her pad.

She slid the listening screen open and leaned forward. "Hi. I'm Dr. Grand. I'm listening." The jiggling stopped, and Nora could hear knuckles cracking like slow popping corn, one after the other.

"Thank you for seeing me on such short notice," the woman said. She sounded husky yet lyrical, as though she had been singing all night in a smoky club. Nora almost expected her to begin to snap her fingers to the rhythm of her voice, which had a subtle accent. Polish? Swiss? Maybe even Dutch. "I know your office has been overextended since the publication of the article. Congratulations."

"Thank you," Nora said, twirling her pen. She knew this was a bad habit, as she wasn't adept at it, and the pen had often gone hurtling into the darkness. Nora had to clamber onto her hands and knees in the pitch black, her glow light too soft to extend into the corners of the room.

The jerking movements of the woman's leg, which she had started jiggling again, punctuated her speech but she made no attempt to quiet it. "I wanted to see you, particularly you, because I think you can help me."

"I'll do the best I can. But you know, I can't help you. I

can only help you figure out how to help yourself." Nora felt herself roll her own eyes as she ministered the mantra, but it was imperative to ensure that patients understood her role in therapy. She was no Band-Aid.

"Okay, sure. However you want to work. I guess I'll just tell you why I'm here."

Transcript of Patient F78A

I did something nine years ago. It wasn't a mistake and to this day, I don't regret it. But I regret how I approached it. That's partly why I'm here, to try to make things right. I'm at a point in my life where I'm ready to get serious with someone. I've dated a little bit, but I have finally met someone who makes me really happy, and my daughter likes him, too. She deserves a solid male figure in her life. Don't get me wrong…we've done great, just the two of us. But I can't move forward if I don't address what happened. I should probably back up to where it first began.

My career as a model started early. I remember having intellectual ambitions once. I don't want to be ungrateful, or pretend that the facts aren't the facts. I am beautiful. I'm lucky. I don't know what it's like to be overlooked or ignored because I've always stood apart. I'm sensitive about the fact that for some time, I also stood out for my brains. But once I was discovered, I started to travel down the modeling path, forgoing *kohuke* even though I loved it because it would give me cellulite and skipping cross-country skiing with my friends because it would accentuate all the wrong muscles.

But before you start to feel too sorry for me, know that I haven't lost out on everything. There's so much

I have received over the years because of my looks. I don't think it's fair, but that's the way of the world. It surprised me that it's not just a male thing. Women, too, would give me what I wanted, and I could get away with practically anything. I certainly haven't suffered.

When I first stated modeling, everyone I worked with said I was talented. That's another common misconception, that just because you have a look, that you'll be a good model. That's just not so. You have to learn the trade as much as you do anything else. You have to make it into a career; it's not just a side effect of your looks.

For a few years, it really seemed like this was my future. But then suddenly, things seemed like they were drying up. It was like my feet were in wet cement, trying to make my mark, but it was drying faster than I could move forward. Every time I almost extricated myself, another model slipped ahead of me. There's no explaining it. It's not that I'm ugly or fat or my eyes are too wide apart. Casting agents just want a certain "look." They can't explain it. They know it when they see it, and apparently for months, mine wasn't it. My agent and booker tried to get me jobs, but the Carmen Kass look was out for the time being. And while I know it's irrational, as a seventeen-year-old, I couldn't have felt less attractive. I needed to do something to pick myself up.

All my friends in high school were dating and having sex, but contrary to what it may look like, I was stalled. Papa was always afraid that my modeling would catapult me into the next generation, that I would grow up too fast, and I'd miss out on my childhood. But as a model, I hadn't had one date. All the male models were

too beautiful, truly good-looking, but there was nothing sexual about them. They were sculptures to look
at, not to touch. But in my very own house, there was
this high school kid who was staying with us as part of
a program. He was in my house for four months, no
strings attached. While he tried to play cool around
me, I could tell that I made him nervous. He blushed
when I spoke to him and flirted with me, and I knew
I could have him if I wanted. He was right downstairs.
I didn't even have to cross Toompuiestee.

After it happened, and Mama took me to the doctor over the summer, I was naturally frantic. But then
after some time, I realized it was my way out. I didn't
have to be in a situation where I had failed anymore,
where I felt transparent and second-rate. With a baby,
I had an excuse, but I also had a chance for reinven-
tion. I couldn't stay in Tallinn and sit back and watch
all the girls with the right look surpass me. I had to go
somewhere new, to the opportunity I'd been afforded
before I got pregnant, where they could look upon me
like a brand-new entity, exciting and fresh.

I never thought Papa would be as supportive as he
was. It was his idea that I go to Moscow. I had some
savings from my jobs, but he gave me the bulk of my
seed money and called some of his friends, who found
me the apartment where I lived until Claudia was born.
It was his dream to entice Ema there; that she would
want to help me and be closer to her grandchild, so that
eventually she would want to relocate to Moscow and
leave Tallinn behind. And she did. But once I started
on my own, I knew I had to continue on my own in
order to prove my strength to myself.

Before I got pregnant, I would see models that were

also mothers in the hallways at casting calls and I'd look down on them, laughing inwardly at how pathetic they seemed. They seemed so much older than me, wearing more makeup than they really needed in order to hide the fact that they had ten years on the rest of us. Some of them even brought their kids into the casting calls because they had no other choice. Those were the ones I actually felt really sad for. I couldn't help but go over and play with their children while they were audition-ing. One time before I had Claudia I even botched an audition so I'd help their chances of getting the job. They never did, poor things, not when they were com-peting against teenagers who had the dewy, fresh skin of the young, and longer, lithe bodies that hadn't held the fruit of a child. You can always make someone look older, but when you try to look younger, it's always so obvious and so sad.

When I first arrived in Moscow with that little seed in my belly, I realized with a jolt that I would have to be one of them. I imagined my days with horror, stand-ing in those same dank hallways, clutching the sweaty hand of my small child, feeling terrible because I felt so embarrassed having to tote her around and feeling even worse for feeling embarrassed. That is, until I began to rely on Ginevre and Sasha and their friends and their extended network.

They taught me how to work the system pretty quickly. Shortly after Claudia was born, I fired Viktor and hired an agent the girls recommended, who could practically guarantee magazine work. That's where the money is. Everyone thinks it's in runway, but the only perks of runway are that you get to keep the clothes. I had to pay her a much higher percentage, but it was worth it. I started small, modeling for book covers, bus wraps, food packaging. I graduated to makeup, shampoo ads; I was the face of a Russian national hair salon chain. The jobs kept pouring in; I was constantly working. I wasn't picky at first; I took the work when I got it, because it was that income over those few years that kept Claudia and me going. I'm raising Claudia to try to be as self-sufficient as possible, but there's a large part of me that wants to spoil the living hell out of her.

The group was not only supportive; it was smart. We'd all finagle things so that we wouldn't go after the same calls, so as not to incite rivalry and create division amongst ourselves. Some of us were taller, some shorter, some had a Eurasian look, some had an Anglo look, some were only being called in for legs, some for backs, some for runway, some for skin. But these women, these single mothers, we all became one another's families when we had no other, or that we'd been ousted from, or in my case, when we wouldn't allow ourselves to rely on them.

Looking back, I can't help but wonder if my behavior was cowardly. At seventeen, I thought it was the polar opposite. I thought I was being brave, by dealing with my problem myself. After Papa helped me secure the little bedsit three miles from Red Square, I refused any additional financial support from either of them. And while I wouldn't allow Ema to move in like she would have liked to in those early days, they visited frequently and got to know their granddaughter.

Even when I first saw Claudia, I was discouraged by how much she looked like her father. In fact, it infuriated me. I'd read that biologically, babies resemble their fathers so that they aren't abandoned or eaten by them.

Such a primordial notion, I'd thought to myself. I understood it, though. Because if he had had any inkling of where I was and what had happened to me after our one afternoon tryst, I feel fairly certain that he would have done the right thing by getting on the first plane to Moscow to be by our sides.

I say fairly certain, because the truth is, I didn't know him all that well. He was a guest in our home for a few months when I was a teenager. I didn't really make an effort while he was staying with us. I always liked him though, even though I stayed on the periphery. Mostly I liked the idea of him—just like the exchange program he was participating in, I'd thought he would be good for the family like a pet or a color TV or a tree house we could all build together in the backyard. It was like he could be our reverse family project. Somehow I miraculously believed that he would cheer Papa up from his mopey citizenship issues. I thought he might help my brother start to stand on his own two feet by listening to him and showing him how to be brave. Maybe I knew him better than I thought, because ultimately he ended up accomplishing those things.

And there's what he did for me. He doesn't know it, but he gave me hope that I could be more than just a body. Ironic, isn't it? Because being pregnant is just that: you're providing a body for another being to live in so that it can grow strong enough to come into this world. But he gave me what I needed when I was starting to doubt myself, and needed to feel alive. I've been forever grateful to him for comforting me that afternoon, for giving me Claudia, who has given me more joy than anyone could ever hope for.

I feel silly even saying it, but just in case it's not clear,

I'll say it out loud. It's Nico. It was him all these years, and I have kept it a secret because truly, what was the point? We were both basically children, and I didn't want to ruin his life with this information. Truth be told, I didn't know whether or not I would ever be able to face Nico again until things got serious with my current boyfriend, Javier. I didn't know whether or not I'd ever be forced to.

And so I've begun to prepare. I've actually rehearsed it, like I have for certain auditions where I have a line or two, replacing "Boys, come in for dinner," with "Oh, what a surprise. It's been years. In fact, your trip changed my life more than you could ever imagine. And here she is," and with that, I imagine that I will push Claudia forward.

In the interest of full disclosure, I'm not here because I want anything from him. I'm not seeking money or anything of the sort. Claudia and I are doing really well together. But she has a right to know who her father is, but not if he's not willing to be in her life or at least play a role in it. I can't subject her to that kind of pain at this point. Everyone should know the truth, including my partner, my daughter and her father. I think it's only fair.

I would have been happy to tell you this in the light, face-to-face, without any distractions. Not that I don't love the concept of SafeSpace; in fact, I think it's brilliant. The truth of the matter is, I didn't need to speak to a therapist. I needed to speak to you. We've never met, but I need your help to approach Nico. You're his sister. I need to know if it's okay to tell him. How should I do it?

I know this is a lot to handle, so I don't want you to respond right now. I will make a follow-up appointment in two weeks, and maybe we can discuss the situation more together.

★ ★ ★

The next morning, Nora sat very still on the edge of her bed, wrapped in a towel still damp from her morning shower, the ends of her hair dripping down her back like tadpoles. She felt unhinged. She had grappled with this knowledge on her own for nearly twelve hours; longer than she had thought was humanly possible. She had sat through enough broken ethical code hearings in the wood-paneled room at U Michigan to know that was the last thing she wanted to do in her first few years of her own practice. The session had been shocking, but it was what had happened afterward that had succeeded in toppling her completely.

After patient number F78A's jarring account, the woman exited SafeSpace, leaving Nora cloaked in the darkness, stunned beyond belief. Nora needed a drink. Eleven in the morning didn't quite merit a slug of whiskey, so she settled for coffee. The state-of-the-art coffee machine that Nora had installed in her private office worked too well sometimes; she no longer had the excuse to step outside to grab a cup of coffee, take a walk around the block and clear her head. But she had to leave.

The old-school diner stood on the corner like a lighthouse. Nora walked toward the counter, but she was distracted by a little girl's voice speaking in French. The girl had her hands folded over a white ceramic diner cup, and her top lip was covered in whipped cream.

"N'est-ce pas, Maman?" The woman had her back to Nora, but she could see the girl's face clear as day as she dipped her head back down to the mug and took another sip. It couldn't be. But it had to be. The girl's face was not only clear as day, it was also as clear as her brother's face. The girl had Nico's face. The woman with her back to Nora had to be Mari, who had just left the office. But how could she recognize a

face she hadn't even seen before? What kind of prosopagnosia was this, where she recognized faces she didn't know, but could also see other people within them? The whole thing was shocking: that Nico had a daughter, that she could see his face within hers. She didn't know where to begin.

The memory riled something in her, and she crouched farther over, allowing her hair to drip over her head onto the carpet below. Behind her, Shahid sat up, rubbing his eyes and his beard simultaneously, creating that wonderfully comforting scratching sound that Nora had come to equate with him.

"Hey," he said, his voice creaky with sleep. He reached over to catch some of the rivulets that were trailing down her back between his fingers. "What's wrong?"

Nora shook her head. "Just struggling with something from work. An ethical situation." Shahid had heard this before, many times. Nora was as sensitive as they came, and she often adopted her patients' challenges, dragging their depression home with her like a sack that she left by the door and glanced at from time to time while chopping vegetables at the butcher block in the kitchen. Sometimes she went into a trance-like state, staring at an invisible spot upon the ceiling, at which point Shahid had learned that she was just thinking about a particularly difficult patient and what she could say to help. He had learned quickly that the best way to support her was not to dig deeper and ferret around— that only made her more tense and snappy—but to be here for her, physically. So that morning, he scooted forward in the bed and wrapped his arms around her from behind. She felt the coarse, curly hair on his chest moisten against her back. She leaned into his embrace and felt his solidity hold her upright. She was so lucky to have him, she thought, to have someone who trusted so wholly the bizarre nature of her work, who inherently trusted her.

"Want to talk about it?" he asked, his lips against her shoulder.

"I don't know," Nora said.

"Nor, you can't carry it all on you all the time. Tell me."

"Okay," she said, turning around to face him. "I need to talk about this. But no names."

NICO

New York City
April 2012

Last night, the one name on everyone's lips had been Nico's. The entire theater had shouted for him, pounded their feet and demanded that he come forward and address them, the way he always had through another person's voice. He'd stood back in the wings, completely overcome by the noise, his senses feeling overwhelmed like the one-and-only time he'd dropped acid in college. It was a rally for the announcement for mayoral candidates for the City of New York, and he'd been waiting in the wings, waiting for Mike Raimi to accept his nomination. Mike, simultaneously, had been climbing the ranks of state government, mentoring Nico along the way. But when the name was announced for the Democratic Party, Nico was stunned when he heard his name. Mike smiled at him conspiratorially from backstage, encouraging him forward. Someone pushed him softly out from behind the wings onto the platform, where a podium was set up and he was expected to speak. Somehow this had all happened so quickly; he hadn't prepared anything. He was a speechwriter with nothing to say.

As Nico pivoted himself out of bed using his buttocks as ballast, he could hear his BlackBerry buzzing from the bedside table. He must have slept through half a dozen phone calls and messages. He couldn't do this anymore—sleep through things. He had to be on all the time, or hire someone to be on for him. Did he even have that power? Did he even have a budget?

He lay back in bed, turning the little ball on his phone over and over, scrolling through messages of congratulations and messages of support and elation and offerings to help. There was one from the senator's former chief of staff who wanted to come work with Nico; could they meet for coffee in order to discuss the details? There were dozens of inquiries from the press—they needed a comment from him, some quotes, anything to work with that they could sculpt into news. There was an email from his mom, from Toby, from Leo. He opened them all in the order he received them and read them hungrily.

You're doing it! We're so proud of you. Call you later to find out how we can help, but we're behind you 100%. I'll force everyone in the office to wear the pins. Send some over as soon as they're made.
Love, Mom

Dude, I could hardly believe the news. Mayor? As in Gracie Mansion, Secret Service, the whole shebang? Do you have time this week to grab a beer? I want to hear all about it.
Toby

Nico—Paavo phoned me this morning to tell me that you are running for the mayor of New York City. That is a very high title. I wish you all the best.

Paavo is seeing a girl but he is being very secretive about the whole thing. From what little I have gathered, she was in the program with you all. He and his colleagues have been working like dogs for CallMe. It's live now in Estonia, Prague, Latvia, Moscow and Lithuania and now they are talking about moving into Turkey. He may move to Istanbul to set it up. It all sounds very important, just like you.

You know how I hate US politics. But knowing that you are on the other side of the ocean working for your country makes me believe that it's not such a bad place after all, that maybe there is some hope for America. So do well. Get elected and show the rest of the world that you're not all hopeless capitalistic pigs. (STD.) Did I use it properly?
Affectionately, Leo

And there was a voicemail. "Nico, it's me. Call me. As soon as you can." He replayed it. There was no element of excitement in Nora's voice. It was as flat as a piece of paper. Her tone held no celebration in it, no congratulation in the least. In fact, it was almost didactic with elements of the priggishness she'd assumed when they were younger and she was put in charge when Stella and Arthur went out for the evening.

Nico felt split down the middle, like the satyr painting at the top of the staircase in the MoMA that always made him feel edgy. One half of him was on fire—he was so prepared to accept this new political challenge—while the other half felt doused by Nora's blasé temperament. He vacillated between responding to the emails and calling Nora back. He wanted to revel in the news, in the celebration, but there was something in Nora's voice that made him dial her number. She picked up on the first ring.

"Where the hell have you been?" His sister was agitated. He could tell that she was pacing a worn path over the carpet in her office. "I called you three times."

"Relax," Nico said. "I slept in. It was a late night." He

waited for her to ask why, in case she hadn't turned on the news in the past eight hours. But she was silent. "Is everything okay? You feeling all right?"

"I'm fine," Nora snapped before softening. "I mean, physically. I'm okay. Things have been nutty in the office. We've had a deluge of new patients because of that article."

"That's awesome." Nico yawned and stretched his arms overhead. He didn't like where this was going; the call was supposed to be about his professional successes, not hers. After all, the Grand family had gathered in the Flatiron loft and toasted Nora's success the week before. "Really great news. I'm happy for you, Nor."

"I'm not calling to gloat. I'm calling because...ah fuck. I really can't even, shouldn't even be telling you this. Doctor-patient confidentiality and all. But... I have to tell you."

Nico felt his strength falter. This wasn't Nora being dramatic or seeking attention. He remembered the same quaver in her voice when she had returned from the hospital and he had held her in his arms, allowing her to breathe in his scent and record the memory of her brother in the only way she knew how then. "What's going on?"

"Have you heard from Paavo lately?"

"You know I haven't. Not since that weird email and my desperate moves to get back in touch with him. He hasn't even contacted me since I went to Tallinn. Why, what'd he say?"

"Well, now I think I know why. It's not really about Paavo, though. It's...shit. Here goes. Mari is in New York. Mari Sokolov." What other Mari was there? After Nico tumbled into bed after the celebratory drinks at McKeegan's, Mari flashed across the television screen like a siren. She had been the last thing he'd seen before he passed out.

"Really? Last I heard she lived in Moscow. She might even be back in Tallinn."

"Well, twelve hours ago, she was in New York City."

"She's probably got a job here. What does it matter?"

"It matters that twelve hours ago, she was sitting in my DR."

"Wait, what?"

"She came to me as a patient. And I shouldn't even be telling you this, but you're my brother."

"Well, she probably saw your fancy article. I can imagine the number that modeling does on your psyche. She needed someone to talk to. Random that she found you out of all the psychs in the city."

"It wasn't a coincidence, Nico." On the other end of the phone Nora huffed an internal battle within herself. "Fuck, I'm going to get my license revoked."

"Oh my God, Nora, spit it out."

"I think you should look her up. You should meet. She's modeling, working Fashion Week. I think you should just go find her and talk to her yourself. I can't say anymore. It's not my business."

"You're sure as hell making it your business," Nico growled. "Scale of one to ten, how important is this? Do you have any idea about my news? Do you have any idea where *my* career is headed? Do you even care?"

Nora sucked in her breath. "That is so unfair, Nico. It's just bad timing—it's all happening at once. It took me aback. I saw the announcement last night, and I'm so excited for you, and I want to talk about that, I really do. But I'm having trouble dissociating from this news right now. Can you respect that?"

Since the accident, Nico had learned to respect Nora's feelings a thousandfold. Over the years, he'd often disregarded his own emotions and prioritized hers. He, after all, could recognize his friends and family. He didn't need written clues, or a distinguishing mole to be the difference between a familiar face and a complete stranger. But perhaps he had conceded his feelings enough. Nora was a big girl; she was a psychologist. She took care of *other* people; why should Nico feel as if he had to continue to protect her? And the jargon that came with being related to a therapist—respecting me, hearing someone out, understanding your subconscious— he had learned to identify the language, but it didn't make it any easier to stomach.

"Life or death situation?"

"Life."

Now Nico was taken aback. He'd meant the question to be answered with a yes or no. He narrowed his eyes and pushed the hair out of his face. His throat was closing in on him. He needed water, and then coffee, in that order. He squeezed his eyes shut.

"Good or bad?"

"Guess it depends on how you look at it." Nora's voice hadn't lost its caginess. There were secrets trapped within its timbre. Aside from the frustration of wanting to know what Nora knew that Nico didn't, Nico recognized how Nora's ability to keep secrets had truly distinguished her as an exemplary therapist. She'd kept secrets from the start—as children, never ratting Nico out, learning tidbits about him as an older sister might that his parents never would and keeping them close to her heart through the ages. Of course, a psychologist had multiple strengths and skills—asking the right questions, helping people to feel comfortable, understanding human nature, for goodness' sakes—but secret keeping was one of the main reasons that people sought out a complete stranger in whom to confide their deepest, darkest fears and thoughts. And her ability to not let her emotions meddle with cold, hard facts was what made her stand out.

But timing was not one of Nora's strong suits; she needed time to figure things out, to work through faces and identities like a tangled ball of yarn, starting with a dimple or a cluster of chin hairs, before she could narrow down a friend or acquaintance. And for Nico, time was essential. He had an instant to seize and create his career, to barrel through without a second thought. It was like Coach had drilled and trained into his boys—the reason for being so light not only on your feet, but quick to think was so you could seize the opportunity for a takedown the moment the window opened. It didn't matter if you were faced with someone far more talented than you, someone better skilled, even someone who weighed more. If that someone sneezed, blinked or hesitated in the slightest, the window was open and it might close again forever. Nico had to seize this moment, this hesitation, this one time when the world was behind him. The opportunity was like an eclipse; he might never see it again. It wasn't the time to delve into the past, or trifle with irrelevant matters. He could track Mari down once he'd begun putting things into place. He had a campaign to run.

NICO

New York City
February 2014

It is bad enough being late. Nico lingers by his apartment door for a good hour, running his fingers over the teeth of his keys and weighing the pros and cons of attending the Hallström 40th Anniversary Reunion Celebration. When he finally locks the door from the outside and makes the mad dash for a taxi only to sit in bumper-to-bumper traffic for what feels like an interminable time but is actually fifteen minutes, he feels the cons column climbing nearly as high as his cab fare. After an infuriating search by a lethargic security guard at the entrance of the United Nations, he marches down a long hallway toward the entrance to the General Assembly Hall.

A buzzy blonde catches him subtly by the crook of his elbow. "Sir, can I get your name?"

"Nico Grand."

She frowns, ticking her finger down a long list. "We have a Nicholas. Is that you?"

Perhaps she's too young, but he is relieved that she hasn't recognized him or his name. She is standing next to a table that holds a few scant name tags. Nico scans the remainders and points.

"That's me," he says.

"You missed the welcome mixer and they're about to start. From where are you joining us?"

"Just downtown," Nico mumbles.

So it is bad enough that he is late, but worse that he has only journeyed a few miles north from his SoHo apartment, while most of the already-seated alumni have flown in from other parts of the country and the far reaches of the globe, negotiating borders and visas while he has only had to manage his conscience and his cowardice. He is late, and about to tiptoe upon the precipice of what could possibly become a major showdown. But Nora's wedding is the following weekend; now is Nico's chance to make things right.

"I know things have been weird between you and Paavo," Nora had said. "But he's my friend, too, and I want him there."

"Of course," Nico had said. "He should be." Five years have passed since the two men have spoken. So here he is, at the Hallström 40th Anniversary Reunion Celebration, desperately hopeful to make amends. Nico has sent multitudes of unanswered emails into cyberspace, left plaintive messages on Paavo's voicemail until finally, the ultimate rejection pinged dolefully into Nico's inbox, The following message to: <paavo@callme.com> was undeliverable, dropping Nico's dignity like a deadweight onto his chest.

"You can go ahead," the blonde says, pointing to the solid paneled doors. He pauses outside, letting his breath condense against the cutout glass circles that peek into the imposing room. He has been here before, on a school trip in grade school and of course during the private guided tour that was set up by Hallström. It hasn't changed since; the grand gold column with its embossed United Nations seal still sprouts from the center of the room like an oracle. The wooden paneling encircles the room for optimal acoustics. Great negotiations have been made in this space, peace kept in multiple missions, countries unified, heads of states honored. So there is no reason it can't serve as the hub for two grown men to resolve their differences.

Alumni of the Hallström program now occupy the seats that are usually filled with diplomats. As he slinks inside, Nico looks upon the sea of unidentified heads that face forward, watching a reedy gentleman in a perfectly fitted suit balancing awkwardly on the dais, tapping a microphone and shaking his head. Nico skims the room and thinks he spots the back of Pyotr's head, and Malaysia's and Anika's and Tomas's.

Barbara Rothenberg has been given a throne in front. She hasn't been associated with Hallström for years. With the new administration in place, Nico has read that she'd stepped down from the position at Hallström, and as she turns her head to glance not-so-surreptitiously at the audience behind her, Nico thinks he catches an air of resignation about her, as though her resignation hasn't been her choice. Next to her is Herman Hallström himself, hoary yet dignified, his spine curved like a nautilus shell. He sits clutching an ancient wooden walking stick, its head carved like a lion's, the mane smoothed and coiffed by constant handling. As a few sycophantic alumni approach him timidly, he raises his head regally and shakes their hands, nodding but remaining tight-lipped throughout the greetings. And there, at the end of one of the long tables in the middle, is Paavo. Next to him is an auburn head, which might be Sabine. Or perhaps it is Paavo's wife. Nico will learn later that they're the same person and feel a sharp twinge in his chest that Paavo hasn't even told him they'd been dating, much less invited Nico to the wedding.

Nico walks down an aisle toward the stage and slides into an empty chair at the end of a row. He clutches the program that an usher has forced between his sweaty fingers, letting his eyes trail over the afternoon's schedule of events, speeches, awards and more speeches. He tries to remind himself that Hallström is just a silly school program. It wasn't supposed to be life changing. It wasn't supposed to matter in the long run. Twelve years ago, Nico had entered the home of a complete stranger and then the Grand family had invited Paavo into theirs. The program was supposed to last a year. Their relationship was supposed to last a year. No more.

The man on the platform clears his throat, glancing up across the expanse of the room. Nearly all the seats are full, and all the heads turn toward him with rapt attention.

"Students, administrators, distinguished alumni and honored guests," he begins. "On behalf of the NEA and the UN, we welcome you to the new Hallström 40th Anniversary Reunion Celebration." A crack of applause ripples across the room and Nico finds himself leaning forward in his seat to see whether or not Paavo is joining in. He isn't.

"I'm Melvin Peabody, the new program director of the new Hallström. At its height in the 1970s," Melvin continues, "the Hallström Student Exchange Program for Understanding Relations across the Cold War Divide was one of the most sought-after, competitive programs of its kind. Gaining entry within its hallowed halls meant guaranteed admission to some of our member countries' premiere academic institutions. If the revered Herman Hallström vouched for you—" here, he nods his head in reverence toward the first row of seats "—your future was sealed in gold, opening doors to the likes of Princeton, Oxford, the Sorbonne. The Hallström Student Exchange Program for Understanding Relations across the Cold War Divide opened doors for students, but it also forged invaluable relationships between the young people of estranged countries, cementing lifelong friendships, establishing business relations, and perhaps even a romance or two?"

The room titters. Nico watches Sabine lean her head against Paavo's own. "The Hallström program has historically chosen the best and the brightest for the program, watching its students go on to glory. We boast four Nobel Laureates, two Pulitzer Prize winners, seven heads of state, far too many statespeople to count, and two Tony winners." Melvin pauses to wait out the applause. "And now that a new partnership has been formed, between the National Endowment for the Arts, the United Nations and Hallström, we intend to uphold that reputation. Our goal is to build upon the existing program that fosters relations between countries, but to enhance it by simultaneously ensuring that the arts, those much-neglected pillars in today's education, are given a priority within the cross-cultural dialogue."

Nico and Paavo were exactly the type of students for which Hallström had originally been founded, those tenacious, curious ambassadors of goodwill; young, agile minds that would help to rebuild the bridges that had fallen and broken down between countries; students who were in it for the experience, rather than what they could glean from it.

"While the program will continue to uphold the tenets that the original Hallström program put into place, in addition to visiting embassies and dignitaries, students will also visit museums, artists' studios and cultural centers. And we have worked to open these opportunities to South and Latin

America as well as western parts of Africa, though while I must caveat that these programs are still in pilot testing, we will have two students joining us from Mali in the new school year." Melvin shifts his papers and peers down at the front row once again. "We would be remiss not to mention a few people without whom we wouldn't be sitting here today. Barbara Rothenberg, program director for Hallström for twenty-nine years." Barbara lifts her head and smiles tightly toward the stage. "And of course, our very own Herman Hallström." The old man remains in his seat but lifts his cane in the air to the sound of raucous applause.

Nico opens the program again. There are two more hours before they will break for lunch. He feels the weight of the past twelve years begin to settle upon his shoulders, as though he has put on a heavy coat. Right now, time is a welcome factor. Time will help him compose himself and prep to face Paavo and answer for all that has happened.

Before the ink dried finalizing the sale of the Hallström program to the National Endowment for the Arts and the Understanding of Neighbor Nations, aged Herman Hallström stipulated that the original countries be included in the merger, and had succeeded in adding Ukraine. However, he has lost the battle over retaining Russia, as world relations with the federation have become strained and thorny when Russia neatly overtook Crimea in an effort to protect its Russian-speaking population from the ill treatment of the rest of Ukraine. It is a surreal time in the world; it feels as if Russia has been skulking in its hemisphere of the world, gaining back its strength, adding muscle, putting on weight and is staring down some of the underdogs from the former Soviet Union, pitching for a fight.

In fact, Estonia is rumored to be the next target; with its

large ethnic Russian minority, Russia is adamant that language should not be used in Estonia to segregate and isolate groups. The border town of Narva has been getting antsy and divisive and Nico has called Leo to ask after his parents.

"They're tough birds," Leo said on the phone, sounding nonplussed. "It is all nonsense. Putin is too big for his pants. He wants to begin a new cold war. We've been going back and forth on this language debate for nearly two decades now. Now Russia will save the day for all us Russian-speaking Estonians? I know better than this. I studied long and hard to be taken seriously in my own country. I live here, and will continue to live here. I refuse to be bullied by that crazy Kremlin man." Leo went on to tell him that his Russian allegiance was softening, that he spoke only Estonian at home now, that he had sold his Lada for a new Volvo.

Herman Hallström has maintained that while Russia is being a bit of a bully, there is no better time to strengthen the bonds between the youth of the respective countries, to bolster ties that have been weakened in the past few months. But the board has remained rigid and he has been outvoted. Russia will no longer be an active participant in the Hallström program. There will be no more exchanges between the United States and St. Petersburg. There will be no more Pyotrs.

Nico can see Pyotr now in the very first row, leaning forward, his forearms on his thighs, looking down at the ground as though he is concentrating very hard or completely zoning out. His girth seems unchanged, and when he turns his head, his perpetual sneer appears to have gone slack. He seems softened somehow, as though the years have melted the bullish resolve within. Nico sees Anika, Tomas and Malaysia, but there is no sign of Evan. He remembers how soft he'd been, how he'd shaken when Barbara had ripped his book into two equal parts at their first orientation, how Nico had worried about how Evan would fare during those few months in St. Petersburg with only Pyotr as his guide. Nico scoffs softly and shakes his head. That was years ago. They have all come miles since then. He isn't even sure that Evan remembered it, wherever he was. Did that year matter as much to any of the others? Did Hallström imprint upon the lives of the other students as it has upon him and his family?

Everyone has served a purpose, taking on their specific role during the one-year program, and some of them even beyond. Paavo has been Nora's navigator, helping her chart her future by helping her turn a cognitive disorder into her destiny. He has encouraged her to approach situations with a new understanding after the accident. Prosopagnosia or not, he helped her recognize herself and her capability. He had helped her identify her abilities, helped her see beyond what that tiny little slip of damaged brain tissue could never undo to build a strong, successful woman who might never have existed without him.

Nico had been Paavo's protector during that year of high school. While he'd wanted to shield Paavo from the threat of a mob of bullies, Nico can't deny that he had encouraged him during wrestling practice out of pure guilt. So he'd amped up his bodyguard role and welcomed Paavo into the fold, helping him learn some holds, while building up his upper body strength and his confidence for when he returned home. It was on the football pitch in Kadriorg the summer after he returned from New York that Paavo made the acquaintance of Jaak Alver and Riki Part, the two founders of CallMe, and together they had discussed their visions of creating a future that narrowed the world through internet-based communication, bringing them all to the forefront of the technological revolution in Estonia. It had likely given him the courage to act with Sabine. It had pinioned his doubts and allowed him to soar.

Nico had been Mari's solace on a very low and lonely day, a day that Mari could never remove from the recesses of her memory because there was proof of its occurrence. But on that day, she had needed Nico more than she had ever known.

But where does that leave Nico? After that traumatic phone call from Mason Landry divulging that a scandal was hovering over Nico's potential election to Mayor of the City of New York, the scandal that he'd fathered a child and never supported her or her mother, the news had spread like the plague that gossip was. It had made its way into polling booths, onto webpages, text messages. He'd lost the election. Not by much, but numbers don't matter when one loses. Nico has since slunk from the spotlight, taking the time to lick his wounds and salvage what is left of his dignity. He has made the obligatory—and difficult—call to Leo and Vera, who have known for some years now that Nico was the one who had fathered Mari's daughter. In fact, when he visited Estonia and found only the parents in the house in Kadriorg, they had assumed he had come looking for her. They had been far too nice to him on the phone, assuring him that it was okay that he hadn't known. He'd been so young, after all.

But that was just it, he'd argued. He had been complicit in an act that had resulted in a child, a child he hasn't known about for most of his adult life. His daughter is a thousand miles away and he hasn't met her. Over those days, Nico learned—mostly through Nora—that Mari has raised his daughter single-handedly, shaping her into a self-sufficient young girl who speaks fluent English, Russian, French and Estonian, while simultaneously nurturing her own burgeoning modeling career.

Instead of acceptance and empowerment all those years ago, he now learns that what he should have felt was shame. What he should have felt was shock. He should have claimed responsibility. But Vera and Leo haven't mentioned a thing about legality, about requirements or expectations. They have told him what they know about Mari and her life with Claudia. They have spoken of Claudia's aptitude for languages, about her zeal for travel, how she is on her third passport after the first two have been filled with stamps. They have told him about Mari's commitment to her little girl and how driven she had become when she learned she had to support two. But they haven't asked him for a thing since the truth has come out. They told him what they knew. But if he wants more, he will have to speak to Mari.

Once the fervor of the scandal had died down, Nico found that he still couldn't reach out to her. Each time he picked up the phone to dial the number, or tried to type out an email, his muscles and joints felt frozen, like a car stalling on a busy highway. On many levels, he felt as he had all those years ago after he'd returned to New York after the first semester of Hallström, when he'd written and deleted countless emails to Mari.

Mari, I hope you're doing well. I'm sorry we didn't get to say a proper goodbye.

Dear Mari—there has to be something that people say in situations like these. Do you know what it is? If so, please tell me.

He couldn't imagine what he might say to her now, how futile whatever words he might choose would sound when he said them out loud. Instead, he has tried to pick up the pieces of his own broken life. Chastened, he has reached out to clients he had written for on the side while he'd been working for the senator, and has picked up some freelance jobs along the way. His reputation and talent preceded him. His client roster is strong enough for him to start his own communications agency, the Mighty Pen. He isn't the star he once was, but he is slowly rising.

He tries now to focus on the keynote speaker, a current student who is reading an essay aloud. It is a piece that she has written for her acceptance into the program, and the new Barbara Rothenberg, a small, perky woman with a matching bouncing blond bob, introduced it as one of the most groundbreaking essays she has ever received during her short tenure as program director.

"It's not enough to learn about these things in books, or watch movies. Most of the time, those aren't even true to how cultures go. Most of the time, we aren't getting a true sense of people, their hearts, their souls," the student reads, beaming as though she has created the program herself. Nico remembers Barbara ripping the cultural book in two pieces on the first morning of Hallström orientation. He can hardly believe that happened, and yet, it is arguably the most important thing that could have happened. It forced him to not take Paavo or anyone else in the program for granted, to not just read a book and regurgitate it back. It has forced him to get to know Paavo for who he is, and to understand that he is a person and not just simply a representative from Estonia, that his family, as strange and cold as they once had been, weren't secretive and suspicious nor were they KGB spies. It had forced Leo to understand Nico for who he was as they bonded over an esoteric language that even stubborn-as-nails Leo would champion one day.

Quakes have succeeded in shifting plates so that the geology of the earth will never look the same again. Tornadoes have blown through towns, decimating them to dust. Yet these two families have somehow survived, holding on steadily through the storms, gripping pieces of driftwood in order to stay afloat. But they may not have to drift forever. Because that morning, as Nico had deliberated in the foyer of his SoHo apartment, he knew he couldn't even consider facing Paavo at the 40th Hallström Reunion without taking some responsibility. He'd tossed his keys onto the table by the door, pushed his shoes off one after the other—a habit he'd acquired after those few months with the Sokolovs in Tallinn—and sat down at his laptop. This missive was not something to compose while in transit or on a tiny device where the letters appeared shrunken and insignificant. This was a plea, a bridge and an extension, each abashedly long overdue. He wrote as though he'd known what he wanted to say all along, letting his fingers guide the way. He wrote two missives. He sent one and printed the other.

And then what? There was no chance in hell that they'd be one big happy family. He is sure he doesn't want that, and she certainly doesn't appear to, either, not after the years of independence she has insisted upon. Perhaps he can apply for that job at the Estonian embassy. Maybe he can even take the Mighty Pen to the Baltic, offering his services to politicians, celebrities, maybe even models. There are so many opportunities to consider. Because the one he knows he wants is to be part of Claudia's life somehow. Once he meets her, he knows there will be no turning back, and he prays that Mari will be open to it.

Sabine is shifting in her seat, turning her head, looking bored. Nico catches her eye and she smiles at him, shaking her head softly, though he can't tell if the look is for showing up late to the reunion or for all he has not done over the years. He smiles back and points to the hallway, signaling that they will connect after the speeches.

Nico opens his phone to check his email again, but it remains empty.

He thinks of his parents in their sprawling apartment and how fiercely they love him. He thinks of Ivy and everything they have put themselves through in order to accomplish so little. He thinks of the look on her face as he finally had to put the phone down that Election Day and tell her the truth. How she stood up and walked out of the room, didn't return his calls for a week, and then finally agreed to meet him at a coffee shop to officially end their relationship. He thinks of Mari and that December afternoon, the light sprinkling in through the shades, the urgent way she had pulled at his collar and the resigned look she had on her sleeping face as he left the room and clicked the door shut behind him. He thinks of Paavo—a riddle-obsessed teenager who spent years shrinking into himself after being taunted and haunted by a group of insignificant lowlifes. He has changed the world. He has scored the prettiest girl in the program. He has overcome. There is so much that Nico wants to say to him, but there is more that he wants left unsaid. He wants the girl's keynote speech to go on forever; he wants her to have written pages and pages, flipping them over and over like a neverending wedding toast.

But the girl wraps up, and as the applause continues like a waterfall, Nico rises and walks into the hall. He, too, has a speech prepared. It sits folded in his pocket, ready for its audience of just one. He stands with his back to the wall, a tide of Hallström alumni teeming around him, and feels for the paper nestled against his leg. He starts to second-guess himself, as he does before every speech is sent off to every client. Could he have phrased it in a more eloquent manner? Has he chosen the right words to say what he truly means? Does he have what it takes to approach Paavo in the first place?

But there he is, Nico's Estonian exchange partner, stepping into the hall with the same look upon his face that he wore when he waited in the baggage hall at Brandenburg Airport, unsure which boy had been assigned to him. Nico waits for the current of alumni to bring Paavo toward him. Sabine is nowhere in sight, and Nico is both frustrated and grateful for her absence.

They can reach to touch one another now, initiate an awkward handshake, even grapple if one of them is quick enough to take the other down to the floor in an unexpected hold. Nico smiles and Paavo nods back, though it's not an unfriendly gesture. Paavo has reticence in every movement, hesitance in every gesture. Nico removes the paper from his pocket and hands it to him before either of them has the chance to say anything.

Dear Paavo,
Technically, I am stronger. I've worked out for years. I've bench-pressed and pulled deadweights and squat-thrusted and run for miles. I can do a hundred push-ups and twenty-five pull-ups in a row without breaking a sweat. At least, I used to be able to do that.

But today you have to be stronger than me. You have to go beyond my foibles. You have to embrace the insecurities that I have hidden behind for years. It'll be a more difficult task than any opponent I've ever wrestled or any weight I've ever lifted. I know that you're a bigger person than me, because I don't know that I could forgive myself had the situation been reversed. And I don't want to take advantage of your kindness, but on some level, I have nothing else left to rely upon.

Just because I was strong didn't mean I was confident. My experience with Hallström gave me a whole new kind of strength. My semester in Estonia made me feel infallible, and I wanted to help people the way that I hoped I helped you. But it also made me think that I could get what I wanted, that I could attain a level of superiority that no one should be allowed.

But my actions resulted in hurting you, in changing Mari's life, in potentially estranging her from Estonia—though, in honesty, that was something she wanted long before I ever entered the picture. Regardless, it made her life a lot harder and she shouldn't have had to shoulder the burden alone.

Please understand that I never meant to hurt you, or Mari. I was young, but youth shouldn't be an excuse or an alibi. I take full responsibility for my actions. After all, if I remember anything from junior year physics, it's that every action has a reaction.

So, I hope you'll be kind enough to bestow the answer to this riddle upon me now:

It may only be given, not taken or bought. What the sinner desires, but the saint does not.

Paavo blinks, and looks down at the ground. He folds the paper back along the same lines and puts it in his pocket. His face breaks into a smile, the likes of which Nico has never seen on him before. When he looks up, his mouth is pursed, as though he has already uttered the word. But Nico has to lean in to hear him speak.

PAAVO

New York City
February 2014

"Forgiveness."

★ ★ ★ ★ ★

ACKNOWLEDGMENTS

They say that the second child is much easier than the first; I wish it were true of the second book. I couldn't have written this without:

Dear friends and family who nurtured, bolstered and elevated me throughout: Maya Frank-Levine, Shabnam Salehezadeh, Adele Kudish, Manil Suri, Prajwal Parajuly, Nikhil Mitter, Bindu and Joyshil Mitter, Marcia Riklis, Daniella Hirschfeld, Kean O'Brien, Vibhuti Patel, Ed Adams and the 115th Street New York Public Library, and the gracious folks at Harlem Mist.

Joska, Gabi, Gery and Zsofi Molnar in Budapest: once strangers, now family. There would be no story without your unharnessed ability to love.

Ed Dadey at ArtFarm Nebraska, for the invaluable time and space to clear my head, leave it all behind, and just write.

Priya Doraswamy for believing from the very beginning.

My awe-inspiring MIRA team, including Emer Flounders, whose sunny attitude makes anything seem possible. Erika Imranyi, whose keen literary instincts make everything better.

New friends in Estonia, a tiny country with a large heart: Liina Normet, Scott Diel, Mahesh Ramani, Taivo Lints.

Kamala Nair, your unwavering friendship and conscientious advice have buoyed me from the very first page.

Jennifer Field, I can't imagine life without the levity of your humor, your infallible encouragement, your steadfast support.

Nalini Nadkarni, for your incessant, fierce love: of me, of books, of words.

Maitreya Padukone, for more than just happening to be there; for truly *being there*.

Rohit Mitter, for supporting me: intimately, inexorably, ineffably.

Neil Padukone, for a whole lot more than you will allow me to publish; for reinforcing me in far more ways than I can begin to express.

Nina Padukone, you are the strongest person I know. Thank you for championing and pushing me every single time I wanted to give up, and inciting an insatiable, fiery ambition deep within the recesses of my soul.

Salma Padukone-Mitter: I wrote much of this book while I was expecting you. I cannot thank you enough for being a gentle, serene tenant on the inside and for inspiring me to be the best version of myself every single day since you emerged. I can't wait to see how *your* story unfolds.